ROCK THE BOAT

BY:

Carol Edward

Published by
Ace Lion Books
June 2017

Ace
Lyon

Published by
Ace Lyon Books
Acelyonbooks.com
First Edition
Cover Design by S. M. Savoy
Carol Edward Rock the Boat
ISBN 978-1-947122-10-9

Contents

ROCK THE BOAT

-1-
Everything Perfectly Aligned

Sergeant Michael Evans sat at the counter of a local diner and snatched a menu, his stomach growling. Two of his squad joined him. Just back from a four-month tour in Iraq, all three were tanned and starving. The waitress arrived while he read the menu.

"Well, let's see here…" Inger slid a gnarled finger down the menu and paused. "Gimme the pancakes and eggs. And, I'll take a steak, medium rare, with hash browns." He handed the menu to the waitress. "Put a side of bacon and sausage with that. And toast," he added as the waitress laughed.

Franton chuckled and said, "Make that two."

The waitress giggled. "For you, sir?"

Mike lowered the menu and gazed into the most beautiful blue eyes he'd ever seen. Framed by thick black lashes, eyes the color of a clear summer sky met his.

"Yeah, what they're having."

When she glanced up from the pad in her hand, her smile froze, and a blush tinted her high cheekbones.

"Um, right. Anything to drink with that?"

Mike leaned forward as his gaze traveled her. A white t-shirt showcased full breasts, while a short, black skirt encased slim hips and long, tanned legs. "What do you suggest?"

She took a step toward him until she leaned forward over the counter. Soft, pink lips parted as white teeth bit the plump bottom lip.

Never in his life had a woman's mere presence affected him to this degree, and he shifted uncomfortably in his seat.

Damn, he needed to get laid soon, and by her.

They stared at each other for a moment.

Inger snickered and turned it into a cough, one work-roughened hand rising to cover his face.

The flush on the girl's cheeks deepened, and she straightened. "Um, coffee?"

"Sure." Mike would've agreed to anything and realized he was grinning like an idiot.

Not that she appeared to mind. Quite the contrary, the sexual tension vibrated so thick between them he thought he could draw her close for a kiss and she wouldn't protest. The thought of pressing his lips against her made him throb, and a low moan escaped him before he could contain it. He hastily cleared his throat.

"Coming right up." The girl sounded breathless, and her nipples showed through the thin cotton of the t-shirt, glimpsed for a moment before she whirled away and scurried for the kitchen.

Mike cleared his throat again as she hurried away.

"Holy crap, dude, I thought you were going to drag her over the counter," Inger said and snickered.

"Fuck that, I thought she was gonna crawl over it." Franton slapped Mike's back. Cool blue eyes shadowed by thick black eyebrows tinged with gray smirked at him. "Wouldn't mind sharing that one with you."

Mike grinned, hiding a wince. The one time he'd shared a girl with Franton hadn't gone well. Franton lacked finesse, and the girl had been bored and faking it. Without passion, he might as well masturbate, which is what he'd ended up doing. While Franton humped the girl in the bed, he'd masturbated to a memory of sharing a girl with his best friend Nick two weeks before. Now, that girl had been into it. Nick had got her engine going really good before he took over. Just thinking about that night made his cock throb again.

By the time the waitress returned with their order, Mike had himself under control.

Unfortunately, she'd had time to regain control too and managed a professional friendliness with everyone.

When they finished, a different waitress handed them the bill. Bright blue nail polish on press-on nails, more appropriate for a teenager than a thirty-year-old woman, tapped the check after she set it down.

"What happened to our waitress?" Franton asked and gave Mike a small smile.

"Off shift, but I'll be sure to give her the tip." The new waitress tilted her head to the side, dyed blonde curls bouncing, and winked at Franton.

Franton leaned forward and lowered his gruff voice, his threadbare flannel shirt parting to show his hairy chest. "Maybe you could help me then? I'm just back from overseas and looking for a date tonight. The steakhouse on sixty-three serves a mean margarita."

The waitress giggled. "Sure, I'm Alice. If you're serious, pick me up here at eight."

"Alice, I'm as serious as a heart attack, and me and you is going to have a real good time." Franton stood and fished in his worn jeans for his wallet. He left a forty-dollar tip, and they headed out.

"Smooth," Inger chuckled.

"Pfft, worked, didn't it?"

"True..." Inger glanced back at the restaurant and then at Mike. "Too bad you waited too long. That other one sure looked interested."

Franton slapped Inger on the shoulder. "Don't let that innocent look fool you. Mike's planning a reconnaissance right now. Tomorrow, he'll be back here getting her number."

Mike snickered, tossed his keys, and caught them in one hand. He winked at Inger. They knew him so well. "Man, I got a waiting list a mile long."

"Hook a brother up." Inger ran a hand over his balding head and then crammed on a blue cap he took from his back pocket.

Mike chuckled again. While Inger would be his first choice for a man on his six in a firefight, his thin build and leathery, wrinkled complexion made him the last pick for scrounging companionship.

Mike slapped Inger on the back. "Join me at the gym sometime and put some meat on those scrawny bones. Women like a man with a little muscle."

Inger punched his shoulder hard. Mike laughed and rubbed it. Thin and wiry, five inches shorter, seventy pounds lighter, and ten years older than Mike, Inger still packed a mean punch. The oldest corporal Mike had ever met, Inger managed to lose every promotion he got within months for fighting. He was a certified CFL, and Franton was following in his footsteps.

"Mike, no matter what I do, I'm stuck with this face. Some men get all the luck," Inger said.

Franton snickered. "Yeah, but at least he's willing to spread his good fortune around. And I don't mind being second choice."

Mike left his friends bantering at Franton's beat-up truck and returned to his small apartment where he napped for a while. After every mission, it took him a few days to decompress. Too antsy to relax after his nap, he decided to go for a run. Experience had taught him the best way to adjust to a normal life was to live it, to be in the crowds and embrace the noise. If he lingered in the quiet, he would start jumping at shadows.

He threw on an old sweat suit, strapped a knife to his ankle, tied his sneakers, and headed out the door.

A popular place for runners, the boardwalk teemed with activity. People of all ages and skill levels moved along at varying speeds.

On the pier, by the steps leading to the sand, he took a moment to stretch. Pale sunlight lit the sand in streaks of pink and rose as day gave way to night. Joggers in the distance kicked up puffs of sand while couples sat on blankets spread out on the beach. Cool and crisp, the late September air not conducive to swimming or sunbathing left the sand mostly deserted. From here, Mike could run two miles and then climb onto the boardwalk and run home with plenty of time to shower, change, and meet the guys at the club.

He'd just started the second mile when he saw her. The waitress from this afternoon was doing yoga on a mat spread on the sand. A t-shirt, so worn it was almost transparent, covered a light-gray sports bra and yoga pants.

"Wishes do come true," he muttered as he approached.

"Hi, remember me?"

Startled, she jumped up, and her eyes widened.

Mike grinned as perfect skin smooth and fine as porcelain flushed.

"Your friend Alice has your tip; I was disappointed not be able to give it to you."

The flush darkened, and Mike almost laughed aloud. While he hadn't meant a double entendre, the reaction made him smug.

"Ahh, thanks," she murmured, as she glanced up and down the beach. People jogging in the distance seemed to reassure her; at the sight of them, her shoulders lowered.

For the first time, he realized she had an accent.

"Irish?" he asked in surprise.

The lilting melody of her voice was soft, only noticeable as a brogue on certain words.

"Aye, I came here to go to school. My da was an American." She licked her lips and glanced away. Self-manicured fingers rose and rubbed her arms as if she were cold. Each short, rounded nail was painted a different color.

"Was?" Mike scanned her feet as he spoke, and sure enough, the toes matched the fingernails, each a unique color.

"Aye, he passed three years ago when I was eighteen. I never really got a chance to know him. My parents divorced, and I lived with my ma."

Again, she glanced away, surveying the area as white teeth nibbled her bottom lip.

"And your mom lectured you about the dangers of speaking to strangers."

To his delight, she giggled and held out her hand. "Ashlee Conner."

"Mike Evans." Mike took her hand,

intending to shake it, but as soon as he touched her, his intention changed. The hand in his trembled when he kissed it.

"Enchanted," he said, meaning it.

Every fiber of his body wanted to grab her and kiss her, to lay her on the mat and make love to her, to feel her perfect skin against his. Without conscious decision, his grip tightened.

"Alice is meeting my friend Franton tonight. You know, the guy with eyebrows." Mike wiggled his, and she laughed. "How about dinner? We could meet them, that way your mom has nothing to complain of."

"Aye, yeah, okay." The blush rose from her neck this time, and she winced.

"The diner at eight?"

Still blushing, she nodded.

He hesitated and then stepped closer and tipped her chin back with one finger. Eyes glued to hers for any sign she didn't want him to, he bent down slowly as her lashes fluttered closed, thick black lashes shading her cheek as she leaned towards him. The kiss was quick and gentle, and he felt it to the soles of his feet.

Her soft sigh when he drew away caressed his skin.

"Mmm." The indistinct sound he made caused her to shiver and step closer. Not one to miss an opportunity, he placed a hand on the small of her back and pulled her against his chest. This time, he gave her a real kiss that left them both gasping. Soft and warm, her body curved against his, a perfect match.

Flustered, she pulled back. "I'm not— I don't—, " she cleared her throat. "I've never..." The red burned across her cheeks as she spun away.

Mike grabbed her arm. "No, it's okay. There's no rush. We can take our time and get to know each other. Sorry about that. It's just…" Not knowing how to explain feelings he didn't understand, he held up his empty hands.

She turned back to him, smiling, blue eyes sparkling. "You're exactly the man my ma warned me against."

At that moment, Mike knew he was lost. The smile, the sunset, the girl, everything was perfectly aligned. The grin on his face deepened, and he traced the curve of her cheek with one hand. "No. I'm not."

❋ ❋ ❋

Three months later, Mike arrived at Ashlee's dorm room as he had almost every night since he'd met her. Sidney, her roommate, let him in. Mike bit back a grimace. Sidney made it abundantly clear she was available and willing and took every opportunity to try to form a wedge.

"Ashlee's with Kurt in his room and they've been in there for hours. I wonder what they've been up to?" One red lacquered fingernail tapped his chest while the other hand twirled blonde extensions around her fingers.

Mike stepped back. "All right, I'll wait in the hall."

"No need."

Mike yanked his hand away when she grabbed it and tugged him toward her bed.

Sydney glared, brown eyes narrowing, red lips pouting, and put her hands on her hips. "Fine, wait for the frigid little bitch."

Mike laughed. He'd run into a lot of girls like Sydney in the past and happily taken advantage of the fact they always wanted what someone else had. Although, Sydney took competition to an entirely new level, or maybe she was so aggressive because he was so uninterested. "Make up your mind, is she a whore, or frigid? Cause the only bitch in this room is you."

Before Sydney could reply, the door opened, and Ashlee entered followed by a red-headed boy Mike assumed was Kurt.

Ashlee smiled when she saw him. The smile lit her eyes.

Mike returned the smile.

Her hand rose to touch the small red scar on her arm, and her smile widened.

Kurt put the books he carried on the desk by the door, mumbled goodbye, and fled.

Ashlee kissed him, somehow managing to put happiness in her kiss. His own kiss was hungry. He hoped her smile indicated she was ready. The birth control implant she'd gotten in her arm last week gave him hope. Without another word, he took her hand and pulled her after him, leading her to his truck.

In the truck, she climbed into his lap and kissed him again. "I love you," she murmured for the first time before kissing him again.

"Will you marry me?" Mike heard himself say.

Instantly, tension filled the vehicle, both shocked by his proposal.

"No, I mean yes. But, no, you don't need to marry me." Flustered, Ashlee climbed into the passenger seat. She rose a trembling hand to push her dark hair behind her ear, the other pressed against her chest as if he'd made her breathless.

Mike chuckled and leaned over, kissing her neck, cupping her breast, running his thumb over the erect nipple. To his surprise, he wanted her to say yes, wanted it badly. "Well?"

A low moan was his answer, and she

dragged his t-shirt up, hands wandering over his chest, then lower. When she touched him through his jeans, she moaned again. The sound went right to his groin, making his pants uncomfortably tight.

"Don't leave a guy hanging, Ash."

"Take me to your place."

Mike pulled back. "Is that a yes or no?"

"Yes, but you know that. I can't refuse you anything, but you needn't marry me. I'm ready now."

The horn let out a sharp bleat as she climbed into his lap again and she giggled. Giggles that died away as she kissed him. The heat of her kiss warmed his soul.

"Okay, but—"

"Can we talk about it later?" Breathy and low, her breath skimmed his cheek as she spoke. "The voice of my ma saying, 'a good Catholic doesn't have sex out of wedlock' is ringing my ears. Ma has a lot of issues on everything though and me da always told me to trust my heart, and my heart wants you. I love you, Mike."

"Yeah, later, right. My place now?"

"Uhhuh." She continued to kiss him, breathing harder as his hands roamed.

"Ash, I can't drive like this."

"Sissy," she murmured as she slid over to

the passenger side, kneeling on the seat so she could continue to kiss him.

"Good thing I only live ten minutes away," he muttered as he started the car.

No woman had ever made him wait before. Not since his first time had he been this nervous and excited. The thought of getting her naked in his bed and teaching her what he liked and finding out what she did, made him groan aloud.

The past two months had been torture, stopping at kissing and light petting. Ashlee was passionate, but her mother's voice in her head inhibited her. She always drew back before things got too out of hand with a worried comment about what her mother would think. Mike blessed her father. When Ashlee committed to something, there was no turning back.

Breath coming hard, she kissed his neck, her hands dropping to his waistband and undoing the top button of his jeans.

Mike was amazed he hadn't killed them or received a ticket on the way to his apartment. Before he'd unlocked the door, she had his pants unzipped with her hand in his boxers, caressing him.

As he kicked the door shut, he pulled her shirt off, then his, while she undid her jeans and shimmied out of them. Wet, warm, and welcoming, a sigh turned into a moan as he slipped a finger inside her under the blue panties.

He unhooked her bra with one hand while the other fondled her, sliding through the wetness, rubbing the small sensitive nub. Both her hands pushed his pants and boxers down as he kicked off his shoes. She pulled away to remove her sneakers and pants.

"You're sure?" Mike searched her face. Emotions showed as if written. Love, lust, and nervousness, anchored in trust.

For an answer, she threw her arms around his neck, and legs around his waist. No doubt she was ready. Damp panties teased his erection. He carried her to the bed, ripping the underwear off and pushing her into the mattress. Wide eyes stared up at him as she spread her legs and he guided himself into her tight opening.

In his fantasies, when he pictured this moment, he took the time to caress her, but he couldn't wait.

A shivering moan escalated to a breathy scream as he entered her fully, and she jerked her hips against him.

Watching her face, he slid from her body until just the tip of his penis remained inside, then eased back.

Tears clouded her eyes as she moaned his name.

Faster and harder he thrust as she arched against him, straining. The way she responded to him, the sounds she made both surprised and aroused, filled him with heat like never before in his life.

"Let it happen," he whispered as he leaned down to kiss her breast, the bewildered look on her face making him chuckle. Eyes closed now, she moved with him, her body tense. "I love you, Ashlee. That's right, come for me. Tell me how you like it." He shut his eyes and went faster and harder, making her moan deeply.

"Was that a good moan?" On both hands, he balanced over her, unmoving.

"Oh aye. Don't stop!"

He chuckled and obliged. This time when she moaned, he continued to thrust. "Yes," he murmured as her legs widened, giving him a deeper angle. The slap of flesh on flesh and their panting breaths filled the room. "Come for me, Ash." Mike kept his strokes even and long as she writhed against him and started to keen.

A minute later she convulsed, muscles spasming and body relaxing. "Yes, God yes, just like that!" Mike threw his head back and jerked his hips against her hard with his own release.

Still gasping, he rolled them over, placing her on top, and laughed when he saw her face.

"Don't be embarrassed, that was amazing."

The flush receded from her skin as he kissed her and rubbed her back. On one elbow, he pushed up, sliding her to the side to caress her breasts. The pointy tips were dark pink now. His hand trailed lower, fingers gliding through sticky wetness.

"I should go clean up." Red crept up her neck into her cheeks.

"No, I like it, how wet you are from us." Mike glanced at his fingers smeared with blood from her virginity. The sight filled him with lust. She had ruined him for all other women in one evening. No one else would be able to touch his soul like this. *Wait till he told Nick, he would never believe it.* "You're mine now, Ash, forever."

A dazzling smile lit her face.

"Forever," she repeated in a voice full of love. Her fingers trailed across his back, through his hair, across his chest, stopping on his flaccid cock. Heat followed her touch, and his cock engorged under her hand.

"So many things I want to do with you." His gaze on her face, he rubbed her clit. "Too soon?" His hand stilled when she winced.

Again, she blushed. "No, it feels good, but I need a shower."

Eyes intent on hers, he lifted his hand to his nose and sniffed. "No, you smell amazing and feel even better." Two fingers slipped inside her as he resumed, rubbing. "Trust me, I like it. Come for me again. I want to watch you, and when you come again, I'm going to make love to you." He smiled as her legs parted and she bucked against his hand. He kept talking, his voice deep and low.

This time when she came warm wetness coated his fingers, and she screamed when he entered her. Able to gauge her response better now, he didn't stop his hard thrusts. When he finished, tears trickled across her cheeks, and she pulled him down on her, wrapping her legs around him, hips still jerking against him.

"Oh, dear Lord, if I didn't already love you, I would love you now," she murmured.

He laughed. "Can we talk about that proposal now?"

The smile she gave him reached his soul.

-2-
TELLING IT LIKE IT IS

"Nick!" Mike waved a hand as he pushed through the crowd.

"That's 'Sir' to you." Nick grinned, and grabbed Mike in a headlock, ruffling his hair.

Mike laughed and gave him a quick hug. "Looking good, man, not even a limp."

"A-holes still won't let me go back to work. Too many damn pins holding this leg together."

"Well. You know what they say." Mike shot Nick a sidelong glance as they pushed through the crowded airport to the baggage claim. "Those that can't do— teach."

Nick snorted and punched him in the arm. "So, what've you been up to while I was gone? The guys shipping out soon?"

"Yeah, a few months of training bullshit, and we go over again in January, and as to what

I've been up to… well, first I have a favor to ask."

"Sure, consider it done." Nick snatched his duffle from the luggage carousel and frowned and yanked it back when Mike tried to take it from him. "The favor?"

"Yeah." Mike surprised himself by blushing. He glanced away, clearing his throat.

"Ho ho, consider her done," Nick said and chortled when the blush deepened.

"No, it's not like that. Well, it is, but isn't."

"That's crystal clear, but I speak Mike, so I deduce this girl is special, you really like her. Dateable special, not just a screw, but you want to, um, rock the boat."

"I married her."

Nick stopped dead and gaped at him.

Mike grinned. "Congratulate me; I got married three weeks ago."

"Holy shit, are you kidding me?" Nick pulled back and stared at Mike's flushed face. "You aren't fucking kidding me. Well, congratulations." A frown wrinkled Nick's brow as he resumed walking.

"About that favor…. " Mike said.

Nick stopped walking again, the frown deepening. "Man, a wife… well, I ain't no homewrecker. Jesus, Mike, what kind of girl did you marry?"

"No, Ashlee isn't like that. She was a goddamned virgin when I met her. You'll like her, Nick. She's sweet and funny, and her name suits her; she can burn you right up. Sex with her is fucking amazing. She'll do anything I ask."

"Well, good for you." Nick resumed walking.

Mike placed a hand on Nick's arm. "I was hoping you two would hit it off. While you were gone, I really missed you, man. Stay at our place, in the spare room, and get to know her. The apartments for couples are much nicer than what we had."

"And she's cool with that?"

"Absolutely, she's making the room comfortable right now."

"That isn't what I meant, or am I misunderstanding?"

The flush on Mike's cheeks deepened. "No, you understand me, you always did. Ash is amazing, but I miss sharing with you."

"And she's cool with that?" One dark-blond brow lifted, Nick stopped and faced Mike again.

"To be honest, she doesn't know."

Nick rolled his eyes. "Where the hell did you park your heap anyway."

"Handicap parking." Mike laughed when

Nick glared. "Give me the damn bag and let's get out of here."

Mike snatched the bag, hurried to the truck, and threw it in the back. A snort of laughter at Nick's disgruntled expression, made Nick glare as Mike took the handicap sticker from the windshield and tossed it in the glove box.

Eyes closed, Nick leaned his head back in the passenger seat and ran a hand through his short, blond hair. "So, you want me to what, go home with you and seduce your wife?"

"Sort of. I want you to go home with me and make friends with her, and then I'll break it to her. The worst she can say is no."

"No, you, moron, she might kill you or kick your ass to the curb." Nick opened his eyes and sighed. "Mike, you could ruin what you have with her."

"She loves me. That won't change, and it's not like I'm going to cheat on her. Wait till you meet her, and we'll talk about it again, but if you could stay there while I deploy that would rock."

"Mike, I'm flattered, but you're not thinking things through." Nick held up his hand as Mike started to speak. "How do you see this playing out? You call me when you're in the mood, and I pop over, and your wife will be cool with that?"

"Well…" a frown on his face, Mike glanced at Nick, then back at the road.

"How thrilled will she be with you when I'm on a date or turn you down because I have a girlfriend of my own? Jesus, Mike, this isn't some girl we pick up in a bar and share for a night. This is the woman you'll spend the rest of your life with."

"Damn, you're right, but man, those were some good times."

Nick chuckled. "That they were, but that's done for you. Married man now, remember?"

"Yeah." Mike heaved a heavy sigh.

✳ ✳ ✳

Ashlee greeted Mike with a deep kiss and Nick with a shy smile. "Welcome, make yourself at home. Mike's told me a lot about you. I've made your favorite for dinner, and I hope you like it as much as Corporal Franton's."

"What?" Nick glanced at Mike, sighed and then laughed. "For real, you told her black beans and rice was my favorite?"

"It's not?" Ashlee glared at Mike while Mike laughed and slapped Nick's back.

"Wait till you try hers, it will be. Come in and grab a drink while I throw your bag in your room." Still chuckling, Mike headed down the hall as Ashlee offered Nick a beer.

❋ ❋ ❋

"Oh, my God, Ashlee, I can't believe this is black beans and rice; it's really good." Nick scooped another large helping from the bowl as Ashlee beamed at him.

"What's your real favorite? I'll make it tomorrow."

"Steak and potatoes, boring but there you have it." Nick leaned back in his chair and rubbed his flat stomach.

"Tomorrow's the game, honey." Mike stood, kissed her cheek, and picked up his and Nick's empty plate.

"Leave it." Ashlee took the dirty plates from Mike's hand. "Go visit with your friend. I know you missed him. And, I didn't forget about the game. I have snacks all prepared. Chicken asparagus dip, taquitos, chili with green pepper salsa, and cookie brownies." She smiled and turned to Nick. "Make me a list of things you like, and I'll pick them up when I go shopping."

Nick exchanged a grin with Mike behind her back as she grabbed the dishes. The list would be long indeed if he listed everything he'd like to do with her. Mike had married a beauty with long chestnut hair, full lips, and brilliant blue eyes. The flowered print dress she wore showed off her narrow waist and slim legs. Pert breasts, standing high and firm, begged to be caressed. Nick swallowed hard and shifted in his seat.

Mike's grin widened.

Ashlee was exactly as Mike described, sweet and funny and as he didn't mention, devoted to him. So in love, it was nauseating. Kind and considerate to Nick, he ceased to exist when Mike walked in the room. Not that she was rude, but the glint in her eye and body language said clearer than words how much she wanted Mike.

Over the next weeks, Nick tried not to hear them in the room next door. An impossible task in a house as small as theirs. The giggles that changed to smothered moans got him hot and frustrated.

Mike had shared lots of girls with him over the years, but this one wouldn't go for it. And damn, Mike would be a fool for trying and breaking her heart. If she were Nick's girl, he wouldn't share with her with anyone.

With a strangled moan, he grabbed his pillow and jammed it over his head to stifle the sounds from next door.

For three months now he'd been living with them, and Nick had never been so jealous in his life. Not when he caught his high school sweetheart kissing the guitar player, his hands in her pants, or when Mike took over his position as squad leader and he'd been assigned desk duty. Everything about Ashlee excited him, from her musical voice to the way she hummed while cooking, so happy in the simple task it was contagious. Just being in the same room with her made him happier.

The chair rocked he sat down so hard. Mike was an idiot. Hell, Nick was an idiot to not move out and cut strings with this mess. Anyway he figured it, someone got hurt. Three was a crowd for a permanent thing.

Keys rattled in the door, and Ashlee entered, carrying two big bags of groceries.

"No, stay there, I got it," she said and kicked the door closed with one foot. She smiled as he started to stand. "The grocery store had a great special on hamburger, so I bought twenty pounds. What do you think of Swedish meatballs for game day? Tonight, I'll make a meatloaf and maybe meatballs for the freezer. Oh, and I picked up more of that honey ham you liked." Ashlee set the bags on the kitchen island and began putting the groceries away still chatting.

Once everything was away, she grabbed a beer for Nick and soda for herself and sat down beside him. "Want to go do yoga with me later?"

"No class this afternoon?"

"No. Professor Wayne canceled his classes for the next week. His wife had a baby."

"Yeah sure." Nick closed his eyes and rubbed his forehead.

"Hey, you okay? Leg bothering you?" Immediately concerned, she leaned over him and felt his brow with the back of her hand.

Two weeks ago, he'd gotten sick with chills, fever, aches and pains, and ever since she'd been a mother hen, worried he'd relapse. While looking after him, she'd seen the scars on his chest, and they horrified her. The scar from the leg surgery hadn't bothered her as much even though it was bigger. Something about the gunshot wounds freaked her out.

Normally, he liked the attention, but right now with her breast pressed against his arm as she felt his forehead was a little much. Not while he was sitting here debating his options with her. *Try to seduce her? Steal her away from Mike? Talk Mike into sharing her for a night? Move out and find a girl of my own?* That last option held no appeal.

Ashlee had spoiled him. More and more he wanted what Mike had; a loving wife to greet him when he came home. Someone kind and sweet who really cared about him. Not someone – Ashlee – he wanted her.

But, if he'd learned anything in this last year it was that sometimes, no matter how hard you tried, you didn't get what you want. Bad timing could screw up your entire life. If he hadn't jumped after Mike when he'd fallen through the floor, a routine patrol turning to shit in seconds, Mike would be dead and Nick would've been the man in the restaurant.

Instead, Nick was shot five times saving Mike and in the hospital when Mike met Ashlee. Not that he would hesitate again. And not just because those men in the basement would've had time to arm that rocket launcher and take out half his squad. Mike was not only his best friend but a teammate, and it was Nick's job to protect them.

Franton and Pauly had covered him while he dragged Mike's unconscious body out of the building while bleeding from his wounds. Nick left four of the attackers in the basement dead. Franton and Pauly killed the other two. A haze of yelling men, rough hands, and pain clouded those memories.

The squad had humped their unconscious bodies out of there. Two miles on their backs at a run. But now, here he was, and Mike had everything Nick wanted.

On impulse, he hugged her, resting his chin

on her head, breathing in her scent. What the hell was he going to do? Whatever it was, he needed to decide before Mike left in two weeks so he could tell him face-to-face.

Mike was his best friend and a tough guy, but Nick was bigger and stronger. Nick snorted softly to himself. What did he think he could do, fight him for her? Life on the streets had taught Nick to fight dirty. Sure, he would win, but Ashlee wouldn't be impressed, she would be angry.

The quickest way to get her to despise him would be to hurt her husband. *Unless I disappeared him permanently.* Nick groaned and put his head in his hands disgusted with himself for even considering murdering his best friend.

Ashlee hugged him back for a moment, ran a gentle hand over his hair, and then rose and brought him a glass of water and the bottle of Tylenol.

"Thanks, sweetheart. Just a headache. Let's go get some air." Nick stood and grabbed the yoga mats from the closet by the front door.

A grin on her face, she joined him. Nick followed her from the apartment a deep scowl lining his brow. He'd fallen in love with his best friend's wife, and she was too damn sweet to ever leave Mike, especially for her husband's best friend.

The next day, when he came home, Ashlee jumped up from the kitchen stool, rubbed her face, and scurried to the stove.

"Dinner is in an hour and a half." Thick with tears, her voice cracked.

"What's wrong?" Nick hesitated and then hugged her. She leaned on him a moment before pulling away and wiping her eyes.

"Nothing, it's stupid, I know he's a soldier and has to go back."

"Ahh, two weeks?"

Tear-filled eyes met his, and she nodded.

Nothing he could say would ease her, so instead, he helped prepare dinner. Neither of them spoke.

After super, Ashlee retired to the bedroom to read while he and Mike watched a game. At the kitchen island, Nick glanced down the dark hall. A light showed on the bottom of the closed bedroom door.

"I'm glad you changed your mind, Mike. As much as I want her, Ash is too sweet. You'll break her heart. And I can't live here and be celibate. When you deploy, I'll stay and look after her, but you need to–"

Mike got himself a beer as he interrupted. "Yeah, I agree my first idea sucked, but I haven't changed my mind. Just taking the time to consider my options. You're right about Ash not being into a casual thing, but I could talk her into a permanent relationship. The trick is how to do it. My original plan, of the two of you here for months getting to know each other when I go, won't work. She would never cheat on me, and if she developed an attachment, she would deny it to her dying day. No, this has to be my idea. But, you like her, right? I mean...."

Mike peeled the label off his beer bottle and took a big swig. "Could you love her? Not just a quick screw, but a real relationship?"

Nick's heart leapt. "Look, if we're going to do this, you have to share her completely. I'm not settling for being part time or once in a while. Can you hack that? When you come home, and we're in bed together? Or when we're watching a movie, and she cuddles with me, not you? And don't forget, you'll be gone for months at a time, and I'll be here with her."

Mike stalked away and stared out the window, his back rigid. "Hardly seems fair, does it? You get all the fun, able to come and go as you please, while I..."

"Man, you're such an idiot. Nobody is making you do any of this, it's all your choice. And shit, man, if you want to divorce her, I'll take your place in a heartbeat."

"And share her with me?"

"Hell, no! When I marry, my wife won't be a toy for my friends."

"Well fuck, you're right, I'm an ass." Mike left the window and grabbed himself another beer. After offering one to Nick, he flopped on the couch and put his feet on the coffee table. "If I said yes to all that…" Mike took a sip and glanced at Nick.

"Can't just say it. You need to mean it. Ashlee's a beautiful woman. Any man would be lucky to have her. And really, talking about this is kind of pointless; she'll never go for it. She's the type of girl who needs to be in love to have sex. How are you going to feel if she falls in love with me?"

Mike snorted and smirked at him as he rubbed a hand through his short, dark hair. "Pretty cocky, aren't you?"

Nick shrugged. "Just telling it like it is."

Mike chugged the rest of his beer. "What about you? How will you feel when she says she loves me? Or was this going to be one sided? Make her fall in love with you and string her on? String us both on?"

Nick snickered. "Are you proposing to me too?"

"You wish." Mike rose and got another beer. "That's as complicated as shit. Can't we just have a good time? Bottom line here, Nick, if I can talk her into it, are you interested or not?"

"Fuck, yeah." Nick grabbed a beer and slapped Mike on the shoulder.

"Well, wish me luck. I'm going to try to convince her tonight."

Nick laughed, then grimaced and stared at the bedroom door, but it stayed closed. Gray eyes steady he met Mike's brown one's head on. "Mike, if she were mine, I wouldn't share her with you."

"Good thing I found her first then, huh." Mike chuckled, slapped Nick on the back, grabbed another can of beer and a bottle of cheap strawberry wine that Ashlee liked, and hurried to the bedroom.

Nick snagged himself a beer, wishing he was a fly on the wall in there. After finishing his beer, he headed to his room to pack. No way was this working out like Mike thought. One week with Ashlee and he could see that. Mike was too accustomed to girls falling all over him, but Ashlee wasn't the swinging type.

-3-
PLEASE, ASH, FOR ME

Nervous tension in his shoulders, Mike refilled the water glass with wine and handed it to Ashlee.

"You're going to get me drunk." Eyes sparkling, she gazed at him over the rim of the glass.

"Hope so."

Mike finished his beer and pulled her close, her naked body warm against his. The mirror in the corner bounced her reflection to the bigger mirror leaning on the wall by the bed. Her expression now revealed raw desire.

Thick, black lashes fluttered to her cheek as her head tipped back, and breasts jutting out, nipples hard and eager for his touch. He caressed her a moment, observing the hardened peaks. Blue eyes opened and stared into his in the mirror, and together they watched his hands on her breasts while she sipped her wine.

When she went to place the empty glass on the nightstand, he took it from her, refilled it and placed it on his nightstand.

"Sit here."

He patted the bed between his legs, and she smiled and knelt between them, leaning down to kiss him.

"Face the mirror, honey." A mix of anticipation and dread swirled in his gut. *Man, I hope she agrees.*

He didn't think his asking would be enough to strain the relationship permanently. Nothing he'd asked her to do, or did to her, had upset her before. Granted, this was a request of a completely different sort, but she enjoyed sex with him, initiating it as often as he did. If he tired before her, she would sigh with disappointment. The thought of Nick watching her come for the second time got him so hot beads of semen seeped from his cock.

A half-smile on her lips, she turned and leaned against his chest. He kissed her neck as his hands roamed over her. "Let's talk a few minutes, okay?"

"Do you have to leave earlier?"

Both her hands grabbed his arm, holding it across her breasts her worried gaze, meeting his in the mirror.

"No, but, Ash, no matter where I am, or how far apart we are, for days or years, I'll never stop loving you."

"Me either." Slow tears trickled down her cheek.

Mike wiped them away with his fingers. "No need to cry, honey."

"I'll be lonely without you." Sadness replaced her excited look. Her grip tightened clutching his arms, pressing him tight against her.

"And I'll miss you too," he whispered against her hair. "But no matter how lonesome I get I won't cheat on you. Let's make some memories I can bring with me."

Mike handed her the glass, waited till she sipped and then took a deep breath.

"You don't have to be alone. Nick is stationed here."

The lack of reaction told him she hadn't understood his intent. They had talked about getting sex toys, and she was for it. She loved to see him come on her breasts while he stroked her with his fingers. Nick was the ultimate toy, is all he needed to do was convince her.

"And, I'm glad he's staying with us, but it's not the same." She leaned over and placed the glass on the nightstand, then arched her back against him, wiggling against his hardness. Soft and breathy she whispered, "Let's make a really good memory tonight."

Mike smiled and licked his lips. "Ahh, you know I like to watch."

For answer, she ran her hands over her breasts and rubbed her nipples while staring into his eyes in the mirror.

"Mmm." Mike made an aroused sound and kissed her cheek, his gaze locked on her in the mirror.

A smile on her face, she tipped her head back and moved his hands onto her breasts.

His gaze on her could make her wetter and she would willing masturbate or suck him while they observed in the mirror. If he could talk her into trying, Nick watching would excite her.

Deep and low he whispered in her ear. "Not many people know this, and it doesn't mean I don't love you."

Her body tensed and her eyes flew open.

"When I say I like to watch, I mean everything. I want you to have sex with Nick while I watch."

"What?" Shocked, her eyes widened, and her hands dropped to her lap.

"Please, Ash, for me?"

Tears trailed onto her cheeks as she scrambled away, clutching the sheet to her breasts.

Mike held out his hands to her. "Okay, I'm not handling this well. I see that, but don't freak out here, nothing's changed."

"Nothing's changed?" Her voice shook. "Are you gay?"

"No. I want to watch that's all. Would it matter if I was? Would you love me less?" A frown on his face now, Mike leaned back against the headboard.

It didn't bother him if Nick touched him during sex, but he didn't encourage touches either. A touch or two was inevitable when sharing one woman. Nick's hands or cock didn't turn him on, the girl's response to them did. By this time Nick would've made a pass if he were interested, he had enough opportunity, so he was pretty sure Nick felt the same.

"No, I… No." A trembling hand rubbed her face as she returned to the bed, crawled to him and hugged him tightly, resting her face on his. "Nothing will change that, but you shocked me."

He stroked her hair and held her close. "Yeah, it's not like that's easy to say. I wanted to wait and give you guys time to get to know one another, but then… well, I thought if you fell for him, you would feel all guilty and conflicted and never be able to enjoy the sex guilt-free. And, I'll be gone for months and you two could—"

"Wait, you want me to have sex with your best friend while you watch *and* while you're not here?" A sob caught in her throat as she jerked away from him. "You're giving me away?"

"Never, Ash. I'm sharing you. What we have is so amazing, better than anything I ever imagined, but we can have more. Try it for me, and I swear, if you hate it, I'll never ask again."

Lips compressed in a tight line she faced him. "What if I love it? What if we want to run away together?"

"Then I'll come too. It's forever for us, Ash. Please." Mike framed her face with his hands and kissed her long and deep.

Her voice quavered when she spoke. "I want you to be happy, but I don't think I can."

"Okay, fair enough. How about if we start out slow? Do whatever make's you comfortable. Can he come in?"

"He knows? You talked about this already?" Ashlee pulled away again as her voice rose.

"Nick and I have shared in the past. Not like this," Mike added hurriedly when she paled.

Mike hesitated. Never having to talk a woman into a *ménage à trois* before, he was unsure of what to say. In the past, he and Nick had picked up the girl together, making their intentions clear from the start. Nick used to say girls loved the contrast of them, Nick with his rugged, blond good looks and Mike with his boyish charm, dark hair, and handsome face.

"Never with someone I love."

"You love him?"

"Yes, but not for sex."

"Isn't this sex?"

"Yes, but… I'm sorry, I'm not explaining well."

Mike pulled her close, curling his fingers in her hair and meeting her eyes as a blush heated his cheeks. For this to work, he had to be honest about what he wanted and give her what she wanted.

"I want to see your face when you come, hear you moan, push into you when you're all hot and wet from him and feel your orgasm."

"Can't you do all those things just us?"

"Yes, and it's great, but you'll see if you just try it. Seeing him get hard from us will make you hot, I swear it." His body was arguing for him, throbbing against her as he spoke, showing her how excited the thought made him. Instinctively, she pushed against him, which encouraged him.

Ashlee hid her face in his neck, muffling her voice when she spoke. "And if I won't?"

"Then you won't. I'll be disappointed, but I'll live."

Warm breath caressed his neck, and a tremor raced over her.

"No one else ever. Just Nick, none of your other friends ever?"

An eager light in his eyes Mike nodded. "None of my other friends deserve you. Don't take this to mean I don't treasure you, I do. Honestly, it never occurred to me to share you with anyone else. If you fall in love with him too, that's okay. Stationed here he can keep you company while I'm away and I love the thought of coming home to you guys. Just thinking about him watching when we make love after a long absence makes me throb."

"If I agree, I choose when and how?"

Excited and breathing harder, Mike grinned. "Whatever you say."

Ashlee bit her lip, her eyes huge in her pale face. "Okay, but if I change my mind, you'll make him leave?"

"Whatever you say goes." His voice deep and low with excitement, Mike pulled her tight against his chest. "Whatever you want. Nick and I will do anything you want. Let yourself enjoy it, okay?"

A jerky nod brushed against his chest.

"Wait here, I'll be right back."

This was going to be amazing for all three of them. Nick was wrong, he could have his wife and his fun too.

Before she could say anything else, he hurried from the room naked.

A minute later, he returned with Nick in tow. Ashlee huddled on the bed wrapped in the sheet, drinking wine straight from the bottle.

Nick frowned. "Mike, she isn't into this."

"Not yet, but give her a chance."

"Yeah, Nick, give me a chance," Ashlee said bitterly and chugged the wine.

"Mike…" Nick gave Mike a dubious glance and Ashlee a hopeful one.

Mike knelt before Ashlee, taking her cold hands in his. "Love isn't bad, sharing isn't bad, let us love you." After placing the almost empty bottle on the nightstand, he pulled her close and kissed her.

"See, all good," he murmured against her hair as she relaxed against him.

Ashlee closed her eyes and leaned against him as his hands wander, but kept her hands on his shoulders.

Mike pushed her down on the bed, still

kissing her, and she relaxed again. He slipped the sheet off exposing her breasts, and she tensed, hands in fists at her side as her husband kissed her nipples.

"Mike, she isn't enjoying this." Nick frowned.

If she were his, he would never let her do this. The unhappiness on her face upset him. Mike wanted to keep his good times and have a wife, and that isn't how this worked. Nick couldn't deny he desired her though. The hard cock pushing against his waistband was proof of that, and this might be his only chance. Undecided, he stayed and watched.

Ashlee's gaze flew to Nick's face, and a fiery blush covered her cheeks.

"Please, Ash, for me?" Mike murmured.

Ashlee took a deep breath and held out a trembling hand to Nick.

"You don't have to do this. No one will think bad of you," Nick said as he clasped her hand and smoothed the hair from her frightened face.

"No one will think bad of you if you do either," Mike added hurriedly, and Ashlee surprised them all by laughing.

"Kiss me, Nick." Shy and breathy her voice hitched.

Nick smiled, knelt beside them and kissed

her. The kiss built from a gentle touch to a deep exploration. *Mike was right, you could tell what she was feeling from her kiss. Uncertain, shy, and a bit excited.*

Mike moaned, and Ashlee deepened the kiss, Mike's excitement exciting her. Nick wasn't above taking advantage of that.

"I love you, Ashlee," Nick murmured as he trailed kisses across her face and neck.

Beside him, Mike made small encouraging noises as he played with her nipple, rubbing and licking it, one hand rubbing his cock slow.

Ashlee took Nick's hand, pressed it to her breast and sighed when he rubbed the nipple between his fingers. She drew him down for another kiss.

Mike backed away, making room for Nick to lie against her.

"Ash, you should know this is a big deal to me too," Nick murmured between kisses.

Ashlee ran her hands over his back under his t-shirt.

Mike helped him pull it off and then pulled down Nick's sweatpants. "Yes, honey, just like that," Mike said when Ashlee made a small sound of aroused excitement as Nick stroked her nipple with his tongue.

On the bed, kneeling on her left side, Mike took her nipple into his mouth and sucked.

Nick did the same on the right side.

"Oh God." Voice tight and uncertain, Ashlee ran her fingers through their hair.

Mike pulled back and rubbed the nipple he'd been sucking with his thumb. "Enjoy it. Let it happen. I love you. Whatever you want, honey."

"Touch me," Ashlee whispered.

Mike smiled as Nick's hand wandered lower and rubbed her clit. Hands pressing Mike to her breast she arched against Nick's fingers. When Mike reached down and spread her wider, she moaned and placed one hand on Mike's cock stroking it in rhythm with Nick's fingers.

The soft writhing under Nick's hands and excited breathing encouraged him. Purely a physical encounter for Ashlee now, he would do his best to ensure she enjoyed it. Ashlee had a loving nature. He hoped soon she would come to him out of love, not to please her husband.

Nick kissed his way down her body till he reached her clit and began licking.

When she was panting, Mike lifted her and slid inside from behind then sat and used his hands to hold her knees back and spread her wide again as she sat on top of him on the edge of the bed with Nick kneeling before them.

Nick chuckled and continued licking her in short swirls as Mike's hips moved slowly. A good man to share with, Mike always had a good sense of what the girl and he would enjoy.

Ashlee came with a long keening sob. He let Mike enjoy her orgasm a moment, before lifting her off him and sliding inside her.

Her wide blue eyes locked on his.

Nick balanced above them on two hands, kissing her neck and breasts as he made love to her, trying his hardest to convey his love through his body.

Mike still laid beneath her, supporting her upper body, whispering words of love and encouragement both his hands on her breasts as Nick picked up tempo.

Mike's hands wandered her body, his breath coming in excited pants as he whispered in her ear, "This is so good. Let it happen, honey."

"Ohhh." A long shuddering moan and she was rubbing hard against Nick, her leg's wrapped tight around his waist.

Nick threw back his head and groaned with his release. He'd been so caught up in her, he'd forgotten all about Mike.

As soon as Nick's hips stopped jerking, Mike positioned her beneath him, slid inside, and moaned loudly.

Nick's hands clenched in anger. She didn't look back or protest. To her, it was just sex. He meant nothing to her. The realization hurt. Pain replaced his anger, and he watched unhappily as Mike fucked his wife.

"God, Ashlee, this is so amazing. You're so fucking hot. Thank you for trying this." Mike came in a few quick thrusts. "See, fun right?"

Ashlee burst into tears.

Nick's anger returned. To Mike, this was just sex and meant nothing while it was breaking their hearts.

A startled look on his face, Mike hugged her.

Nick took her from him and cuddled her, kissing her neck and smoothing her hair. To Mike, this was just fun and games while he Ashlee were deadly serious. How Mike could miss it, he didn't know. Neither were hiding their emotions.

"That was beautiful, thank you for letting me share it," Nick whispered as he rubbed her back.

Hiccups interspersed with sobs, Ashlee shuddered in Nick's arms. "Now, I'm a whore. Mike, I can't. I'm sorry, but I just can't. I'm not the kind of girl that does casual sex."

Nick shook his head and tightened his hold when Mike reached for her.

"Nothing about that was casual and sharing yourself doesn't make you a whore." Nick drew back and wiped her tears with his thumbs. "You don't love me yet, but you will. Someday, you'll come to me because you want me, not to please him. Mike and I will share you, and we'll stay together. You can fall in love with me too. I won't break your heart, and your husband will be happy."

The crying stopped, and she leaned on his shoulder sniffling. "You really love me?"

"I do. If you weren't already married, I would beg you to marry me," Nick assured her and smiled when she laughed.

"He gave me to you," she said sounding angry and confused.

"And it was swell of him to share you."

She laughed again and pushed away, going to Mike. "And you're not jealous?"

Mike brushed her hair back, a grin on his face. "No, I'm happy. If you ever don't love me, then I'll be jealous."

"What about a family, Mike? What if he gets me pregnant?"

"Forever Ash. Till death do us part. All your children will be mine."

No one notice Nick frown.

-4-
KISS THE BRIDE

Ashlee came through the front door and stopped dead at the sight of him, a dark-red flush filling her cheeks.

A hand outstretched, Nick rose from the couch where he'd been waiting. Since their encounter, Ashlee had been spending long hours at school, claiming she needed to study.

"Can we talk?" Nick dropped his hand and approached.

"Sorry, I, um...." Bookbag clutched like a shield before her, she sidled past and ran for her room. "Can't now," she mumbled over her shoulder and slammed the bedroom door behind her.

Nick sat with a thump on the worn blue couch, put his feet on the coffee table, and rubbed his face for a minute as he debated what to do. *Storm into her room and make her talk to him? Leave and never come back, stop inflicting his unwanted presence on her? Sit outside her door and beg?* That one was his favorite, he felt like begging and crying and cursing. Instead, he went to his room and wrote her a letter.

Dearest Ashlee,

Please accept my apology for the horrible way I've taken advantage. No words can express how sorry I am that I've hurt you. In my defense, I can only say that I love you. Mike is more than a friend to me, he's my brother. For years we've shared everything, danger and long patrols with just the squad for company for months on end. That makes for a close bond. One that can't be explained or duplicated in civilian life. Mike and I were closer than most, sharing women.

Those encounters were just sex. No love, no anything except sexual release. Mike and I used to talk about those encounters, bragging and comparing style or the response we could elicit from the woman. That isn't how it is with you.

With you there is love. Honestly, I didn't think of him at all. All my attention was on you. Because I wanted you, I allowed Mike to share you even though *I knew* that isn't what you wanted. Not really. Which makes me a selfish asshole, willing to hurt you for what I want, and for that, I'm truly sorry.

The question remains where do we go from here. If I met you first, I would never share you with anyone, so I'm such a hypocrite to hope that Mike will continue to wish to share with me and you'll agree, but I can't help it. Any way I can have you, Ashlee, any way at all.

As I write this, I dream of stealing you from my best friend and making you wholly mine. A dream I realize will never come true and makes me feel horrible. Never in my life have I been this jealous of someone or coveted what they have this much. If friendship is all you can offer me, I humbly accept. To continue as your lover is more than I can expect or even want if it hurts you in any way. I don't want to rock your boat, make you unhappy or uncomfortable. I wish all good things for you.

Believe that the night with you is one I will treasure for the rest of my life. If it were possible I would make you the rest of my life; have a life with you, a family, a home, be your husband in every way.

With all my love,

Nicholas

Nick folded the letter, slid it into the envelope addressed to her, kissed it, and slipped it under her door.

For a moment, he rested his forehead on the

door. Inside this room, the love of his life slept with another man. A man he loved and at this moment wanted to kill. Hands clenched into fists at his side, he spun around and hurried to his room where he threw himself on his bed, covering his eyes with an arm. Mike wasn't the problem; he was.

Ashlee loved Mike, killing him would solve nothing it would only make them both miserable. If he killed his best friend, guilt would rot his soul. Head in his hands now, he accepted Ashlee would never be his. Fury such as he'd never felt filled him.

Life was so damn unfair.

The soft sound the letter made as it slid under the door drew her eye. Ashlee rose from the bed where she'd been sitting, staring at her open book without turning pages. Bottom lip clenched in her teeth, she opened the letter. Tears welled in her eyes as she read. When she finished reading, she curled in a ball on her bed crying, the note wrinkled in her grasp.

The front door banged open as Mike arrived home. Ashlee smoothed the note and slid into her nightstand drawer, wiped her face with her shirt, and resumed staring at the same page.

A glass of water in hand, Mike entered the bedroom and frowned. Ashlee hadn't greeted him in two days now, paling and rushing away when he kissed her good morning or good night, the apartment filled with awkward silence.

At least she wasn't pretending to be asleep tonight.

Her gaze flitted to him, and she paled before turning her attention back to the book, gripping it so tight her knuckles whitened.

Mike stretched out on the bed and patted the space beside him.

"Come sit next to me, honey, we need to talk."

Hands twisting together, Ashlee sat on the edge of the bed. Mike examined her a moment before pulling her close, taking her book from her and dropping it on the floor.

"Nothing's changed," he whispered as he stroked her hair. "I still love you just as much. What can I say to ease you?"

Slow tears trickled onto his bare chest.

"Talk to me, Ash."

"What am I supposed to do?" The sad confusion in her voice threw him.

A frown on his face, Mike ran his fingers through her hair, the silky mass sliding smoothly over his calloused palms. "What do you want to do?"

"How can you be okay with leaving me with him? God, Mike, I'll miss you so much." The tears turned to sobs, and Mike sighed.

"I'm not sure what we're talking about here. Are you upset because I'm leaving, or because I'm leaving you with Nick?"

"Both." Muffled in his chest, she sounded angry.

Mike tipped her chin up with one finger. "Don't make yourself miserable. There's no shame in liking the sex." A red flush crept across her cheeks. Mike kissed her when she started to speak. "I get it, you were raised in a strict Catholic home, and this situation wasn't something you ever considered, but be honest, you enjoyed it."

The flush darkened.

"Why make it a problem, Ash? If I like it, and Nick doesn't mind, and you enjoy it, why is this a problem?"

White teeth bit her bottom lip, and she hid her face in his neck.

"Is this…" Mike hesitated and cleared his throat. "Are you embarrassed because you want him, or because you don't?"

A shudder traveled her, and her grip tightened.

"Ashlee, if you don't talk to me about this,

no matter how uncomfortable it is, we can't work it out. If you hate him, I'll make him leave. If you want him, just say, and I'll invite him to join us, or you can, or you can go to him without me, but I really hope you don't do that." Mike's voice deepened. "I don't want to miss anything while I'm here."

"I don't understand how you share me so easily. If you wanted another woman, it would kill me."

Mike leaned back and tucked her head under his chin, playing idly with her hair.

"Ahh… Well, I guess because we've shared so much in the past it feels normal when he's there. Granted, those girls meant nothing to me." He kissed her again, sliding his hand under her sweatshirt, the nipple hardening under the lace of her bra. "Honestly, I have no idea why I like it so much. I guess I'm an exhibitionist, but it gets me so hot knowing he's watching and is turned on."

Both hands under her shirt now, he undid the clasp on her bra and lifted the warm weight of her breasts in his palms. "Can he come in?"

Ashlee drew back and met his eyes. "How do you know he wants to?"

Mike laughed. "Believe me, he wants to. Do you want to?" When a fiery blush scalded her cheeks, he laughed again. "That's my girl."

Annoyed, she pulled away. "You're too smug."

"No, I'm happy. If you hated this, I would miss it so much."

The blush on her cheeks settled into two red patches, and her bottom lip trembled as she nodded to him and glanced at the door.

Mike rose, but before he took more than a step towards the door, she grabbed his arm.

"Wait, promise me this won't change how you feel for me." On her knees at the edge of the bed, Ashlee's troubled gaze swept over him.

"Nothing on Earth could do that." He returned to the bed and kissed her long and deep. "Nothing and no one, but don't go getting any ideas. Nick only!"

Guilt and hope warred for dominance in her eyes. "And I can love him?"

"Yeah, whenever you want to."

"No love him, love him." Gaze intent on him, she bit her bottom lip again.

Mike traced the curve of her face with one hand. "As long as you don't love him more than me."

"That could never happen." A soft smile on her mouth, she brought his hands to her lips and kissed them. "I adore you. You've cast some kind of spell on me. I can't believe I'm doing any of this. First, I married you after two months, and now—"

"Now, you're going to make your husband very happy." Mike kissed her again and went to get Nick.

"Ash sent me for you." The grin on his face widened when Nick looked up startled and dropped the book he was reading. "Keep up the good work, and in no time she'll be coming for you herself."

"Mike, I wasn't lying to her. I do love her."

"Ash is loveable, I don't blame you. Everything she thinks and feels is so honest. No manipulation, just truth. On our first date, she told me straight up she wanted me, but wouldn't have sex with me unless she loved me. No stringing me along. And somehow she manages to put what she's feeling in her kiss."

Nick turned away and went to the window, staring out into the darkness.

A few minutes passed in silence. Mike's grin faded. "Are you coming?"

Without turning from the window, Nick said, "You sure you're okay with this? As a permanent thing, I mean?"

"Yes, everyone is happy, so let's go rock the boat."

Nick winced, then laughed and followed

him from the room.

In Mike's absence, Ashlee had changed into the silvery, silk nightgown she'd worn the night she'd married Mike and lit candles. The mirrors had been moved, and the radio was on low. When they entered, she stopped brushing her hair, placed the antique silver brush on her nightstand, and stood.

A shy smile on her face, she kissed Mike and then Nick, resting in his arms a moment. "For this to work it can't be casual for me."

Tense she moved from Nick and put her arms around her husband's waist. Long chestnut hair swung across the small of her back when she tipped her head to meet his eyes.

"Be sure you want to give me away, Mike, because once I commit to him, I'll mean it."

"Honey, I'll never give you away, but I will share you. Do what you need to be comfortable with this." Hair smelling of strawberries tickled his nose as he buried his face in the curve of her neck and kissed it. For a few moments, they stood unspeaking. Finally, Mike stepped back, took her hands and smiled. "You're our beautiful girl now, not just mine."

Blue eyes shiny with unshed tears, she stood on tiptoe and kissed him, then went to Nick.

One hand traced his face as she kissed him. She put her arms around his waist and hugged him, as she rested her cheek on his shoulder.

"Ash, this isn't casual for me, I love you," Nick murmured as he stroked her back, running his fingers through her hair. The thick strands slipping through his rough hands with silky smoothness.

"Will you marry me, Nick?"

"If I could, I would." Nick smoothed her hair back and met her shining blue eyes.

"Say it. Marry me in your heart and I'll do the same. The three of us will be a family forever."

Nick cleared the lump in his throat. To his surprise, his voice cracked when he spoke, and tears made her expression hazy. With all his heart, he wished he'd met her first.

"Ashlee Conner Evans, I take you to be my wife to have and to hold in sickness and in health for better or for worse. I promise to be faithful to you 'til death do us part."

"Nicolas Rossi, I will be your faithful wife, for better or worse, in sickness and in health. I will love, honor, and obey you, as long as we both shall live, so help me God."

Nick kissed her soft lips. "Time will show how much I love you. If I'd known you would marry me tonight, I would've bought you a ring."

"Tomorrow we'll buy a ring you can wear. Not being your wife publicly will be hard for me."

"Hey, what about me?" Mike said in mock annoyance.

"All three of us can go." Ashlee smiled at her husband. "Kiss the bride, Mike."

Nick reluctantly released her.

On tiptoe Ashlee leaned against Mike with her hands on his face, kissing him deeply. Nick put his arms around her waist and pressed against her back, resting his cheek on her hair.

With all his soul, he wished they were really married, just her and him. Mike a friend who came for dinner or to watch the game and meant nothing to her.

Instead, Mike would be a part of their life forever, an important part. A frown settled on Nick's face as Mike hugged her, and he had to resist the urge to pull her away.

How could Mike share her so easily? To Mike, this was just sex and had nothing to do with his relationship with her. Nick didn't know if he could do that.

But if he wanted Ashlee, he had better learn too.

Ashlee was excited, breathing harder and pressing against Mike while she trailed a hand across him. If she enjoyed this, he would too. That thought firmly in mind, he gave himself up to the sensations of his body, determined to ignore Mike and concentrate on her. Whatever made her happy was okay with him.

One of her hands reached down and drifted across the thick hardness in his pants. Nick moaned, a bare whisper of sound.

"Mmm." Ashlee turned in Mike's arms and kissed Nick again, sliding both hands under the waistband of his sweats, fondling him.

Mike slipped the thin straps of the silk gown off her shoulders. Up-thrust breasts kept it from falling off. Mike tugged it until it pooled at her feet.

"Take me, Nick, I want you," she said in a soft, breathy voice.

Nick moved forward, walking her backward to the bed as she continued to fondle him, her breath coming in excited pants. Nick's gaze on her face, his breath came harder at the look in her eye.

Mike undressed as his wife undressed Nick.

She slid down Nick's body with the pants until she knelt in front of him, his erect penis in her hand. One hand held her hair back as she took him in her mouth.

Nick gasped and put both hands on her head as she stroked him with her tongue. Mike held her hair, and she used both hands on Nick. The soft sound of her sucking and Nick's moans filled the room.

Nick stepped back and pulled her to her feet. "I want to come inside you."

"Aye, come inside me." Breathless, her voice was barely above a whisper.

Nick lowered her to the bed. She guided him between her legs and pulled him down for a kiss.

The lilt in her voice now a purring growl Ashlee said, "Let me be on top."

Nick rolled them over.

"Hold still a second." Head tilted, she leaned back, moving her hips a small amount and then remaining motionless, a look of intense concentration on her face. After a moment, she began to roll her hips in small circles. "No, let me," she said as Nick bucked against her.

"Oh God, Ash," Nick muttered, forcing himself to remain still while she continued her slow movements.

"Right there," Ashlee murmured and began to move faster. In minutes they surged together in sync, building up speed until Nick was sliding as hard and fast as he could. The sound of wet flesh slapping together drowned out the radio.

Nick came in long hard spurts before she

did. The excitement on her face made it easier to let Mike take her from him. Mike laid beside them and pulled her on top of him while Nick's hips were still pumping. Without foreplay, Mike started pounding hard, and Ashlee screamed, a low gasping cry, as she came.

Mike continued to thrust in hard quick jerks as she collapsed on his chest. Not finished he rolled her over and pushed her legs back and continued as she writhed and moaned, 'Oh God,' over and over. In a wet rush she came again and convulsed around him. Mike tossed his head back and joined her, hips jerking as he came.

Everyone was quiet as they caught their breath. Mike flopped on his back and threw an arm over his eyes. "Every time I think it can't get better, it does."

Ashlee laughed and snuggled against Nick. "I'm not sleeping in the wet spot. Tomorrow we buy more bedding too."

Nick kissed her as he ran a hand over her breasts. "No one is sleeping anytime soon." A smile on his face, Nick kissed her temple. The strength of her orgasm and her enthusiasm got him hot there was no denying that. Maybe sharing with Mike wouldn't be so bad. He wouldn't be around much. Most of the time he would have her to himself. He didn't mind if she liked to rock the boat once in a while. Hell, he enjoyed it too.

While he pondered, Mike was taking playful nips across Ashlee's breasts, making her giggle.

Hours later, Ashlee fell asleep across Nick's chest. Silken chestnut hair in a wild disarray tangled in his fingers, strands brushing his face. Eyes closed, he ran a gentle hand over her soft skin.

"Mike?" he whispered.

"Hmm." On the edge of sleep, Mike turned towards them.

"Thanks, man."

A quiet chuckle and Mike squeezed his shoulder a second. "De nada. Thank you, for everything. For saving my life and this. Sex with both of you is amazing and agreeing to commit to her is more than I expected."

Mike paused. "You meant it right?" he finally asked in a whisper.

"With all my heart. Ashlee is my wife now too."

"Good, I'll sleep better knowing you're with her; that if I don't return she won't be alone here."

Nick frowned. "Don't say that, man. You can't go into combat like that, you'll get yourself killed."

Ashlee stirred on his chest, and Nick took a breath and lowered his voice when he next spoke.

"Come home to us. No crazy heroics this time. You're a family man now. Think of your family before risking yourself."

Sheets rustled in the dark room and Mike leaned over them and kissed Ashlee's brow and then to Nick's surprise his.

"I'll be careful," Mike said. A small snort of laughter issued from him when he laid back down. "The guys will be so disappointed."

Nick smothered a laugh and Ashlee stirred again, murmured Nick's name, and tightened her grip before relaxing into a deeper sleep. As he drifted to sleep, he made plans to take leave while Mike was away, glad of the opportunity to have her to himself.

❋ ❋ ❋

Ashlee groaned when the alarm on Nick's watch beeped the next morning. "Sorry, sweetheart, duty calls."

Mike rolled over and pulled his pillow over his head.

Ashlee tightened her hold and slid on top of him, kissing his neck and then his lips while one hand trailed down his body to stroke him.

"Stay home with me today."

"I wish I could." Nick groaned and shifted,

sliding into her welcoming warmth. Hips thrusting slow, she moved with him, excited breathing caressing his skin. "Mmm, this is a hell of a way to wake up, Ash."

"Don't stop," she murmured, and arched harder against him.

"Never. Tonight, when I get home, we go shopping and buy wedding rings."

"Yesss." Long and drawn out, she hissed the word, and his hips jerked faster as he came.

She rested her forehead on his and sighed.

Nick chuckled ruefully. "Sorry, sweetheart, I'll make it up to you tonight."

"Go to work. I got this," Mike said and leaned over them, taking Ashlee from behind while she kissed Nick.

Nick eased out from under them and kissed her again, but her attention was on Mike and his surging hips.

Nick slapped Mike's ass, and went to go shower and get ready for work, leaving them alone in the bed. Neither protested, both too caught up. Twenty minutes later, he peeked into the room, finding it quiet and dark. He eased the door closed, and chuckling under his breath, left for work.

-5-
NEVER LEAVE ME

Ashlee wept in Mike's arms the morning he shipped out as she sobbed goodbye.

"Before you know it I'll be back. Don't write me every day. Don't cry yourself to sleep. Be happy. Let me picture you happy, not sad. As often as I can I'll call, but that won't be too often, so don't worry if you don't hear from me for a week or so."

Her face in the curve of his neck, she nodded after everything he said.

"Promise you'll come home to me?"

"I love you, Ash. Forever." With his thumbs, Mike wiped the tears from her cheeks and then kissed her. "Let Nick comfort you," he whispered, kissed her brow, and then pushed her to Nick.

Nick put an arm around Ashlee and slapped Mike on the back. "Take care of yourself, man, and don't kill my squad."

"My squad now," Mike said as he grinned and slapped him back. After giving Ashlee one last kiss, he grabbed his duffle bag and headed out the door.

Nick pulled Ashlee into his lap on the couch and smoothed her hair as she cried. When the tears slowed, he kissed her temple.

"I took the day off, sweetheart. We can do anything you like."

She nodded against his chest but didn't speak.

Nick pulled the throw blanket over her and stretched out on the couch. Early still, the sun had done little more than add a gray tinge to the sky. They'd been up since three a.m. saying goodbye to Mike.

By the time Nick woke, the sun had risen and flooded the room with warm light. Ashlee still slept snuggled between him and the couch. He eased out from under her and headed to the kitchen. The smell of fresh roast coffee, which Ashlee stocked just for him, filled the room by the time she stirred. Mike never touched the stuff, preferring hot chocolate.

Nick was happily surprised when she came to him and slid her arms around his waist, leaning against his back.

"Could we go for a drive after breakfast? A

long drive away from the base? Let's go somewhere no one knows us and be a couple in public."

"Sounds good, sweetheart. Can you miss a few days of school?"

When she nodded, he grinned.

"I've taken a week of leave. Let's go away for a few days."

The smile she gave him was blinding. She took his right hand and raised it to her lips and kissed the silver band on his ring finger. With a matching smile, he did the same to hers. A grin on her face, she went to pack a bag.

For three days, they visited vineyards and stayed in small inns along the coast. At every stop, Ashlee bought cases of wine and blocks of cheese. The bed and breakfast they stayed at was quiet. No other guests had arrived yet.

Mid-day sun streamed through the gauzy curtains. A fire burned in the fireplace, giving the air a smoky scent and warming the room. They'd spent the last day naked in bed, only leaving to eat a quick meal before rushing back. Nick wished they could stay for a month.

On one elbow, Ashlee leaned over him, her brown hair brushing his neck. As was her habit, she kissed the scars on his chest. "I wish I didn't have school and we could stay right here forever."

"A few more months and you graduate. Then what will you do?" Nick twirled her hair around his finger as he spoke.

"Get a job at the best restaurant that will hire me. Once I get enough experience, and save enough, I'll open my own place."

"I guarantee it will be a raging success."

Ashlee kissed him, tracing his face with her fingertips. "I love you, Nick." Brilliant blue eyes stared into his and shone with unshed tears when he smiled.

She'd never said that before.

"Make love to me, Nicky."

Brilliant sunlight outlined Ashlee's body as she leaned over him. The soft brush of her chestnut hair caught up in a ponytail caressed his arm. The words she spoke caressed his soul.

Eyes intent on her face, he whispered, "Say it again, Ash."

A smile lifted her full lower lip. "I love you." Black lashes fluttered closed, as she leaned down and kissed him. The love she felt was clear in the kiss.

A deep sigh escaped Nick as he ran his hand along her velvety smooth skin. Before he could ask her to say it again, she murmured in his ear. She continued to repeat 'I love you,' between kisses as she kissed her way down his body.

A groan escaped him when she reached his cock. Her warm tongue traveled the length of him, swirling around the head of his penis before she sat back.

Her breasts brushed his chest as she leaned over him on her hands and knees. "There's nothing about you I don't love. Promise me we'll be together forever." Her blue eyes met his, demanding honesty.

Nick framed her face with his hands. "I wish to God I'd met you first and we were legally married now; that this was our honeymoon and you were secure in my love for you. In my heart, you're mine. More than anything I want to be yours."

"My Nicky," she whispered as she leaned down and kissed him.

Laying in his arms, she kissed him a long time as her hands wandered. When she finally pulled back, she was breathing harder. Soft excited gasps misted along his skin as she kissed her way down his body again. With her hands and mouth she caressed his cock until he pulled her away.

A soft disappointed sound changed to an excited groan when he pulled her on top of him. Astride his body, she rode him with her head thrown back and eyes closed. Every sound he made caused her to breath harder or move faster, his arousal exciting her. In moments, they were both moaning and calling out.

The difference was indescribable. This wasn't sex. Tears filled his eyes at the emotion he felt from her. Every touch blazed a path along his skin, her love searing him. He lost track of time, neither was seeking release just closeness.

"I love you so much," Nick murmured as he threw her ponytail holder on the floor, and wrapped both his hands in her thick hair.

The smell of strawberries surrounded them. He made love to her slowly, not wanting it to end.

In a hoarse whisper, she screamed his name and shuddered as she came, falling forward over his chest. The inner muscles of her body clenched him. His release was so powerful it left him shaking and panting atop her. When his hips stopped jerking, he rolled them over again.

Warm tears trailed across his neck. He too felt overcome with emotion. Never had he felt so connected to someone.

Without speaking, he rubbed her back and kissed her forehead and neck. One hand tangled in her hair, the warmth of her skull warming his palm. The heat of her love warming his soul.

"My Nicky," she mumbled as she drifted to sleep.

Troubled by thoughts of trying to talk her into running away with him, sleep eluded him.

He would quit his job in a minute and take her away if she would agree to leave Mike. To ask her though risked her leaving him. Loyalty to her husband might be stronger than love for him. Mike would be angry and would likely try to break them up.

He tightened his grip on her. In time, she would love him more, he would see to that. There was nothing he wouldn't do to keep her.

❋ ❋ ❋

On the way home, she curled into his side. When they reached the base, she pulled away and stared out the window, shoulders tense and hands twisting in her lap.

"Hey, we're okay. No public displays that's all. Inside I feel the same."

She rubbed her face, and Nick realized she was crying.

"Sweetheart… I could retire. You could teach me to cook, and I'll work for you."

She snorted a laugh, wiped her face again, and turned to him. "No restaurant on Earth would hire you. I love you, but you can't cook."

"And I love you. Soon, we'll become used to this and won't even notice we can't hold hands or kiss in public."

She bit her bottom lip. "I really want to hug you."

"And I want you too. As soon as we get inside, I'll show you how much."

"That's just it, Nick, I don't want our relationship to be just sex. I want to do everything with you." Tears trailed down her cheeks. She dashed them away and turned back to the window again.

"Okay, when we get home, after I show you how much I want to hold you, let's go do some yoga on the beach."

Half laugh, half sob, greeted that, and she covered her face with her hands.

Nick glanced over and frowned. Neither said anything till they reached the apartment.

"Ash…"

She straightened her shoulders and rubbed her face hard. "No, I'm okay. We chose this, and I wouldn't trade you for anything."

Nick nodded and grabbed her bag.

Life settled into a steady rhythm and Nick had never been happier. A few of his coworkers teased him about being boring when he turned down all invitations for double dates or going to clubs. Most of the people he worked with were new acquaintances so didn't realize what a big change his lifestyle was.

Comfort and softness had entered his life for the first time, and he loved it. Never, in his entire life, had someone loved him like Ashlee did, wholeheartedly without reservation.

To this point, Nick had been surrounded by hard men doing a violent job, and it suited him. He hadn't even realized there could be another way, not until Ashlee. Care and kindness filled her every touch, which he tried his hardest to return, so grateful to have her in his life.

To his few old friends he lied, blaming his injuries on not wanting to go club hopping and they immediately dropped the subject.

Nick realized to preserve his cover he needed to act normally so invited friends over to watch a basketball game. When he told Ashlee not to cook for them, she frowned.

"Who's coming?" she asked.

"Trent, Angelo, Winters and a friend from work you haven't met yet, Francis Dawn, but call him Frank."

The frown on Ashlee's face deepened. "And they asked me not to cook?"

"God no, but, sweetheart, if I were here as a roommate, I wouldn't ask you to cook."

"Okay… But if I knew, I would offer."

"Sweetheart, it's just simpler if you don't cook. Treat me like a friend. Like you did when I first moved in."

Tears filled her eyes, and she clutched him, resting her forehead on his chest. "I hate this, pretending I don't love you."

Nick sighed and hugged her tight. "Me too."

On game day Ashlee went shopping. Nick greeted his friends, handed out beer, and ordered pizza.

"Damn, Ashlee isn't cooking?" Trent asked as he flopped into the recliner and kicked his feet up.

"Nope, sorry. When Mike gets home, I'm sure she will again."

"When do they get back?"

"Three more months."

Ashlee came in carrying grocery bags and waved the men back to their seats as they started to stand. "I got this. Sorry, I didn't realize you had company. How about I whip up some snacks?"

"I wouldn't say no." Trent grinned at her, and she smiled back.

"You wouldn't happen to have the ingredients for that chicken dip thing you made last time I was here?" Angelo asked hopefully.

"Coming right up." Ashlee grinned at Angelo, put the groceries away, and humming happily, began cooking.

In forty-five minutes, she had dip, chips, and an assortment of snacks on the coffee table and kitchen island. The smell of cake filled the air and a pot of sauce simmered on the stove.

"Man, I could get used to this," Frank said as Ashlee handed him a cold beer. "No wonder you stay here with them. If you get a bigger place, I'd rent a room. What the hell are you going to do when you get a new assignment and have to leave this behind?"

Ashlee paled. A pinched expression on her face, she glanced at Nick then away." Keep an eye on my sauce, Trent, I need to run to the store." Without waiting for a reply, she rushed out the door.

An hour later she returned with fresh bread that she cut up and placed on the counter.

Trent had rescued her cake.

Big bowls of pasta and meatballs were placed in front of everyone. "The sauce is better if it sits a day, but help yourselves to cake and more pasta."

Nick glanced at her. Since her return, she hadn't acknowledged him at all, pretending great busyness. Still pale, her eyes were red, and her hands shook.

"Stay as long as you like. I'm going to my room to catch up on schoolwork. Good night."

Lips pressed tightly together, she hurried away.

"She okay?" Trent turned to Nick, a surprised look on his face.

"Probably a migraine. She gets them sometimes. Or, we bore her silly. Ashlee isn't much into sports."

"Never saw her leave before, she always hangs out for the entire game."

Nick laughed. "For Mike, not the game. Pass me the parmigiana."

Trent handed Nick the cheese and dug into his own pasta with a happy sigh.

Nick stirred his food around and then excused himself to hit the head. Instead of going into the bathroom, he snuck into the bedroom where he found Ashlee crying.

"Sweetheart— "

"It never occurred to me, but you knew. You lied. This is just a temporary thing for you. How could you?" Ashlee used an edge of the blue comforter wrapped around her to wipe her face.

Nick sat beside her on the bed, and she hunched away from him. His heart sank.

"No, I never lied. If, and this a big if, Ash. If

Mike gets stationed somewhere else, or I do, then I'll apply for a transfer. If I don't get one, I swear to you, I'll retire. You're my wife, and I'll never leave you. Please stop crying. Nothing's changed."

To his dismay, she stopped crying, but clenched her teeth and glared at him. "Go away, Nick."

"Ash...."

"Go away!" she screamed in a furious whisper and pulled the blanket over her head.

Nick kissed her head or at least where he thought her head was. "Damn it, Ash, this isn't fair. I can't stay in here. Remember that I love you."

Nick returned to the living room, grabbed a beer and stood at the counter to drink it. When he thought he had enough control over his expression, he resumed his seat and faked interest in the game.

The game dragged on interminably.

"Got a date or something?" Trent nodded to the watch on Nick's wrist.

"Huh?"

"You're checking your watch every five minutes."

"Oh, no. Mike was supposed to call today, and I'm a little worried."

"Ahh... no wonder she ran from the room

crying. Tell her not to worry. You know how the phones are there. Broken half the time and a line a mile long the other."

Nick nodded and drank his beer. On the screen, someone made a good play that he didn't see. He let the excited comments wash over him, going through the motions of interest. He hated the pretense too.

It was late by the times his friends left. As soon as the door closed, he hurried to the bedroom. Ashlee had cried herself to sleep. Tear-streaked cheeks and mussed hair, she clutched Mike's pillow to her chest.

"Sweetheart." Nick kissed her cheek and smoothed her hair back. Bloodshot eyes glared at him. "Damn, I'm so sorry that took you off guard. But I meant what I said— we won't be separated."

Nick laid beside her and stroked her back, slipping his hand under Mike's sweatshirt she wore. Warm skin trembled under his hand as her breath hitched. Tears in his eyes, he clasped her right hand in his and kissed her ring.

She sobbed and clutched him.

"Don't let Mike take me away from you, Nicky."

"Never. You and I will be together forever." The tremble ceased, and he leaned over, pushing her into the mattress to kiss her. "I've been dying to do that all night."

A moan turned into a gasp as he ran his hand across her breast under her shirt, stopping to roll the nipple between his fingers. He kissed her again until she panted and fumbled with his belt.

The sweatshirt thrown in a corner, Nick used his tongue, licking and sucking the pink tips until they stood out hard and dark rose, then worked his way down her body as she writhed.

Her skin tasted sweet. Pure. She was all of those things and more. Laid there beneath him in just loose sweat pants Ashlee smiled up at him, love shining in her eyes. The sweat pants followed the shirt thrown into a corner.

His heart thudded in his chest. He'd never get used to the way she gazed at him. The mix of trust, love, and lust that was just for him. Still fully dressed, he spread her legs and licked until she came, the taste of her excitement intoxicating. The sweet, and somehow at the same time sexy, way she begged him to take her, thrilled him like never before in his life.

Hard and thick, his cock throbbed, making his jeans uncomfortably tight. One hand rested on the pulse pounding in her thigh, the other caressed her breast, the warm weight filling his hand.

"I love your breasts," he murmured as he ran his hand over them, fondling each and squeezing lightly. Released from the confines of a bra, her breasts jutted conically, not rounded, the tips hard peaks.

He squirmed back up her body and began sucking the rosy nipples as her back arched and her hands pressed him closer. He made love to her with his hands and mouth, telling her how much he loved her and promising they would be together forever before finally sliding inside her.

A low continuous moan came from her as she clutched his ass, pushing him deep.

Panting and moaning himself, he thrust into her. She was so wet his thighs were damp, and he made a loud squishing noise on every thrust. When she bucked against him with her orgasm, he let himself come as warm liquid trailed over his balls with her release. Her hands still pressed him tight against her as her body relaxed.

A soft disappointed sound brushed his ear when he slipped from her body, changing to a contented sound when he slid two fingers into her wetness. Inner muscles spasmed around his fingers as her orgasm continued.

Nick breathed in the scent of her skin, which was damp with perspiration and him, holding her close, two fingers still inside her. No one had ever responded to him like this, with such total abandon and trust. The enthusiasm for which she greeted his advances and reciprocated filled him with lust. Too soon for his body to respond, he used his fingers instead.

"Oh God, Nicky." Ashlee keened his name as he rubbed inside her, harder when her muscles clenched, soft and light when they relaxed. Her hips jerked against his fingers uncontrollably as she screamed his name and came again.

Legs shaking and panting hard, she crawled onto his chest, burying her face in his neck. "Never leave me," she murmured and sighed in contentment when he hugged her tight.

She fell asleep there, relaxed and happy. He held her for hours without sleeping, deep in thought.

-6-
A WOMAN OF REAL STRONG OPINIONS

"Something wrong, sweetheart?" Nick asked as he entered.

Ashlee gave him a wan smile.

Normally, when he came home, she was in the kitchen cooking, textbooks or cookbooks spread out on the kitchen island. Always she greeted him with a hug and a deep kiss. Today, she slouched on the couch, not a book in sight just a crumpled piece of stationary discarded on the coffee table.

"My ma wrote, and she wants to see me." White teeth nibbled her bottom lip as she handed him the paper.

Nick sat beside her and read the letter, his frown growing deeper with every word.

"Aye, she's that crazy. As soon as I could, I came here to be with my da instead. I know I'm supposed to love the woman, but she makes it so hard."

"Well, you can't go, not alone, and Mike won't be home for another month."

"I don't want to go at all, but she's my ma."

Nick read the letter again. "Will you be safe there with her?"

"Oh aye, she stopped trying to beat the devil out of me when I got big enough to hit back."

Nick winced. "I didn't realize… I mean, you said you were brought up strict Catholic, but I didn't think people like this still existed. Mixed marriages are common here. Is she really this upset because Mike isn't Catholic?"

Ashlee let out a snort of laughter. "I might as well have married a devil in her view. Mike won't be welcome there, so I'm writing her back and telling her if she can't accept Mike and treat him decent, I won't be returning to Ireland."

"Do you miss your home? We could vacation there without telling your mother."

"Wherever you and Mike are, is my home. Honestly, I don't think the woman ever loved me. She hated my father so much, taking me was her way of punishing him."

Ashlee rubbed the small scar on her arm where the birth control implant was. "When we have children, what will we do?"

"I don't know, but we have time to decide."

Ashlee smiled and climbed into his lap. "True, but I want your child someday, Nick. Holy mother of God, my ma would freak if she knew about you or this." Again, she rubbed the small scar. "Thwarting Gods will, you know. A secret devil worshiper I've become. Orgies and taking the Lord's name in vain. If she had her way… well, I'd be a nun cloistered away to save me from burning in Hell. No man allowed near to cause me to sin."

"She hates men then?"

"With a passion. Except for the good fathers of course. But she's convinced men all have one goal."

Nick laughed. "And she wouldn't be wrong, but some of us love too."

"Oh aye," Ashlee's voice deepened. "Some of you love very well."

✳ ✳ ✳

Two weeks later, Nick pushed the door open with an elbow, both arms full of groceries.

"Hey, sweetheart, I picked up the peppers you asked for—"

"Nick, we have company." The strained sound of Ashlee's voice had Nick's head spinning to her as his hands clutched the bags tighter.

A woman with dyed black hair caught in a

tight bun on the back of her head, not a hair out of place, perched on the couch beside Ashlee. She sat ramrod straight with her legs crossed at the ankles and a teacup in her hand.

Age was difficult to place. The pinched haughty look on her face aged her, but Nick guessed late forties. Ashlee was taller and slimmer with a more delicate bone structure. The only real resemblance was the eyes. Brilliant blue eyes that on Ashlee sparkled with life and love, and on her mother appeared cold and hard.

"Oh, hello, I didn't realize you had a guest. This must be your mother." Nick kicked the door shut with one foot and continued into the small kitchen where he set the groceries on the counter.

Ashlee jumped up and joined him, helping to put the canned goods away, giving him an anxious glance.

Nick gave Ashlee a reassuring smile and a wink, left her in the kitchen, and offered a hand to her mother.

"And you must be Nicholas Rossi, the husband's friend. " Margret Conner frowned and shook his hand with her fingertips, then wiped her hand on her shapeless black dress, which hung on her stocky frame.

"Now, Ma, I just told you Nick lives here.

And yes, he's a good friend of both my husband and me."

"It's not proper to be living with a man not your husband. Not that you have a proper husband either, but that's water under the bridge. No need to be completely outside propriety though. American mores or not, some things just aren't done."

Ashlee sighed and leaned over the counter with both hands braced. "Mother, Nick lives here, and that's the end of it."

"Oh, aye, and I get no say in the upbringing of my only child. The minute you came here I knew this would happen. Disregard the teachings of the church for a life of ease here in the states. You're just like your father."

"Da was a good man." Ashlee took a deep breath and straightened, going to her mother and taking her hands. "Let's not fight over my father. Whatever your issue with him, you must have loved him once to marry him and remain married all this time."

Margret snatched her hands back and rose, tapping her foot encased in clunky black shoes. "Divorce is a construct of man, God doesn't recognize it. Marriage is a sacrament that once entered into can't be undone. God doesn't condone your marriage, child. Please, reconsider and come home. Don't make the same mistakes I did and fall for a handsome face. Learn from my suffering."

Ashlee snorted and leaned back in the chair. "What suffering, Ma? Da supported you till the day he died and never once did you attempt to reconcile. The letters he sent, you burned unopened. The calls you refused for both of us. That was your choice, not mine. And cruel. What right did you have to take me from him and deny me access to him, or him to me?"

Ashlee waved her hands and took a deep breath. "Never mind. As you say, water under the bridge, but this is my life, and Mike is my husband. Stop speaking ill of him when you've never even met him. No matter what you say, he'll always be my husband. Always, Ma! You're welcome to visit, but not if you speak ill of Mike. This is his home, and you'll respect him whether he's here or no."

Margret placed her hands on her hips and glared. "Needs must if I'm to see my child. Wait, daughter, when you've a child of your own and see them making a tragic mistake and they turn from your guidance. Now, where am I to sleep?"

Ashlee rubbed her eyes as she jumped to her feet. "My room, Ma. Nick stays in the guest room."

Nick picked up the small black suitcase by

the door and headed to the bedroom, trying to wipe the frown from his face.

Ashlee had made the bed that morning. No evidence remained of his presence, and his frown deepened. In the bedroom he shared with her there should be some sign of him.

The room lacked personal belongings of any type. No brick-a-brack decorated the dressers, only one picture sat on a nightstand. A wedding portrait. Mike in his dress uniform and Ashlee in a pale pink gown, both looking scared and excited.

None of Nick's clothes hung in the closet or lay on the floor. An almost overwhelming compulsion to mess the room, make his mark on it, made his hands clench. Ashlee was his, and he wanted everyone to know it. The world thought she was Mike's. Not even her mother knew different. A hot wave of jealousy rippled his skin, leaving him feeling flushed and sick.

Margret followed him into the room. "Leave it. Thank you. The trip was tiring. If you don't mind, I'll nap before dinner." Her hand on the door, she gestured him out. Another wave, this time of anger, coursed over him. This room was his.

Nick nodded and left her in his bedroom.

Ashlee glanced up from the kitchen counter where she'd spread ingredients for dinner and winced. She leaned over and peered down the hall, then kissed him quickly, hurrying from his embrace to resume the cooking, a scowl on her face.

"Sorry, Nick. I had no idea she was coming. The sight of her on our doorstep shocked me."

"How long is she staying, Ash?"

"No idea, but not too long, I wouldn't think."

Nick sighed and hugged her, resting his chin on her head. "Not your fault, and she is your mother, but I hate we can't be together in our own home."

Ashlee's grip tightened, and she burrowed her face in his neck as she nodded. "I always hate that, Nick. Not being yours. No one knowing what I feel for you. The guys teasing you about dating or trying to set you up and having to pretend I'm not wildly jealous."

"Oh, sweetheart." Nick drew back and framed her face with his hands. Tears filled her eyes. The ones that trailed on her cheeks he wiped away with his thumbs. "I'm sorrier than I can say that I hurt you."

Down the hall, the door opened, and Ashlee jerked away from him, wiping her cheeks on her sleeve, then running cold water in the sink and washing her face.

Nick stood in the center of the room, not knowing what to do.

Margret didn't come in. She entered the bathroom and shut the door.

"I'm so sorry," Nick whispered and plodded to his room.

Dust puffed from the bedspread when he flopped on the bed. He hadn't slept in here for months. Experimentally, he bounced on the mattress, and it creaked, a loud metallic squeal. Shit, even if he fixed the damn bed she couldn't sneak in right across the hall from her mother. An arm thrown over his eyes, he laid there and moped.

The smell of pot roast and potato filled the room. After heaving a heavy sigh, he went to join them for dinner.

Margret was complaining about the laundry as he entered the kitchen.

"—Not decent." Margret glanced at him and stopped speaking, her lips compressed.

Ashlee rubbed her temple as if she had a headache. "Ma, stop already, it's just clothes. Which I wash." A sudden giggle surprised Nick and by her mother's expression, annoyed Margret. "Nick doesn't care if I see his underwear. Believe me, he's just glad he needn't do his own washing."

Nick laughed and sat at the counter. "Clean laundry is one of the best things about civilian life. That, and the food. Mike must dream about these meals." He winked at Ashlee, and she giggled again.

Margret glared at him. "Hmmph."

Ashlee offered her mother wine, which she accepted. Margret sipped the wine, then gestured at the living room. "Where do you eat dinner? No proper home lacks a dining table."

"At the counter here, like this, or in the living room, whichever we prefer. The apartment's too small for a dining table. Where would we put it?" Not glancing up from the salad she was preparing, Ashlee missed the sneer her mother directed at her home.

Nick didn't miss it but said nothing. Every moment he liked this woman less.

Throughout dinner, Margret complained. Complained about everything, the flight over, the weather, the food. Constant criticism phrased as advice that set his teeth on edge.

"Ashlee, the meal was wonderful as always. Thank you." Nick gave a hostile glance to her mother as he rose and brought his plate to the sink. "Go visit with your mother. I'll do dishes."

"Ashlee Claire Conner, that is no way to treat a guest! Haven't I taught you any manners at all?" Margret jumped up and snatched the dish from Nick's surprised grasp.

A glower on his face, he plucked it back and leaned over the sink. "I'm not a guest. I live here."

Ashlee put a hand on his arm a moment after she placed the dishes she carried on the counter.

"Ma, Nick doesn't mind. Let's me and you go talk and get reacquainted. I haven't seen you in four years."

Margret huffed and flounced to the living room and again sat ramrod straight with her legs crossed at the ankle. "Tell me of your studies, child."

Ashlee spoke about her classes and school friends, and Nick realized she never had any friends over. Since 'marrying' him, she'd kept herself isolated. A deep frown on his face now, Nick sat at the counter listening to them speak. Something needed to be done about that.

"Tomorrow, I'll accompany you and meet your friends. High time for me to be more involved. I let your father keep you from me when I should've come and demanded you return." Margret waved her hand as Ashlee began to speak. "No. No need to rehash all that. Mistakes are plentiful enough for everyone. Let's move on from here. The letters you sent leave me interested in seeing your school. It won't be an inconvenience, I hope?"

"No, Ma, of course not. Tomorrow I'll show you around the campus."

"Very good." Margret rose and nodded at Nick. "I'm off to bed then, good night." Another nod to Ashlee and she marched from the room.

As soon as the door closed behind her mother, Ashlee exhaled loudly and flopped back in her seat.

Nick chuckled and sat in the chair across from her. "A force of nature your mother. A woman of real strong opinions."

Ashlee grabbed a couch pillow, hugged it, and heaved a deep sigh. "Oh, you don't know. She's being real polite, and it's making me a bit nervous."

One eyebrow lifted and the corner of Nick's mouth quirked. "That was polite?"

Eyes closed and head tipped back on the couch, Ashlee nodded. "Oh aye, excruciatingly polite. Not once did she tell me to sit straighter, or speak in a more decorous tone." Ashlee sat up and cracked a grin at him.

"When I turned sixteen, I begged my da to take me, and I'm sure he nearly had a heart attack when I arrived. I was so intoxicated with my new freedom, I was a bit of a wild woman."

A smile tugged at Nick's lips, and he let out a sharp laugh.

"Oh aye, you canna picture it, but I assure you, I was a handful, staying out late, loud music, and dressing— as me ma would say – the complete slut. The poor man was way over his head, but the very soul of kind acceptance."

Tears sparkled on her eyelashes. "I forgive my mother for the harsh upbringing. In her view, she was trying to bring me up right, but no matter how hard I try, I canna forgive her for taking me from me da. To deny me contact with him was cruel. Never mind how it hurt him. Every year he came, and when I ran to him, she would make him go."

Ashlee rubbed her eyes and laid her head on the seat back. "I would cry and cling to his leg, and he would beg her, but the law is the law, and he had to leave. And once he left, she would beat me for clinging to him. When I was seven, she had the property fenced and gated so he couldn't reach the door unannounced and locked me in my room when he was due to come.

"I used to love that house. The shore is so close you can smell the salt air and hear the seagulls. Every day I went down to the beach and explored. No other houses are close; all my friends were imaginary. Once that fence went up, it made the house forbidding instead of quaint. A twelve-foot fence is a might imposing. You couldn't even see the house from the road; the gate blocked the view completely. After that, it felt isolated. Not a castle on a hill, but a cold, stone prison."

Nick leaned forward and placed a hand on her knee. "She beat you?"

"Oh aye. Had a stick in the kitchen and carried a wooden spoon. Believe me, I was a most obedient child." Ashlee sat up and patted his hand, a small smile on her face. "Don't go feeling sorry for me. Discipline is different here. Even the teachers there would give your palm a good whack if you weren't performing to their standards. Granted, my ma was more enthusiastic than most, but she stopped when I grew big enough to hit back. From the age of twelve to sixteen we lived together without hardly speaking.

"My poor da…" Ashlee stifled a laugh and glanced towards the dark hallway. "I'm ever so grateful I got the time with him I did. Patrick Conner was a wonderful, loving man. To this day, I've no idea why he married my ma, although I can see why he left her. She's a terrible hard person to love."

Nick laughed, leaned forward, and kissed her.

For a moment, she returned the kiss, then pulled away and glanced guiltily at the dark hallway again.

Nick sighed and rose. "I love you, and I'm

more grateful than words can express you take after your father," he whispered as he ran a hand along her cheek.

A pillow still clutched to her chest, Nick left her alone on the couch and went to his lonely bed.

-7-
ACCEPT THESE FACTS

Ashlee drove her mother to the school in the morning and gave her a quick tour.

"What dorm did you stay in?" Margret gazed about with wide eyes, which narrowed on the girls in shorts and tank tops sitting in the grass.

"This one here." Ashlee parked in front of a four-story, red brick building and held the door for her mother. "My friend Kurt still lives here… and my old roommate. Would you like to meet them?"

Friends greeted Ashlee and said hello to her mother as they rushed to class.

"Kurt and I take a bunch of classes together. He's one of my best friends here."

Her mother made a noncommittal noise and followed her into the elevator. The ride to the fourth floor was silent. Ashlee knocked on

Kurt's door.

Kurt opened the door in sleep pants with no shirt; a grin lit his face when he saw her.

"Ash! You haven't stopped by in ages." He gave her a hug then turned to her mother. "This must be your mom. Nice to meet you. Kurt Brennan." Kurt held out his hand. "Ash and I met our second year."

A delighted smile on her face, Margret kept Kurt's hand in hers. "You've a touch of the Irish about you boyo."

Kurt laughed and ran a hand through his red hair. "More than a touch. Grandad brought the family over from Dublin when my dad was six-years-old and still speaks the Gallic to us young 'uns."

"So, you're a proper Catholic then?"
Ashlee winced. "Ma!"

A half-smile on his lips, Kurt winked a bright green eye at Ashlee. "On Sundays, ma'am."

The smile on Margret's face faltered then firmed. "It's so nice to know Ashlee had some good Christian friends." She released Kurt's hand and turned to Ashlee. "Will your old roommate be Irish as well?"

Kurt snickered and covered his mouth with his hand. "No, ma'am. Sydney is as American as apple pie. I admit the name can be misleading. With a name like Sydney O'Hare one expects an Irish ancestor or two, but as far as I know, she has none." Kurt turned to Ashlee. "Give me a minute to dress, and I'll meet you in the common room, and we can take your mom for one of our famous breakfast tours."

Ashlee laughed, nodded, and led her mother away by the elbow as Kurt closed his door.

"Breakfast tour?" Margret lifted a quizzical brow.

"A string of food carts we bought from as we ran to class in the mornings. We always slept late and had to rush. Since I married Mike, we haven't of course."

Margret stopped and faced Ashlee, her lips in a tight line and nostrils flaring. "That nice boy was a lover?"

Ashlee stopped shocked. "What? Kurt? No, never. He's a good friend."

"Who you sleep with?" Margret sniffed and turned away.

"Ma, don't be ridiculous. Kurt has always been a friend, just a friend. And so what if he had been a lover? Jeez, you can be so narrow-minded and judgmental. Can't we just have a nice day?"

Margret smoothed her black dress. "Yes.

And I don't disapprove of Kurt. On the contrary, a nice Catholic boy would be welcome."

"Ma, I told you a billion times I'm married to *Mike*, drop it already, okay?"

"Ashlee," Sydney said in a mocking tone as she came up behind them.

"Oh sorry, Sydney, didn't see you." Ashlee took a deep breath and rubbed the heels of her hands across her cheekbones once then introduced her mother.

"Sydney and I were roommates for a few months before I married."

"A pleasure, Miss O'Hare." Margret held out her hand.

A smirk on her face, Sydney shook Margret's hand. "I never believed they were just friends either," she said in smarmy voice. "Ash never came partying with us without him."

"Sydney!" The glare Ashlee directed at Sydney had no effect except to widen the smirk.

"Relax, I'm kidding. No one can blame you for dumping Kurt for Mike. Mike's a hottie."

Ashlee crossed her arms and tipped her head. "Kurt and I never dated, never!" She threw up her arms and spun away. "Oh, who cares anyways? Come on, Ma. Nice to see you,

Sydney."

Ashlee took her mother's hand and dragged her to the elevator.

Margret glanced back as Sydney knocked on a door and kissed the boy who answered, laughing as she pushed him into the room. Lips tight, Margret turned back to face the elevator door.

"That girl was your roommate?" Cold and contemptuous, her voice laced with disapproval, Margret scowled at Ashlee.

"For the last few months. My original roommate transferred when her family moved. Stacy was a really nice girl, and we still keep in touch. You would like her, Ma."

"Hmmph."

Ashlee sighed and pushed the down button.

"So, how'd it go today?" Nick handed Ashlee a soda and flopped down beside her on the couch in their living room.

"Long… the day was excruciatingly long. I'm surely bound for Hell, breaking all these commandments. I can't wait for her to leave."

Nick laughed and patted her knee. He wanted to kiss her, but her mother would be back any moment, the sharp rap of her high heels announced her imminent arrival.

Ashlee jumped up when her mother arrived

and scurried to the kitchen to serve dinner.

After dinner, they watched a movie together that none seemed to enjoy. Margret headed to bed after giving Nick a pointed glance.

Nick waited until the bedroom door closed with a soft thump before pulling Ashlee into his arms. Not giving her time to speak or retreat, he kissed her hard, pressing her tight against his chest.

More than anything he wanted to feel her naked body against his, not for sex, but for closeness. Not feeling like he belonged with her was killing him.

A moment later she pulled away. "Nick..."

He heaved a heavy sigh and left her in the living room. In his room, he tossed and turned for two hours before giving up. On tiptoe, he snuck down the hall.

"Nick," Ashlee hissed in a whisper when he appeared.

"Shh, you'll wake the dragon," he murmured as he stifled a chuckle and knelt beside her on the floor, glad she missed him and couldn't sleep without him either.

Ashlee reached for him, running her hand under his t-shirt, her kiss hot and deep.

A low moan escaped him. Wrapped in a blanket, wearing a t-shirt he'd left in the laundry and a pair of old sweatpants, she'd never looked more beautiful to him. He slipped his hand beneath the t-shirt to caress her breast while he cradled her head.

The nipple hardened and her back arched as she pressed his lips to hers, deepening the kiss.

"Oh God, Nicky, we can't." Panting hard, she pushed him away.

"I know; I just need to touch you." His voice lowered. "I want to touch you everywhere."

A shivery breath of a moan met that statement, and she sat.

He squatted on his heels. "Could we—" He'd been about to say sneak away when the light flipped on.

"What's all this then?" Margret's gimlet stare flicked over them.

Ashlee bolted to her feet, her hands clutching the blanket in fists.

"Not the proper thing at all, is it, young man? Take yourself out!"

"No! Nick lives here, Mother." Ashlee took a deep breath and squared her shoulders. "This is my home, and he stays if I say so."

"Listen to me, young lady. Anyone can see this leading to trouble. He goes, or I call your husband myself and warn him. The man might no be a Christian, but I am. And the good Lord knows this is trouble. Or is it already too late? Are you already committing adultery with this man?"

Ashlee paled and grabbed Nick's arm.

He didn't remember moving to her side. The venom in her mother's tone surprised him as if she relished the opportunity to rant. If a stranger spoke to Ashlee that way he would beat the crap out of him, but this was her mother, and he wasn't sure what to do or say.

"Well, young lady?" Margret's gimlet stare traveled them.

Ashlee suddenly laughed, a hard, bitter laugh. "Yes, it's too late. Nick and I are in love and go ahead, call Mike. Call whomever you please. Nothing will change that." Ashlee dropped the blanket and kissed him.

Automatically, Nick's arms closed around her.

Still in his arms, she turned to her mother who stared open-mouthed.

"Mike already knows. How my husband and I live is no one's business, and I don't need your approval. I'm sorry, Ma, I wish I could be the kind of daughter you want, but I can't."

"What's that supposed to mean— he knows? Are you divorcing already?" Margret pinched her bottom lip with two fingers then dropped her hand, clenching them into fists at her side. "Ashlee, divorce…." She trailed off and took a deep breath before starting again.

"Daughter, the marriage with Michael Evans isn't sanctified by God, but that doesn't mean you can have sex with whomever you choose. As much as I would prefer you to marry a Christian man, a good Catholic, I can't condone this… fornication," she finally spat.

"No, you misunderstand. I'm not leaving Mike for Nick. I'm sorry that you dislike Mike so much when you've never even met the man. Yes, Nick is technically Catholic, but he isn't a church-goer. Neither of us is. Honestly, Ma, because of you I will never be Catholic. My children won't be Catholic."

"What are you babbling about?"

Ashlee sighed and rubbed her forehead. "Accept these facts, mother. Mike and I are married. Nick and I are in love, married in our hearts. My husband not only knows but supports this. In fact, it was his idea. At no time will I become a good Catholic or a Catholic of any sort."

Margret paled and swayed. "Worse than I considered," she mumbled, then shouted, "Repent daughter! This isn't love but lust. The devil's dirty lust and it will lead to destruction. If not here on Earth, surely in Hell."

"Ma—"

Margret ignored her and ranted, yelling bible verses between insults in an increasingly sharp tone.

"Enough!" Nick bellowed and grabbed Margret's arm, pulling her towards the bedroom. "My wife isn't a whore, and she isn't damned. Keep your filthy thoughts to yourself."

Nick continued speaking over Margret's increasingly loud insults. "Stay in this room until you can speak civilly or get the hell out of our house. My wife deserves respect in her home, not foul abuse!"

"Your wife?" Margret spat on the floor. "This is the devil's work and no marriage."

Nick grabbed her and shook her. "Shut up, woman. Think before you utter another word. Ashlee, your daughter, is my wife in all ways that count. Because you're her mother, I can forgive this, knowing what a shock it is. Take time to think before you do or say anything you'll regret."

Margret pulled away and slapped him. "Regret? I regret raising such a creature. Not content to live her own life of sin, she draws in the surrounding people, encouraging them to unholy lust. No child of emine…." Outrage caused her breath to hitch, and she had to take a moment to compose herself. "From this moment, I have no daughter. That foul creature—"

Nick pushed her into the room and slammed the door.

Ashlee stood trembling in the living room. Nick grabbed her hand and pulled her out the front door, snatching her keys from the hook as he passed. "Come on. Let her cool down in private where her shrew's tongue can't hurt us. I'm sorry, sweetheart, I didn't mean to cause this wedge."

Ashlee nodded and got in the car, her face white and eyes shocked and worried. "Can she cause trouble for Mike? Or you?"

Nick shrugged. "Maybe, if she really tries. How hard do you think she'll try?"

"I'm not sure. If I had to guess, I'd say she'll call Mike and rant at him, but I can't see her admitting I'm such a whore to anyone else. Makes her look bad. But I really couldn't say."

Angry at her self-loathing tone, Nick slapped his hand on the steering wheel. "Damn it, Ash, you aren't a whore. That woman is crazy."

Nick turned the car off before pulling out of the driveway and placed a hand on her shoulder. "No matter what she says, or who to, nothing will change how I feel for you. I'm proud of you, never doubt it. For your sake, I wish I hadn't formed this wedge between you, but for my own, I'm happy you claim me."

A snort of bitter laughter was quickly stifled as Ashlee pulled away and stared from her window.

"Childish dreams, Nick. That's all it is. All my life I wanted a mother who loved me. The kind you see on television who praise and care and support no matter what. And I kept trying to please her, even when I never did, not once. I don't like her. God knows I want to, but I don't. So it should come as no surprise she doesn't like me either."

"The woman is impossible to like. No one could blame you." He trailed a hand over her soft hair before gripping the steering wheel again.

"It's still hard giving up the dream." She shuddered, and she covered her face with her hands.

"Oh, sweetheart. I'll love you enough for ten thousand people." Nick pulled her close as she cried on his shoulder.

Margret stormed from the building, dragging her suitcase. Her narrow-eyed gaze narrowed further at the car. Head high, she whirled away.

The next morning Margret took a cab to the university and pounded on Kurt's door.

Half asleep, Kurt answered.

Margret slapped him. "Slake your unnatural lusts with my daughter and pay the price in Hell!"

"What the…?" Kurt lifted a hand to his cheek and jerked back. Doors up and down the hallway opened, and students peered out as Margret shouted.

"My daughter was a good girl until she came here. Whether she influenced you, enticing you to sin, or it was your idea, change your ways, boy, before it's too late. It's too late for the whore I raised, but maybe you can be redeemed. And to think I believed her lies yesterday. Sure, and you're just friends. You answering the door in your underwear and hugging her, mauling her with your eyes. I saw the lustful way you stared."

"Look, Mrs. Conner, I don't know what you're on about, but Ashlee and me—"

"Makes no never mind to me, boy. I came to warn you. You think you're special to her when nothing could be further from the truth. She's not content with only one man. Don't go getting ensnared with her. Repent while you can." Margret's scathing gaze raked him, and she spun on her heel and stalked off.

A few boys came into the hallway, laughing as she left, while Kurt's roommate congratulated him for landing Ashlee after years of pursuit.

"It isn't true. Ashlee and I never dated or anything. Her mom's a nut. Who does that anyways?"

Sydney gave a low, throaty chuckle. "Told ya she was a slut. The good girl act was just that, an act."

Kurt rolled his eyes. "Slut, really? How many guys on this floor alone have you fucked?"

Sydney turned red, and Kurt laughed. "Never mind. I don't have time for you to count that high. And who the hell cares anyways? Fuck whoever you want. Just leave Ashlee out of it. Why ruin her reputation because you have none?"

The girl staring out the door opposite laughed, the laugh growing as Sydney glared. "He's got you there, Syd. Every girl on this floor knows about you. If you don't want a reputation, keep it in your pants." Still laughing, the girl shut her door.

Sydney slammed hers.

"Jesus, no one tells Ashlee about this, she would be mortified." Kurt sighed and closed his door.

- 8 -
I'm Not Warning You Again

When Nick and Ashlee returned home, her mother was gone. Before she'd left, she'd dumped the kitchen garbage in their bed. Ashlee's shoulders hunched when she saw it. Nick cheeks heated in furious anger. He pulled Ashlee from the room and slammed the door.

"Don't worry, or even think about that. By the time you get home from school, it'll be cleaned up. I'll call Mike and warn him. Please, sweetheart, don't let her pettiness ruin what we have. Go shower, and I'll bring you clothes."

A kiss on her brow followed by a light shove toward the bathroom and Ashlee reluctantly left his side.

As soon as Ashlee left the house, Nick stripped the bed, throwing everything away, sheets, blankets, and all. Then he called Mike and left a message that Ashlee's mother had visited and wasn't happy and Mike should call him as soon as he could.

All day long he expected Margret to show up at his work and make a scene. But the day passed like any other. Part of the day he spent on the range, showing the new recruits the correct way to hold a rifle and shoot.

The job usually interested him. As much as he missed combat, the thrill of the chase, a stalk that ended in violence and bloodshed, life with Ashlee made up for that. The life he led now, teaching and going home to her at night was good, and he wouldn't trade it. Not even for his old command.

The peaceful existence he lived now was a shock for him. Never before had he had peace. An abusive home life and indifferent parenting led him to gang life as a child. Wanting something more, something better, he'd joined the service right out of high school, serving a full tour then attending sniper school and serving another, all on the front lines. First in Afghanistan then Iraq.

The middle east was his playground. He was comfortable there with the hard life and hard men and had expected to die there violently someday. Then an injury sidelined him, replacing one life he loved with another

The only thing he would change about his life was Mike. Not that he minded the sex, he liked the sex, he minded the sharing of her life. Not being able to claim her publicly was a problem, one he needed to solve. For her own good, they needed to change. The isolation of her life with him wasn't good. He'd been so caught up in his own life he hadn't noticed the lacks in hers till now.

The office chair creaked as Nick swiveled side-to-side; end of the day paperwork sat untouched on his desk. To fix the problems in his life, he needed to be her husband, nothing else would do. The problem was Mike would never agree unless Ashlee asked. And even then… he ran the risk of Mike saying him or me.

The risk would always remain no matter how she felt for him, Mike was her legal husband. Children would trump marriage to Mike. If he could get her pregnant, he could convince her to marry him for the sake of their child. At least he hoped he could. The implant in her arm was a problem. With no way to remove it without her knowledge or consent, he was stymied. Nick sighed and stood. This problem wouldn't be solved in a day or here. He headed home.

Outside his apartment building Steven

Wrint, a friend of Mike's, hailed him.

"Hey, Nick, I was wondering if you guys are gonna watch the game this weekend?"

"Trent's hosting this week." Nick paused. Steven seemed oddly excited, shooting him glances from half-lowered lids.

"Yeah, okay, I'll call him. I actually stopped by to see Ashlee."

Nick tensed. The grin on Steven's face made him edgy. "Really?"

"Well, I heard some news I thought she might want to hear herself. Mike's coming home next week for two weeks."

"Really?" Nick repeated louder. The grin on Steven's face was now a full-blown leer as if his internal thoughts were completely disjointed from what he said aloud. "How do you know?"

"Cut the orders myself." Steven tapped his wrist. "Aide-de-camp now for the big man himself. Once the doc clears my wrist, I'll rejoin my unit, another six months or so."

"Good of you to come tell her." Nick gestured Steven to proceed him.

Steven paused before the elevator. "What about you, Nick? Will you be moving out before he gets back?" Steven snickered. "I met her mother. That woman is a certifiable nut, but if she speaks to Mike, well, I'm sure he'll kick your ass from here to the middle east."

"Goddamn it!" Nick pulled Steven aside, away from the open elevator door and glanced around. "Where the hell did you meet her and what did she say?"

"Relax, I can keep a secret. She didn't go to headquarters if that's what you're worried about. I won't say a word. Wouldn't mind being friends with Ashlee myself."

Nick clenched his fists. "It's not like that. Don't talk about her like that."

"Sure, sure, whatever you say. Her mom seems to think otherwise."

Nick grabbed Steven by the collar and shook him. "I'm not fucking around here. What did she say and where? Mike's your friend, man. That woman can ruin his career."

"Nah, I ran into her here like five minutes ago. Her and a blonde chick, Sydney something or other. Anyways, she was going off about her daughter fornicating, I kid you not. That's the actual word she used, fornicating and enticing men to the devil. She saw me punch for Ashlee's apartment and grabbed my arm, warning me I'm going to Hell and the entire time the blonde is smirking behind her hand. Anyways, the mother finally storms off. The blonde stayed, seemed convinced I was one of Ashlee's lovers. We got a date for later."

Steven paused and leaned against the wall beside the elevator. "So, what's going on? Are you and Ashlee?"

"No, not that it's any of your business."

Steven glared and pushed away from the wall. "Fine, not my business. Lie all you want, but as you said, Mike's my friend. Why should I keep quiet for you? You're the only one who's career is on the line, screwing another officer's wife. Sure, he'll be embarrassed, his new wife couldn't wait a few months and—"

Nick punched him in the stomach. Steven let out a sharp oof and doubled over as Nick held up his hands and stepped back.

"Sorry, man, lost my temper. Look, it isn't like that. Ash and I… shit." Nick rubbed his fingers through his hair. "This goes no further, and you say a damn thing I'll swear you're a fucking liar."

Steven grinned, a hard shine in his eye, and leaned against the wall, one hand rubbing his stomach. "This better be good, Nick."

Nick snorted. "Fuck you. Tell Mike. Just tell him privately. Don't embarrass him. He knows already."

"Like fuck he does. You living here with her— No fucking way."

Nick nodded slowly. "That's what I'm telling you. We share her; he knows, and it was his idea."

Steven lurched upright. "No fucking way!"

"Look, don't tell anyone. Pretend you don't know. Ashlee would be embarrassed too, not just Mike."

"How the fuck did you talk him into it. How'd ya talk her into it? She doesn't seem the type at all."

"I didn't talk them into it, he offered, and she isn't the type. Ashlee is sweet and loves me. She loves Mike too and did it for him, but now, well, it's more. She loves me, and I love her."

"He fucking offered?" Steven lifted an eyebrow and then peered at the elevator with a speculative gaze. "And she agreed, just like that?"

"Don't even fucking think it. Mike and I are tight. It isn't casual. Touch her, Hell, even think about touching her, and I'll kill you."

"Don't get your panties in a twist. Can't a blame guy for being interested; she's a nice piece of ass."

Nick clenched his fists so tight his nails bit into his palms.

Steven slapped him on the shoulder and scratched his balls. "I'm chill, man. Only room for two at the inn, I get it. And you're the home fires. Wish I had me a friend like you. Go off to war, come home to a nice cozy house, the woman ready and raring to go with no bull crap. Mike's got it made. You do all the husband bullshit, and he gets all the pussy."

"Steven… I'm not warning you again. That's my wife you're talking about, not some street whore."

Steven grinned and waved both hands. "Right, got it, you two are serious." Steven snickered. "Well, you three."

"Leave her alone, man. I hear one fucking word of this anywhere, and I know what hole I gotta plug; you get me?"

"Will do. Tell her the news yourself. Man, you lucky son of a bitch. Bet that news gets her all hot. Glad I got a date tonight." Still chuckling, Steven headed out.

Nick glared after him. "Well, fuck," he muttered and rubbed his forehead.

Not knowing if he'd made things better or worse by confirming Margret's rant, he headed upstairs to tell Ashlee Mike was coming home.

-9-

NICK AND I ARE SO HAPPY YOU'RE HOME

Nick drove Ashlee to the airport and waited in the car.

Mike arrived on a military plane and was welcomed by a grinning Ashlee. He dropped his bag and swung her into his arms while she cried and covered his face with kisses. Other soldiers greeted their wives and sweethearts in much the same way.

Bag in hand, and an arm around his wife's waist, they headed to the car. Ashlee leaned hard into his side, still kissing him with both arms around his waist. At the car, she crawled in the backseat with him.

"Good to see ya, man." Nick glanced in the rearview mirror and grinned.

Neither looked up at him.

"You too," Mike mumbled as he slid his hands under the dress Ashlee wore. A wide smile lit his face when he found nothing except

Ashlee underneath.

Ashlee straddled his lap, leaning back to undo his pants and free his rising erection. One hand on his face the other his cock, she kissed him as he hardened in her hand. A low moan came from her.

"Ash…"

"Mmm." She made an indistinct sound and sat astride him, both sighed deeply.

"Man, I could get used to this," Mike murmured as Ashlee swayed on top of him, rolling her hips, hands braced on the seat back, making love to him in the back of the car.

For a few minutes, only the sound of heavy breathing broke the silence in the car.

"Oh God," Ashlee groaned and wriggled harder. Her orgasm made her cry out and throw her head back.

Still hard inside her, Mike kissed her neck and undid the top buttons of her dress while she arched her back, jerking slightly with her orgasm. Once he'd undone enough buttons to free her breasts, he put his hands back on her hips while his mouth sought the pink nipple and sucked.

"Ahhh." A sound of contentment as his tongue danced across her nipple escalated into a breathy hum of desire.

Mike's hips jerked with his orgasm, and he

buried his face in her breasts, breathing deeply.

"I missed you, honey."

"Me too, Mike, so much." Both her hands pressed him to her breast. "Nick and I are so happy you're home."

Nick smiled. Even now with Mike's cock inside her, she thought of him, and her home was with him. In her heart, Mike was coming home to them, not her.

Mike caught it too, because he glanced up, a scowl on his face that smoothed when their eyes met in the mirror. A slow nod and a rueful smile crossed his face before he kissed Ashlee's cheek, working his way down her body.

"You two are going to get me arrested. Cover up back there," Nick said as he pulled up to a stoplight.

Ashlee's excitement excited him. Nick had been worried he would really resent Mike making love to Ashlee, but he was looking forward to the three of them too. Two weeks of hot sex with his best friend and then Ashlee would be all his again. He didn't know how Mike could stand leaving her with him, but he was glad he did.

Ashlee giggled and clutched her dress closed. Mike chuckled and pushed her down in the seat, kissing her breasts, taking each nipple into his mouth and sucking for a few seconds before moving to the next one.

"You hard yet, Nick?" he asked.

"Damn straight."

Mike chuckled again. "Ash, I been dreaming of you sucking me while he fucks you till you can't do anything except moan. Then I want to trade places and watch him come on you while I come inside you. How's that sound?"

"Oh aye, I can do that." Deep and low, Ashlee purred her response, the sound going right to Nick's groin.

Nick glanced at them again in the rear-view mirror. "Keep talking like that, and I'll only last a few minutes. You want long and hard we might have to do this again."

"That's good too," Ashlee said and moaned again.

"What's good? I can't see you. Was that comment for him or me?"

"Both." Ashlee giggled, the giggle changing to a breathy shout. Nick glanced into the backseat, but couldn't see anything except her head thrown back. Mike's body blocked the rest.

"Oh Jesus," Nick mumbled as he changed lanes. "You have five minutes, then you better be dressed enough to leave this car or I'm pulling you out just like that."

"Mmm." Ashlee made an indistinct noise, and again Nick didn't know if it was for him or Mike.

Hard and throbbing he needed to readjust himself as he drove, opening his fly and letting himself loose from the tight confines of his jeans.

Ashlee leaned over the seat, took him in her hand, and licked behind his ear, causing him to swerve. Both arms around Nick's neck Ashlee's warm breath skimmed his cheek as she spoke,

"Whatever you want while your home, Mike. For the next two weeks, you pick the positions. You're in charge, tell me how you want it."

Mike pulled her back down in the backseat. "Wait your turn, Nick. I get dibs."

Ashlee giggled and whimpered.

Nick drove faster.

The two weeks passed in a blur of fast food and love. The only time Ashlee cooked was Sundays for the games.

Steven showed up for the game and leered at Ashlee all night, making her uncomfortable and Nick angry.

Ashlee's mother hadn't seemed to have told anyone else except Mike, and Mike had told her to fuck off. When she threatened to go to his boss, he told her he would claim she was bitter because he turned her down and had friends that would lie for him. That seemed to shut her up.

Ashlee hadn't heard anything from her except for one letter postmarked Ireland begging Ashlee to come home and repent.

Ashlee had sent no reply. Nick was tempted to send a response but thought better of it. The less he had to do with that woman the better. No one spoke about her mother.

✵ ✵ ✵

"Ash, invite some friends to the game Sunday," Nick said as they sat down to eat the takeout he'd brought home.

Instead of making dinner at night Ashlee used that time to do homework so she'd have more time with Mike.

Ashlee glanced up from the textbook on the counter and pursed her lips. "The only close girlfriend I have lives too far away, but maybe she can come for a longer visit. Sydney chased all my other girlfriends off, but I can ask Kurt."

Mike laughed. "Give them time, they'll come around once they realize Sydney's nowhere near. You can hardly blame them. I never saw someone who wanted what others have so aggressively in my life."

Ashlee straddled his lap on the bar stool. "You were never tempted?"

"Not even a little bit. No one compares to you."

"Such a sweet talker," Ashlee murmured as she ran her hands under his t-shirt. The takeout grew cold on the counter.

✽ ✽ ✽

The Sunday before Mike left, Kurt came over for the game. Mike greeted Kurt with a handshake, then ignored him. Nick spoke with him during commercials, trying to get to know him, wanting to be friends with Ashlee's friends. Steven sat at the kitchen counter with Kurt, ogling Ashlee all night. He was going to have to do something about that.

That night in bed Ashlee complained about Steven to Mike.

"Don't invite him again, he gives me the creeps."

"Really?" He pulled her close and ran a hand over her body, settling it between her thighs.

"All night he stared at me. When he wasn't peeing, that is. That man pees more than anyone I know. He should see a doctor."

Mike chuckled and slid a finger inside her. "Sure, honey, if you don't like him, forget about him, he's uninvited."

Nick said nothing, continuing to undress as

he watched them.

"Your friend Kurt seems nice," Mike said as he rolled to face her and then traced her lower lip with his thumb.

Ashlee rolled her eyes. "You've met him before."

"Really?"

Ashlee laughed and spread her legs wider, reaching for Nick.

Nick smiled and took her hand, crawling onto the bed. While Mike used his fingers, he kissed her, enjoying the excited sounds she made. He reached down and felt her too, and she writhed. Both their hands on her making her so wet he could hear it.

"That's my girl," Mike murmured and kissed her left breast. Nick did the same on the right. Legs spread wide, she thrust against their fingers, holding their cocks in her hands.

"You going to come, Ash?" Mike asked. "Want me inside you?"

"God, yes," Ashlee keened as her legs spread even wider "Don't stop touching me, Nicky."

Nick withdrew his fingers and rubbed her clit instead as Mike slid inside her. The squelch from Mike's heaving hips was drowned out by her excited yell and Mike telling her how hot she was.

Ashlee squirted hard when she came. Warm

liquid trailed over Mike's balls and Nick's hand.

"Fuck yes!" Mike shouted and came, pulling out and spurting on her clit.

Nick pushed him aside and slid into her, going slow, enjoying the muscles spasming around his cock. In minutes she was begging him to go faster and harder, but he kept to the slow pace until she growled in frustration.

Mike laughed from his spot on her left side where he played with her nipples, licking and rubbing them between his finger and thumb.

Ashlee grunted beneath him, a harsh primal sound Nick matched. Body moving in sync with him, she was totally his, calling his name as her orgasm neared and her body tensed. Mike pulled her legs back, and Nick slammed into her as hard and fast as he could while she shuddered with her release. He'd wanted to come on her breasts, see his mark on her, but couldn't hold back. She screamed his name when he came.

Exhausted, he flopped onto the bed on her right side, and she curled into his arms, her sweaty brow resting on his chest.

"That was amazing, Nicky, I love you."

"Hey, what about me?" In mock outrage, Mike slapped her ass.

"I love you too, but your head is gonna swell

soon."

"Maybe in twenty minutes or so… if you're lucky."

Ashlee giggled, rolled over, and kissed him.

The next morning, when they saw Mike off, she didn't cry, only hugged him hard with tears in her eyes.

After Mike had left, she turned to Nick. "Make love to me, Nicky, just us. I missed you."

Nick smiled and kissed her, swinging her into his arms and laying her on the couch. "I missed just us too. Not that sex with Mike isn't awesome but…" he trailed off as her eyes fluttered closed, enjoying his caresses.

Poor Mike, he thought as Ashlee kissed him, the kiss full of love. Mike had sex with her, he and Ashlee made love. Soon he would be able to talk her into having his baby. He wasn't above using her upbringing to talk her into marrying him to raise their child. Maybe on Mike's next deployment so there would be no chance the child was his.

- 10 -
MAN, HE WANTED TO BE MIKE

Steven sat on a bar stool at the kitchen island; a long piece of off-white Formica that formed an L with the rest of the kitchen counter. Stacks of Tupperware with colorful lids lay across the countertop beside half-prepared plates of food. Various size bowls held herbs and chopped vegetables.

Ashlee hummed while she cooked. Not a constant sound, more of a finale as she completed a dish. Attention on her cooking, she barely spared Steven a glance, and he was getting annoyed.

Franton had received a hug when he came in and Inger a bright smile. Frank a laugh and a special drink handed to him right away. He got shit. A curt 'hello' and ignored. All night Ashlee brought dishes to Franton, asking his opinion, or staring at him eat.

Steven swiveled on his seat and examined Franton. The man was big, not muscular like Mike, but husky and old. At a guess, Steven thought he was late thirties to mid-forties. Franton had graying black hair and the bushiest eyebrows he'd ever seen. *Dude must be hung like a horse for her to fawn over him all night.*

Steven's gaze flitted to Inger. Thin, wiry and old, older than Franton, and the man was downright ugly. Ashlee sat beside him laughing at something he said. When she rose, she patted his hand. Without acknowledging Steven, she returned to the kitchen counter and resumed cooking.

Steven tried once again to make conversation. "This chicken is really good. What's it called?"

Gaze on the dough she was rolling out, Ashlee didn't look up as she answered.

"Barbeque chicken."

A hot blush flushed his cheeks. *Bitch was trying to make him look stupid.* To calm himself, he focused on the game and took a sip of beer.

"Back in a sec, gotta pee."

Face still red from anger, he set the beer on the counter and headed to the bathroom.

In the hallway, he glanced back. No one was in sight, so he entered her bedroom and hurried to her dresser. Three minutes later he returned to his seat, a pair of her underwear tucked in his pocket. Everything in her drawers was exactly as she left it. One hand in his pocket fondling the panties, he leaned forward and gestured to the bowl of ingredients she was mixing. "So, what's that you're making?"

"The filling for the stuffed bread. It'll be ready in an hour. Would you like more chicken while you wait?" A smile on the corner of her mouth that didn't reach her eyes, Ashlee glanced at him, then returned her attention to the bowl.

"No thanks. Want some help? I can mix it up real good."

Red crept into her cheeks, and she whirled away, taking the bowl to the furthest counter. "No thanks, I got this."

With hurried movements, she spread the mixture onto her dough and threw the loaf into the oven. After washing her hands, she sat in Mike's lap.

Mike hugged her absently, his attention on the game. Ashlee snuck peeks at Nick who jerked his gaze away. Steven snickered. When Nick glanced at him, Steven nodded at Ashlee and lifted his beer bottle in a toast. Nick glared, and Steven snickered again, then faked watching the game.

Steven offered to go buy more beer and slipped Ashlee's keys from the hook by the door.

Thirty-five minutes later, he returned and set the beer on the counter. The copied keys were wrapped in the panties in his pocket.

Ashlee began putting the beer in the ice chest. Steven took the opportunity to touch her, pretending to help, rubbing his thumbs over her hands, grabbing her wrist. Lips in a tight line, Ashlee left him to finish putting the beer on ice and sat with Mike again.

Nick gave him a heated glare. Steven shrugged and headed to the bathroom.

Thirty minutes later, Ashlee resumed cooking at the counter. Steven tried to make conversation and was once again rebuffed.

Again, he headed to the bathroom and instead entered Nick's room. The rest of the evening was the same. By the time he left, he was furious. The heated looks Ashlee gave Nick were unmistakable. As soon as the door closed behind everyone, she would have his pants off. Hell, maybe she was just waiting for him to leave. The way she was acting so chummy with the other three, maybe they were playmates too.

He slapped the steering wheel with one hand as he stroked himself through his jeans.

He needed a woman. Sydney didn't answer his call, *probably out banging someone else, the dirty whore.*

A hard smile on his lips, he closed his eyes and tipped his head back. Sydney was a hot piece of ass. The dirtier he talked, the kinkier he was, the wetter she got. They had a date Wednesday. For now, he would go downtown and buy himself some company.

Later that week, on the way to pick up Sydney in his crappy car, Steven stopped outside Ashlee's apartment.

Nick hadn't invited him to the game this week either, but he'd gotten Mike to offer. The dirty looks Nick shot him amused him. The security on this place was nonexistent, stealing and copying the keys had been child's play, and sneaking back in to retrieve the USBs even easier. Already he had hours of footage of the three of them.

The video he got, *holy crap.* The footage was so much more than anticipated. What he expected to see was Ashlee sneaking into Nick's room behind her husband's back. Instead, the camera in Nick's room only showed him changing. All three of them slept in the same bed. Nick hadn't lied. Mike knew and approved.

What luck running into her mother like that.

He would never have suspected otherwise. If Nick hadn't said Mike knew and approved, he never would've put in the video. He hadn't decided on his approach yet. Play it sweet like Nick or pushy like Mike. Ashlee ignored him at the last game, getting her attention was proving harder than he thought.

He reached down and rubbed his cock as he leaned his head on the window. That shit was fucking hot, and he wanted to play too.

Man, he wanted to be Mike, telling them both what to do, running the show. Head tipped back, he rubbed faster, jerking his hips, imagining he was the man in the video. Yeah, she would like him better, he could be harder, and she liked it hard.

Sergeant First-Class Nicolas Rossi always the big man on the squad, pretending to be tough as nails while in reality he was pussy-whipped. Anything she asked him to do he did with a smile on his face. Mike was more his style, telling her and Nick what he wanted, and she lapped it up, all big blue eyes and open legs. Man, he wanted to get him some of that.

A loud, drawn-out groan as he came fogged the window. He reached over and grabbed a wad of napkins to wipe himself off. "See you soon, honey." Steven blew a kiss towards the apartment building as he drove away. He had a date to get ready for.

That morning Steven had collected the recordings and edited them at work. From the back, in the dim light of the bedroom, he could be mistaken as Mike. Mike was more muscular and a hair taller, but the camera Steven had hidden behind the mirror, and the one in the ceiling gave good views without showing Mike's face. Both men had the same crewcut and hair color.

Nick and Ashlee were clear in the pictures. Nick lay on the bed with his legs spread. Ashlee knelt between them with her ass in the air, taking Nick in her mouth. Then Mike was behind her rough and sudden, and Ashlee was loving it, pushing backward hard.

Steven bought the same bedding they used and filmed himself with the prostitute. Tied face down on his bed as he whipped her ass then fucked her, the camera focused on his expression and the girl's writhing hips. Then the scene cut back to Nick, making love to Ashlee slow and gentle, and in the video, it could be Steven lying on his side, rubbing his hands over her.

It's a fucking masterpiece.

Steven watched it fifty times, and it got better every time he saw it.

Sydney is gonna love this shit.

At eight, he picked up Sydney. Until he'd seen the video of Ashlee with Nick and Mike, he thought Syd was hot. Now he found her sort of boring, just lying back and taking it. Steven kissed her cheek and held the car door for her. She ate that shit up.

"Got a treat in store for you tonight." From the corner of Steven's eye, he glanced at her as she smoothed her skirt and checked for lipstick on her teeth. Sydney turned to him and raised a brow.

"Ash and I are meeting Nick later and having a little party; wanna come?"

Sydney crossed her legs, and her lips parted as she leaned closer. "Ashlee know you're inviting me?"

"No, but she won't care as long as you're discreet like."

Sydney slunk across the seat and slid her hand onto his groin. "Yeah, take me."

Steven took her to his place and offered a whiskey, which she accepted and knocked back like a sailor on shore leave. After two drinks, he pretended to check his watch and make a call. "Let's start without them. I'll get you all warmed up for him, just like Ashlee likes it. If you're up for some rough stuff that is."

"Two men, huh? That's her thing? And she likes it rough?"

"What about you, Syd, you like it rough?" Both hands braced on the couch behind Sydney, Steven leaned over and nipped the side of her neck.

An eager shiver traveled over her as she stood, taking a provocative pose, a foot pointed, and hip cocked. The zipper on her dress slithered down in one long pull, and she stepped out of it naked. No underwear, no bra, just woman. The breasts were fake but attractive, round globes with large nipples. Steven grabbed and squeezed till she moaned and dropped to her knees. He released her tit and gripped her hair, pulling her head back, wrapping the blond extensions around one hand. The other unbuttoned his pants and drew his cock out.

Sydney tugged his pants down and untied his boots as he yanked her hair. As soon as she pulled his pants off, he slapped her, making sure he didn't hit hard enough to mark her face.

"You ever do two at once before, Syd?"

"Yeah, boys though, not men. Boys have no stamina." Low and breathy she growled her response, gazing up at him with eager eyes.

"I can't wait for them. Let's get our party

started." He pulled her over his lap and smacked her ass. At first, she wiggled and sighed, then laid still.

"You hit like a girl," she said, sounding petulant.

Steven stilled. "Didn't want to mark your beautiful skin."

"Sure… saving it for Ashlee, I get it." Sydney tried to stand, and Steven pushed her back down hard, making her giggle.

He held her down while reaching for his pants and freed his belt. Sydney screamed as he beat her. Screamed and squirmed and begged for more.

Excited now, he made her suck him while he shouted insults at her and called her every dirty name he could think of. The skin of her ass was bright red, and he wanted to hurt her more, wanted her to really scream. She was begging him now to fuck her, and he loved it. Deep moans and grasping hands pulled him to her.

The phone rang. A telemarketer, but Steven pretended it was Nick. "Just us tonight, honey," he said as he hung up. The leather belt in his hand swished through the air, making a slithering noise. On the floor before him she whimpered and reached for him, gaze glued to the belt, lips parted and breathing hard.

"Give me what I want, Steven. We can play with your friends another night. We're going to have so much fun together."

"Shut up!" Steven drew back his arm and brought the belt down across her breasts.

She screamed in pain and cowered. "Too much!"

"Just about right, I think." Excited by her fear, he hit her again and fell on her.

Afterward, Sydney slunk to her clothing and tried to dress with hands that shook.

"Aww, come on, honey." On his knees, he crawled to her and pulled her into his arms, kissing her neck as he rubbed her back. "Let's watch some home video, so you can see how a real woman acts."

"Home video?"

"Sure, wanna see Nick and me in action?"

Brown eyes wide and excited, she shook her hair back and licked her lips. "Yeah, show me."

Steven chuckled and turned on his television. The small USB was already inserted. Thirty minutes into the video Sydney was wet and begging for him again. Steven obliged her, his gaze glued to the screen where Mike cut off Ashlee's underwear with his k-bar. Sydney called his name, not paying attention to the screen now.

"Yeah, this is gonna be so amazing, all four

of us."

"Mmm. Can't wait, Steve."

"Me neither, soon, Syd. I'll set up another date, and this time they won't miss it."

✻ ✻ ✻

At the next game, Steven sat at the counter and spent the night trying to engage Ashlee in conversation. All evening she ignored him, talking with her friend Kurt and Nick instead. The way she stared at Nick, he knew they would go at it as soon as he left.

Shit, maybe he should just blackmail Nick, but he doubted that would work. Time was on his side. Mike shipped out tomorrow and Ashlee would be desperate for it soon. A smile on his face, he bid them good night.

The next day he retrieved his cameras, sure there would be a hot new movie to watch. He wasn't wrong. Half the night, the three of them took turns, but he couldn't enjoy it. Ashlee had asked Mike to ban him from the house and Mike had agreed, the fucker. In a rage, he crushed the USB.

Sydney called him the next night, and he made plans with her for the following weekend.

The two of them had a good weekend, but being banned from the Evans household rankled. New edited video of him and the prostitute got Syd real hot, but with Mike away, creative editing was getting harder. He and Sydney watched the same recordings over and over.

A month later, the television screen flickered muted light across the ceiling. Naked, Sydney sat on the edge of Steven's bed, remote control in hand.

Steven gripped her thigh. "Ready to go again?"

Sydney laughed, brushed his hand off and stood, spinning to face him with both hands on her hips, her fake boobs jiggling. "That isn't you in the films. That's Mike."

Steven pushed himself up in bed, letting the sheet fall, exposing his erection. On the screen, footage played of Ashlee with her mouth on him. The older footage never showed his front, but he couldn't resist including this shot on his new tape. *The expression on Ashlee's face was so hot.*

Sydney pointed and laughed. "Look at him. Even from this crappy angle, I can see he has a bigger dick and on your best day you aren't that muscled. I can't believe it took me so long to notice. Where the hell did you get these videos? Who's the girl in yours? It sure as hell isn't Ashlee."

Still laughing, she headed for her clothes.

Furious, Steven grabbed her arm and pulled her back to bed. "What the fuck do you know? I was there, and that sure as shit is me." He rose a hand to slap her face as he yanked her down onto the blue comforter.

"Yeah, sure it is. Whatever you say, Steven." Sydney tossed her hair back and glared, not bothering to rub the red mark he left on her cheek.

On his hands and knees above her, he was so furious he shook. "You don't know what the hell you're talking about!"

Sydney laughed a low, throaty chuckle. "Prove me wrong. Call and invite them to come play. You keep telling me we will, but somehow, they always cancel. A fucking month has gone by, and I never saw them in person once, just video."

Steven slapped her again as she tried to push him off. Excited by her real struggles, he forced her arms down and took her hard while she fought to get away from him. When he finished, he rolled off her and slapped her ass. She glared and ran for her clothes.

"Aww, Syd, don't be that way. Can I help it if Ash hates you? Don't worry, she loves me though, and I can talk her into anything."

A scowl on her face, Sydney paused by the door and turned back, then shook her head, heaved an angry, disgusted sigh, and stormed out.

Furious again, Steven threw his pillow at the door, then began picking up everything in reach. A few minutes later, he stood in the wreckage of his room breathing hard. *How dare that bitch call him a liar? The proof is right there on the fucking screen. Big as life he and Nick are screwing Ashlee.*

All week he fumed. Nick's smug face aggravated him more every time he saw him. Wednesday, Nick's name caught his eye on a report, and a plan was born. Nick would be out of town for five days, leaving him free to convince Ashlee. Man, it would probably be easy too. All he had to do was tell her Mike sent him. Assure Ashlee he was more fun and Nick would do whatever Ashlee wanted. Syd would be thrilled to have new playmates. The four of them would have a really good time.

- 11 -
As Bad as I've Ever Seen

A confusing babble of voices interspersed with sobs and the sounds of a struggle greeted Nick when he entered the emergency room.

The base sported a small hospital with an equally small emergency room. In his ten years of service, he'd never once set foot inside it, mostly because he'd served most of that time overseas.

Since being given his desk job, he'd managed to stay out of hospitals, instead, visiting his doctor whenever his knee injury flared up. Gone for almost six days, he hadn't been back on base for an hour before Trent called, sounding very upset and telling him to come, that Ashlee was injured.

Trent stood outside the cubicle where the commotion was taking place. He wore his MP uniform and a look of horror. When Nick entered, he glanced over to the door and then hurried to greet him.

"Nick, she's hysterical, and we can't reach Mike." Trent looked away and cleared his throat. "It's bad, as bad as I've ever seen and she was calling for you. I thought maybe you could calm her and get her to let the doctors see her."

"What?" Nick's face paled.

Trent had been a combat medic and seen some pretty horrific stuff. Right then, Ashlee screamed Nick's name. The scream turned to sobs and begging for Mike. After taking a last glance at Trent's wincing face, he strode behind the curtain.

Ashlee crouched in the corner of the room with a metal pole in one hand, the type used to hold an IV. The other hand, swollen and red, was tight against her chest, the weight of it holding a shirt closed. A man's shirt, bloody and unbuttoned, hung on her small frame, hanging to mid-thigh. Pants ten sizes too big slipped from her slim hips.

When he entered, she let out a piteous wail, dropped the pipe and threw herself into his arms. A deep moan changed to a gasping sob when his arms automatically closed around her. A weird form of déjà vu overtook him, dizzying in its intensity. Just five days ago she'd flung herself into his arms and moaned and gasped, but the difference horrified.

"Ash, my God, Ash. What happened?" Shocked, he tried to pry her off to better examine her injuries, but she clung to him with hysterical strength.

"Help me." Her voice was a thin pitiful wail.

"Ash," he repeated and smoothed her hair back, drawing his hand away in alarm at the blood that coated it.

"Mike— he's gone to kill Mike, and they won't call him. No one will help me."

She drew back to meet his eyes, her own wild. The right eye was swollen shut and black from bruising. Dried blood held a jagged cut closed on the left side of her face. Another surgically straight cut held together with butterfly tape crossed the cheekbone. The entire cheek was puffy and red with blue streaks. Tears streamed from her right eye, clouding the blue.

Her injuries made him feel sick, and he had to force words past the lump in his throat.

"Calm down, sweetheart. What happened to you?"

"Mike wouldn't just give me away! I know he wouldn't; he loves me. You love me, right?" Hysterical panting and a deep tremor raced over her.

"You know I do. Please calm down and tell me what happened."

"Call Mike. He's gone to kill him."

"Who, Ash? You're not making any sense."

"How come you didn't come save me? Why didn't you come for me?"

Without warning, she collapsed in his arms and screamed when he tightened his grip to keep her from falling.

"Sir, Sergeant, she needs medical attention. Please, Sir." A doctor gestured to the examination bed.

Nick nodded, carried her to the bed, and laid her down.

"Noooo, Nick, please don't leave me here alone, please." Too weak to stand on her own, she scrabbled with her good hand for a hold on the metal rail surrounding the bed and screamed again as she pulled herself up.

Nick leaned over her, using his weight to immobilize her. Her arm went around his neck, and she clutched him, sobbing. He felt like sobbing himself.

When he'd laid her down, the shirt had opened exposing her breasts and stomach. Along her left side, dark-blue and red bruising and shiny, waxy areas covered her breast. Caked blood and small lacerations crisscrossed the left side of her body. The right side didn't have a mark. Still perfect and beautiful with only a few small bruises and flecks of dried blood, the comparison was shocking.

Doctors and nurses conferred over his head and an MP he didn't know asked for information, but he couldn't concentrate. Ashlee still sobbed in his arms, begging him to help Mike.

"Let the doctor examine you, and I'll get in touch with Mike."

"And you'll be careful too? He's crazy and wants to take Mike's place, but he might try to kill you too."

"Yes, I'll be fine. Let the doctors help you. Who did this, Ash?"

"That guy, Steven, Mike's friend, the one that creeped me out at the last game. Nick...." Heavy breathing warmed his ear and sobs choked her as she tried to speak. "He hurt me so bad, Nicky. Don't let him take me again," she whispered.

"Oh God, Ash. I'm here now, and I won't leave you alone. You're safe." Tears filled his eyes, and he blinked them back furiously.

Excited commands between the doctors in the cubicle finally got his attention when Ashlee went limp in his arms. Before he straightened, he kissed her uninjured cheek.

Hands clenched into fists to hide the

shaking, he scanned down her body where a female nurse was cutting off the too-big pants.

"Sir, you need to leave now," another said and took his arm.

"No, I'm not leaving! I promised her."

"Sir…"

"No! I'm not leaving!" He glared at the nurse who licked her lips, bit the bottom one, nodded, then scurried to the other side of the bed where she began cutting off the shirt.

Nick's horrified gaze traveled over Ashlee. The damage continued down the left side of her body. Both wrists and ankles showed heavy bruising where she'd been tied and struggled. Struggled hard. Handprints marked her thighs, so deep and numerous he felt physically ill. Dried blood covered the inside of her thighs, and fresh blood spotted the white sheet beneath her. With the pants gone her feet became visible. Yellow pus leaked from blackened skin mixing with dried and fresh blood.

"Sir?" A hand on his arm brought his horrified gaze away from the damage. An MP held a pen, which he tapped against an open pocket notebook.

Nick rubbed his eyes hard and turned away from Ashlee. "I need to call her husband. Oh, dear God… this can't be happening. Steven

Wrint did this. At least I think that's who she meant."

"What happened?" The officer poised his pen above the notebook.

"How should I know?" Nick took a deep breath and rubbed his face again.

"Why did she ask for you?" The MP flipped his notepad closed and gave him an enquiring glance.

"I live with them. Mike's deployed."

"Sir... how come she wasn't reported missing?"

Nick thought he might vomit. "I didn't realize she was. Jesus, can we do this later? Look at her. She needs me now."

Guilt seared him. He'd gone away and left her knowing Steven was interested and hadn't called her once. Sure, a phone wasn't handy, but he could have arranged for someone to check on her. Instead, he'd left her unprotected and worse, unaware that Steven knew about them. She would have trusted Steven, thinking he was just Mike's friend and nothing more.

Holy mother of God, if he'd just checked on her, he would've known to track Steven down. Not that he considered for one minute Steven would do something like this. Maybe make a rough pass, one he had to stop with violence, but never this. A shudder shook him. Both hands gripped the metal bar on Ashlee's stretcher so hard his knuckles turned white.

The MP tapped his pen a few more times. "Well, it's like this, Sir. My partner and I found her running down the street. Trent recognized her, which is good because we never got her to say who she was. She was hysterical, telling us to call her husband and you, but see and here's the thing. She also kept saying, 'why would they do this to me, my husband wouldn't just give me to him.' So, you can see the problem here, can't you?"

The MP glanced at Ashlee, and his lips tightened. Nick followed his gaze and bit back a sob. While he spoke with the MP, the nurses had flipped Ashlee onto her stomach. Stripes covered her back and the backs of her legs in varying shades of red and blue. A black patch on her left side formed a perfect ring.

"Oh, dear God," Nick gasped and reached a trembling hand to her, ignoring the officers and doctors. Tears streamed unheeded over his cheek. He leaned down and hid his face in her snarled hair. Matted and filthy, her long brown hair appeared wet instead of bloody.

After a moment, he cleared his throat and straightened. "Check for pneumonia."

The doctor glanced up in surprise.

Nick gestured at the black circle. "That's for

water boarding. She'll have fluid in her lungs."

"What? Waterboarding?" The doctor glared and grabbed his stethoscope.

"Yes, you break a rib, and it makes it real painful when you struggle to breathe." Nick's breath caught, and he swayed. The room grew cloudy and the voices far away. Someone had waterboarded Ashlee. No, not someone— Steven. Red flushed his cheeks as a furious rage infused him.

The MP grabbed his shoulder. Nick jerked away and gripped the metal bar on the side of the bed.

"Look, I'm sorry, but can you see my position on this?" The MP gestured to Ashlee's sheet covered form as the nurses placed the clothing they'd cut off into bags. "Clearly, she greeted you with relief, but… the condition in which we found her demands an investigation."

Nick rubbed his forehead. "Yeah fine, but gimme a minute here." Without waiting for an answer, he turned to the doctor. "How bad is this?"

The MP grabbed his phone and headed into the hallway.

The doctor glanced up. "Are you a family member?"

Nick's face burned. Ashlee and Mike were

his family, but no one here would understand that.

"Look, Doc, I have to go call my best friend and tell him his wife's been attacked and brutally raped and beaten. What I need to tell him is her condition. Mike is in Iraq right now. Shall I just say no one can be bothered to tell me?"

Nick glanced at the door as the MP entered again.

The doctor winced and straightened from where he'd been leaning over listening to Ashlee's breathing with a stethoscope. "Tell him she has broken bones. I'm unsure of the exact amount at this time without x-rays, but at least four. Fluid is causing respiratory distress. I suspect she has an injury to her liver and spleen and am running tests now to confirm. Six needle marks on her right arm indicate her assailant drugged her, and we're running a tox screen for that. Once we get those results, we can sedate her and do a pelvic exam where I'm sure there are injuries, but at this moment I can't comment on the severity. The burns on the right side of her body aren't too bad, neither are the lacerations. If she survives, she'll have mild scarring."

"If?" Nick whispered, the room blurring with his tears.

"Her condition is critical. Run down as she is the amount of bruising coupled with pneumonia and multiple broken ribs… Well, any of those injuries could prove fatal. The injuries were inflicted to produce maximum pain. The soles of her feet and her fingernails... This…." The doctor stopped and cleared his throat. "Someone tortured her over a few days, someone with knowledge. The injuries aren't random, but purposeful. Pain management will be a serious issue when she wakes. "

"A few days?" Nick's voice cracked, the room spun, and he fell to his knees, only his grip on the bar by her bed keeping him upright.

The doctor exchanged a glance with the MP

"Oh God, Ash, I'm so sorry I didn't check on you." Nick ran a trembling hand over her uninjured arm. The doctors and MP spoke amongst themselves for a few minutes, leaving him alone crying into Ashlee's hair.

"Let us take care of her." The doctor turned to the nurse and ordered more tests and an operating room made ready, gesturing Nick to move away as nurses crowded the bed.

Nick nodded numbly.

Ashlee moaned, and her lashes fluttered open.

"Rest, sweetheart, you're safe now." Nick

stood and leaned over, murmuring endearments in her ear. "Don't move; let the doctor help you."

Weak and low, her voice shook. "Nicky, you still love me, right?"

"Always, sweetheart."

"He said you wouldn't, but I didn't believe him. Lies… only lies, Nick. Mike wouldn't give me away again."

"No, he never did. Mike loves you."

"Is he safe? Nicky, you still love me…." Ashlee trailed off.

Nick straightened in alarm as she lost consciousness again.

The nurse nodded and pointed to the IV she'd just inserted into Ashlee's uninjured hand. "The doctor okayed a mild sedative, so we can do the exams. Could you please wait outside?"

He raked a hand through his short, blond hair as he nodded jerkily and left the cubicle after kissing Ashlee's brow. Trent waited outside with six other officers. The MP glanced at the messages on his phone and followed him out.

"Trent, I need to call Mike."

Trent gave him a quick one-armed hug and a sympathetic grimace. "Already did, man. They're tracking him down now and will get him on the first flight back here."

"Yeah, okay, but I need to speak with him. Ash says Steven Wrint is going to try to kill him."

"What? Steven did that?" Trent paled and took a step back.

"So she says, but she isn't making a lot of sense. Where did you find her?"

The MP that followed him from the cubicle laid a hand on his arm. "Before we get all chatty, how about you answer some questions?"

Trent glared at his partner, took Nick's arm and led him to a private consulting room. The four other MPs followed, crowding into the small space.

"Sit, you look like you're going to pass out or be sick. Harry, get him some water." Trent pushed Nick into a chair and sat beside him.

The MP with the notebook strode forward until he stood in front of Nick. "Okay, so if you live with her, how come she wasn't reported missing?"

"I left Monday for a refresher course and got back today. I didn't realize she was missing."

"Refresher course?"

"Yeah, since my injury, I teach here on base." Nick pressed the heels of his hands hard against his cheekbones and then glared at the

MP. "Does that matter? Who cares what I do? Is anyone investigating Steven Wrint?"

"Yes, sir. Two teams are at his home as we speak."

"Did you locate him?"

"No, sir, we did not, but we've found evidence corroborating her statement."

"So, why the hell are you giving me the tenth degree?" Nick took a deep breath and ran both hands through his hair, then rubbed his neck. "Never mind. I don't care why. Catch the bastard. And, Jesus, Trent, we can't leave her alone; she thinks he'll come back." Nick's fists clenched so hard his nails bit into his palms. More than anything in the world he wanted five minutes alone with Steven Wrint.

"No, I won't leave her alone, buddy. Someone will guard her every moment until we catch him." Trent slapped Nick's shoulder and rose.

"Mason?" Trent said to the MP holding the notepad and pen.

Mason nodded and slipped the notebook into his pocket, but his narrowed gaze remained on Nick.

Trent turned back to Nick. "Nick, a team will be going over your home with a fine-tooth comb."

Nick stood and dug into his pocket, pulling

out a set of keys that he handed to Trent. "Have at it."

"Come to the station as soon as you can to give an official statement."

"Yeah, sure, whatever, once I know if she'll be okay." Nick pushed out of the room and headed back to Ashlee, but the cubicle was empty.

The orderly cleaning the room called the nurse for him, and she led him to a waiting room. "Mrs. Evans is being prepped for surgery now. Doctor Nerig will be out to talk to you. Were you able to reach her husband?"

"A friend is handling that, but even if I reached him right this minute, it would take him at least a day to get here. He's stationed overseas." Nick paused then burst out, "Ashlee is my family. She and Mike are all the family I have. Please, I need to know she's going to be okay."

- 12 -
AND NOBODY SUSPECTED

Trent glared at his partner, Mason, as they left the hospital.

"What's with that shit? No way is Nick involved." The glare deepened when Mason shrugged and kept walking. Trent grabbed his partner's arm and spun him around. "Or Mike, and don't go bothering him right now, either."

"Get your head outa your ass. Those two are your friends, but so was this Steven guy, right? And you're shocked he's involved." Sergeant Leland Mason glared back. "I get you don't want to believe they could do something that sick, but you heard her. Are we just gonna let 'em get away with that shit?"

"I'm telling you, no fucking way are they involved. Mike's crazy about her, and she's crazy about him. If you saw them together… Man, I'm telling you, no fucking way."

"Fine, but something shady is going on. Mark my words." Mason pulled roughly away, strode to the patrol car, and flipped on the lights. "And hurry your ass up before their buddies get to their house and remove our evidence."

Grumbling under his breath, Trent got in the car. The short ride to Mike's was made in silence. When they arrived, they found the place empty. Food just starting to stink sat on the counter in bowls with colored plastic lids.

Mason stopped and picked a few of the bowls up, cracking the seals and sniffing before making a face and putting them back down. With a glance at Trent, he took a few pictures.

"That's nothing. Ash cooks all the time. Come here on game day, and there are piles of bowls. Ash is determined to create a culinary masterpiece. She's always experimenting." Trent's lips tightened as he walked away from the counter. "Steven was here for the last game and raved about her chili, the goddamn bastard."

"Did he do anything odd or out of the ordinary?" Mason continued to take pictures as they spoke, bagging a glass and plate in the sink and leaving yellow place-cards.

"Not that I noticed at the time, but now that I think back, he spent a lot of time at the counter here. But I thought he was enjoying the food. The first few times I came over I did the same thing. If you sit at the counter, she's always testing stuff on you."

"Testing?"

"Is it too spicy, too salty— you know, asking for an opinion."

Mason nodded and walked away and then opened the closet by the front door and rummaged through it. "Anything else you remember he did?"

"Went to the bathroom every five minutes. And he didn't drink much. Ash replaced our beers every twenty minutes or so, but he nursed his all night. But, I don't know him well enough to judge if that's odd or not."

"That's fucking odd," Mason said. "Who goes to watch a ball game and doesn't drink?"

Mason left the closet and headed to the bathroom. "Hey, what's to say he actually went to the bathroom? I can't see the living room from here, just a corner of the kitchen counter. You say Ashlee handed out beer. Was that on a set timer, or did people ask, or what?"

"On commercial breaks, she hands out food and drinks, and someone usually hits the head."

Mason left the hallway, entering the bedroom across the hall. A typical bedroom furnished with a king-sized bed sporting mussed blankets. Two dressers stood side-by-side with a television mounted above them at the foot of the bed.

Pantyhose were tied to the headboard. Mason photographed it, bagged the hose and placed another yellow place-card. A glass of water and plate with crumbs rested on the nightstand. Again, he photographed and then bagged it, leaving place-cards behind. A cracked mirror hung on a stand in the corner, and an antique mirror leaned against the wall. Trent took prints from both mirrors.

The closet was filled with female and male clothes. Mason opened the nightstands and rifled through the drawers, finding nothing of interest.

"No uniforms in the closet." Trent tapped his bottom lip and headed to the hallway where he opened the closet by the bathroom door. "Yep, here they are. Both Mike and Nick are keeping them here."

Trent headed into the second bedroom, this one smaller. A full-sized bed was pushed against one wall. A small dresser with a mirror over it and a television mounted on a swivel mount stood in the corner. Books and mail were piled on the nightstand near a glass of water with a fine coating of dust floating on top. Small sprinkles of plaster floated on the dust and specks covered the nightstand.

"That's odd." Trent held the glass up, peering at it in the room's light. After a moment's examination, he dipped his gloved pinkie in and examined the dust that stuck there.

"Mason, look at this." Trent held out the glass. "How long you think a glass needs to sit to get dust on it?"

While Mason inspected the glass, Trent examined the ceiling and walls around the bed. Hands on his hips, he stepped back and scrutinized the space again. "Ah ha." Two sharp tugs pulled the light from the wall. Someone had drilled another hole behind the light. Nothing filled the small space now.

Trent placed the light on the bed and headed to the master bedroom. The bedside lamps there came off easily. "This is what Steven was up to." Trent pointed out the small camera tucked behind the light fixture.

Mason climbed on the bed and removed the light fixture over it, revealing another camera. "Proves nothing. Anyone could have placed them. Dust everything, bag 'em and tag 'em. Dust the glass in Nick's room and bag that too."

Lips compressed, Trent went about his

work. "Okay, sure, but why is the one missing from Nick's room?"

"Maybe Steven got bored watching Nick sleep and whack off. Who knows. These cameras aren't cheap." Mason placed the camera in an evidence bag and sealed it. "Okay, smart ass, how did he get them out?"

"Don't be retarded. If Steven was willing to spy on his friends, I'm sure he managed to copy the keys. It would be damn easy. Take Ash's keys hanging on the peg by the door, go out to buy beer, copy the keys, replace the stolen keys."

"Did he go buy beer?"

"We all did at one time or another."

"Right, well, let's tear this place apart." By the end of the hour, they found three more cameras in the bedroom, two in the kitchen and one in the living room. All the same make and model, motion activated, with twelve-hour memory cards.

Back at the station, Mason and Trent dusted the cameras and cards for prints and sat in one of the interview rooms to view the footage. Trent played the first disk, the one they'd found on the bedside lamp.

"We aren't watching this," Trent said as he fast forwarded, making the image on the screen blur as Ashlee undressed and readied for bed. "What do you think we're going to learn?"

Mason shrugged and started the second recording. "How about that? "

He smirked and pointed at the screen where Ashlee jumped in Nick's arms, kissing him and removing his clothing while Nick laughed and kissed her back.

"Oh, Jesus," Trent whispered.

"Motive— a cheating wife," Mason said in satisfaction.

"I don't know what to say, I'm shocked." Trent turned his pale face back to the screen and jabbed the fast forward, skimming the images of one of his best friends cuckolding the other.

Mason started the third recording. "Let's see if we have any other suspects."

Two recordings showed Mike and Ashlee making love. A blush on his cheeks, Trent hit fast forward through them. The last recording made him gasp.

"What the bloody hell?" Trent asked as he leaned forward to view the images.

Mike and Ashlee laid on the bed and Nick walked in, both turned and smiled at him. The audio was a garbled mess too indistinct to make out, but the action was clear. Nick undressed while watching Mike make love to his wife. Ashlee's gaze locked on Nick while her husband thrust into her.

When Mike finished, he picked Ashlee up and placed her on Nick's lap, kissing her while Nick fondled her breasts. Nick laid her back on the bed as Mike knelt, taking one breast in his mouth while rubbing the nipple of the other. Nick began to make love to her while Mike held her legs spread. Ashlee was obviously enjoying it, writhing and placing their hands on her breasts. Trent hit fast forward as Ashlee took Mike's cock in her mouth, his head back, body moving in sync with Nick's thrusts.

"Kinda blows your theory out of the water." Trent flipped off the recording, spinning the micro USB on the table.

Mason leaned back in his seat and rubbed his neck, his lips pursed. "Yeah, I'll admit I didn't see that coming, which in hindsight is pretty stupid. And nobody suspected?"

"No, I mean, I knew they were real good friends, but, no." Trent hesitated. "Mason, if we turn this last recording in, Nick's career is over. Hell, Mike's career is over. They have enough shit to deal with without that."

"How sure are you we have all the recordings?" Mason lifted an eyebrow.

"Does it matter? I can only try."

"Well fuck, you're asking me to destroy

evidence."

"Evidence of what? They committed no crime. Obviously, all three consented. Are you really going to let that son-of-bitch ruin their lives?"

Mason flicked the recording with a finger. "Take 'em, take 'em both. The one where she greets Nick, and this one. Nick's a good guy."

Mason flipped the small chips to Trent and rose. Trent nodded his thanks and gathered up the evidence, sealing it in bags to which they both signed their names.

- 13 -
OUR BEAUTIFUL GIRL

A commotion in the hallway drew Nick's glance to the door as booted feet and indistinct, murmuring voices approached.

Before him, propped on her left side, Ashlee lay covered in a light, white sheet. Machines ticked and hummed at the head of the bed, their steady clicks a comfort. Tubes supplying oxygen and removing wastes connected to her. The one from the latest surgery dripped a yellow, blood-tinged bile into a small sealed container nurses checked regularly.

"Mike," Trent said outside the door.

Nick glanced up again when Mike entered.

Pale and haggard, Mike stopped right inside the door. Still wearing his desert fatigues and flak jacket, his combat boots were covered in dust. His helmet and headset dangled from his hand. He glanced around the room, and then with a shrug, dropped them by the door.

"Mike." Nick's voice cracked, and he had to clear his throat. "Mike," he said again in a whisper. "She just fell asleep, so keep it down. The doctors can't give her strong pain meds yet; her head injuries worry them." Nick turned his gaze from Mike's stricken face to Ashlee.

"Is she..." Mike cleared his throat and tried again. "Her condition?"

"Bad." Tears filled Nick's eyes when he glanced up, and he quickly looked away.

Mike joined him on the other side of the bed. A deep moan followed by a choked back sob issued from him when he saw her face. "Dear God, Nick, our beautiful girl." Dazed, Mike sank to his knees.

Nick rose to let Mike touch her. Blood withdrawal, medication, and the IV had left bruising in their wake on the previously uninjured arm. The relatively bruise free cheek rested on the bed, leaving the broken one visible. With a trembling hand, Mike smoothed back Ashlee's hair the nurses had washed and combed.

"Dear God." A red flush climbed over Mike's unshaven, pale cheeks, settling into two deep-red spots high on his cheekbones. Short, dark brown hair stood on end as Mike ran a shaky hand through it and turned his hollow gaze on Nick.

Nick's lips tightened, and his hands clenched before he relaxed and placed a hand on Mike's shoulder for a moment then pulled back the sheet covering her with a determined rush.

"Motherfucker!" Mike clamped his lips shut and traced his hand down the length of Ashlee's left side without touching her. Shoulders rigid and breathing hard, Mike stalked around the bed examining her. "Motherfucker," he whispered through clenched teeth. When he saw her back, he began trembling.

Nick pulled the sheet back over Ashlee's still form, and she let out a breathy moan, making the machines beep and hum louder. Both men stilled. Neither moved until the machines settled into a steady rhythm once again.

Mike rejoined Nick and knelt, placing his hand on the back of Ashlee's head as tears filled his eyes. Nick rested his hand on Mike's shoulder.

"Don't leave her alone. She's terrified he's coming back for her. I'll leave you with her for a minute." Nick tightened his grip on Mike's shoulder as Mike let out a sob.

"Yeah, give us a minute please." Mike

gulped hard and wiped his cheeks with his free hand as he straightened his shoulders.

Nick nodded and left the room, closing the door quietly behind him.

In the hallway, Nick's old squad gathered, Mike's squad now. All still wore fatigues and flak jackets and appeared exhausted. They spoke quietly to Trent who sat in a chair to the right of the door. Palms placed flat on the wall by the door, Nick leaned his head back and closed his eyes.

Trent stood. "You'll be here if I take a quick bathroom break?" he asked.

Nick nodded without opening his eyes.

Trent slapped his shoulder and hurried off.

"Right," Corporal Franton said as his angry gaze followed Trent. "Denton, you take the first watch. We do three-hour shifts till we frag that motherfucker. Inger, you're up next, followed by Pauly and Jenks."

Nick opened his eyes. "That son-of-a-bitch is my target."

"Does it matter who squashes that cockroach?" Franton lifted one bushy eyebrow.

"No, I guess it doesn't." Nick leaned his head back on the wall again. "Just don't be stupid. Make sure Mike has an alibi."

"Do we look stupid to you?"

Despite himself, Nick cracked a smile.

"Hmmph," Franton snorted and resumed handing out assignments. By the time Trent returned, only Franton, Inger, and Nick stood in the hallway.

"What's the latest?" Trent asked.

"She developed pneumonia, but we expected that. The last surgery went—"

Inside the room, a shriek cut off mid-yell and Nick rushed in. Ashlee gasped and vomited blood while Mike tried to support her. "We need a doctor in here!" Nick bellowed as he raced to Mike's side.

"Honey, no one will get in this room, I promise you! Relax, I'll love you till the day I die, no matter what. I swear it. Nick's here too. We both love you. Doctor!" Mike sounded panicked as Ashlee vomited a mist of red blood, spraying his chest and face.

The doctor ran into the room followed by three nurses.

Nick pulled Mike away to make room for the doctors as Ashlee gasped and sobbed. Five minutes later, the machines resumed their steady beeping and Ashlee lay cleaned up and sedated.

Shoulders tense and lips set in a grim line, Mike turned to the doctor. "Doc, we need to move the bed. She freaked when she couldn't see the doorway."

"This bed is—"

Furious, Mike leaned forward and screamed in the doctor's face. "Turn the fucking bed!" Franton, Trent, and Inger ran in the room.

Franton growled as he eyed Mike's blood splattered face and chest. "Right, where do you want the bed, Mike?" Feet spread and hands on his hips, Franton glowered at the doctor.

"Any goddamn place she can see the door!"

"Yes, fine, give the nurses a minute to arrange it." The doctor's sympathetic glance flitted across them.

Nick squeezed Mike's shoulder. "Go home and clean up. God knows what germs you're carrying. I'll be here."

"Promise you won't let her die?" Mike's voice caught on a sob.

"Yeah." Nick cleared his throat and kissed Ashlee's brow.

"No one is dying except the motherfucker who did this!" Franton grabbed Mike's arm and pulled him from the room. Trent and Inger followed.

An hour later, Mike returned. He'd shaved, showered and wore clean jeans and a white t-shirt. Nick glanced at his filthy clothes. He hadn't changed or left her side for more than bathroom breaks since Trent called him two days ago. Now that Mike was here, he would have to return to his duty. The thought angered him. Ashlee was as much his wife as Mike's, but not legally. As far as the law was concerned, he would be court-martialed if their relationship became known. An affair with another officer's wife would get him a dishonorable discharge at the least. At most, he could apply for leave.

"Okay, tell me." Mike pulled up a chair and sat as close to his wife as he could, burying one hand in her clean hair. In his absence, the nurses had shifted the bed to the other side of the room so Ashlee could see the door.

Nick kissed her brow and then paced. "Steven took her. Seems he got it in his head he wanted to be you. The police found recording devices in our house." Nick's gaze flicked from Mike to Ashlee. Mike nodded, his lips compressing. "Trent stole the, um, incriminating ones. As far as the police know, I'm just a roommate. A good friend," Nick said bitterly.

Mike sighed.

"Well, anyways, the bastard took her on Monday right after I left."

"Four days?" Mike gasped, his face paling.

"Four fucking days," Nick agreed, his hands clenched, and he resumed pacing. "The first day wasn't too bad, considering... Steven thought he could talk her into having sex with him. That if she thought you gave her to him, that you wanted her too, she would. And she seemed sure Steven thought if she had sex with him willingly she would fall in love with him and be happy there with him. That first day and night were in our apartment."

Mike groaned and laid his forehead on the bed.

"That's why he only hurt the left side, your side, trying to force her, but she wouldn't willingly." Nick's voice caught in a sob, and he paused. "Our girl didn't want to be a whore. No matter what he did, she wouldn't…" Nick trailed off and cleared his throat before resuming.

"The second day he moved her. She doesn't know how or where because he drugged her. That's when he tried to force her to change her mind. By the third day, he gave up trying to change her mind and just…" Nick trailed off as Mike groaned again.

Suddenly, Mike jumped up and was sick in the garbage can.

For a moment, Nick left him alone to regain control then hugged him. "We'll kill the bastard," he murmured as Mike cried.

Mike pushed away and wiped his eyes. "Killing's too good. He needs to suffer. I saw her back. Those are marks I recognize, *on my goddamn wife*!" He panted with rage and spun away to pace. "What else?"

"Do you really need the list?"

"Yes, goddamn it! Every sick thing he did, I'll do tenfold to him!"

"Two fingernails, five toenails. The bottom of her feet are cut, burned, and beaten. Three broken ribs, a broken cheek, seventy-two knife wounds, mostly small, shallow slices that shouldn't scar too bad. The knife wounds were all salted or soaked with alcohol, not to help her, I'm sure, but the doctor says it should lessen the scarring."

"And her hand?" Mike nodded to the hand in a cast resting on a stack of pillows.

"She did that herself to get away. Steven chained her to the bed with enough chain to reach a bedpan and left her with a bottle of water and three ration bars. 'To go kill you,' she says. Anyways, as soon as he left, she tried to break free and didn't give up. Four bones in her hand are broken, her wrist is broken in two places, and her arm has a hairline fracture."

Mike's forehead once again leaned on the bed, and his shoulders shook. "Nobody's seen him?" Muffled in the bedding, his voice vibrated with anger.

"No sign, but Trent is guarding her. She's

convinced he'll come for her."

"I hope he does. When I get my hands on him—"

Nick glanced around and lowered his voice, leaning down to whisper in Mike's ear. "Hold it together, man. We'll get the bastard, but we need to be smart about it. What good are we to her if we're in prison?"

Mike nodded without picking his head up.

Nick straightened and moved away. "And more bad news, her mother will arrive tonight." Mike picked his head up and glared.

"Sorry, Mike, I had to call her. She's her daughter for Christ sake."

"That woman hates us. If she gets the chance, she'll ruin us both."

"Tonight, I'll stay home. If I'm not here, you know she'll pretend I don't exist. Admitting her daughter chooses to live with both of us is something she'll never do. Don't worry about that."

Mike leaned back and rubbed his face. "Right now, I couldn't care less."

Nick squatted and put an arm around him. "Me neither."

- 14 -
THE NEED TO DESTROY

Nick stormed into his office and kicked the desk chair across the room. A bubbling anger filled him with the need to destroy. The desire to smash everything in the room to pieces was so strong it left him trembling. He rose both hands to cover his face and screamed in rage, the sound muffled.

"Motherfucker! That goddamned motherfucker!"

He dropped his hands, grabbed the laptop on his desk and threw it against the wall as hard as he could. Delicate computer components tinkled into garbage. Nick stood panting in the middle of the room. Not content with that destruction, he swept everything on the desk to the floor and stormed from the room, heading to the range.

At the range, he grabbed his M9 handgun,

his SDM-R rifle, and two boxes of ammunition. Men on the course gave him a wide berth, keeping their eyes averted and their talk quiet.

Nick ignored them. The violent energy inside him needed release. The Beretta M9 held a clip of nine-millimeter bullets. He slapped the clip in as he raised the gun, sighting and pulling in one smooth motion.

As fast as he could, he pulled the trigger, the sharp rat-a-tat-tat and the smell of gun smoke soothed him. Wide holes appeared in the target from his grouped shots. Hands shaking in anger he released the clip, caught it with one hand, reloaded, slammed the clip back in, and did it again. The target before him shredded in lines. An entire case of ammo flew before he was calm enough to shoot his rifle.

He snatched it up from the corner where he'd laid it and headed to the distant targets. One at a time he loaded and shot. The target at seven hundred yards developed a smiley face. A group of quiet men gathered behind him, passing binoculars back and forth.

Once the pattern was complete, Nick squatted on his haunches and broke the gun down, checking and cleaning each piece. Calmer now, more in charge of his rage, he rose.

"Nice shooting," Inger said and slapped him

on the shoulder. "Pauly is with Mike. Franton is scrounging us a chicken dinner, and I thought you might want to rendezvous after work at his place despite the cockroaches seen there. You know relax a little, catch up, and take in the sights."

Nick's hands stilled, and his eyes widened. A look of furious expectation on his face, he nodded at Inger.

A hard smile on his thin lips, Inger slapped Nick's back and sauntered off.

Nick stood still, thoughts whirling in his head. Inger had found Steven, and Franton was watching him right now. A glance at his watch showed he had six hours of duty left. Six hours to plan. He considered telling Mike. *No, Mike would insist on coming, and he needed an alibi. Steven is mine. My fault and my responsibility.*

A fresh wave of rage coursed through him. He'd seen how Steven ogled Ashlee. Seen and knew what Steven was thinking and done nothing to protect her. If he'd silenced him instead of trying to reason with him, none of this would've happened. But she'd made him soft, and Steven had seen that softness and taken advantage. *Fuck,* if he'd silenced her goddamned mother none of this would've happened.

Her goddamned fucking mother. What the hell am I going to do about her? He took a few calming breaths. *One problem at a time.* First, he needed to find somewhere to take Steven. No way was this happening quick. That bastard was gonna suffer. Suffer hard. Hands clenched into fists, he stalked back to the lockers, turned in his gun, requested his training rifle, and went to teach his class.

His gaze rested on Sims, a local boy fresh out of out of high school and basic. A bit of a braggart, he was always talking about his new girlfriend and rehashing his glory days of high school football.

Nick waited for an opportunity, and it wasn't long in coming. Sims bragged to the man beside him about a girl he scored.

"Bull fucking shit!" Nick said loudly. Not turning to face the boy, he kept his gaze on his gun, doing a field strip while he talked. "Where the fuck did that happen other than your imagination? What, you took her to the barracks, or, no, maybe mommies' house and banged her on the living room floor?"

Sims laughed. "No, Sir, Sergeant, I brought her to Balmore point."

Nick snorted, and a few men snickered.

"I'm telling you, it's a real isolated spot." Between petulant and proud Sims continued speaking. "The canyons there are like fucking deserted and twisty as fuck. Easy to hide a car in. When we were kids, we used to hike in there, check out the caves and shit, but the place is like littered with snakes. No one goes there much and like I said, it's easy to hide a car. Nobody ever interrupted me there. A few times I've seen other cars there, but everyone ignores each other. The cops let you be. Feels real private. Girls relax, not all jumpy about police finding us."

One of the other men asked for directions. The kid gave directions and added embellishments while Nick put the gun back together. As soon as he could, he left the range and hurried to the office where he banged on Frank's office door.

"Hey, man, can I use your computer? I sort of broke mine."

Frank rose, slapped Nick's shoulder, and gestured him to a seat. "Yeah, I heard this morning. Sorry, man. Is there anything I can do?"

"No, and thanks. Just need a computer to finish my work, and I promise I won't break it." Frank nodded, rummaged around a moment in the small closet in his room, opened a briefcase, and handed Nick a laptop.

"Take mine. I can use the desktop." He sat at

his desk and scribbled on a piece of paper a moment before handing the sheet to Nick. "The passwords to log on. How's Mike holding up?"

Nick took the laptop and stood. "Like what you'd expect. Thanks, Frank."

Once in his office again, Nick ignored the mess he'd made and used the laptop to view Google Earth.

Sure enough, Sims canyons weren't too far away. The dirt roads were hard to make out, overgrown and dark. Pines covered the steep hills interspersed with rocky outcroppings.

Nick thoughtfully tapped the key he'd just stolen from Frank. He'd need a truck. One that couldn't be traced to him. And water. *Lots of fucking water.* By the time work ended for the day, Nick had a plan.

After work, he headed to a local Walmart, copied the key he stole, and bought a five-gallon collapsible water jug. Tomorrow, he'd replace the key. *Hopefully, Frank never noticed its absence.*

He stopped at an office supply store and bought a roll of white magnet, paints, and stencils. A stop at a convenience store netted him another water jug, a red gas can, and a case of blue Powerade.

Supplies thrown in the trunk of his car, he headed to Franton's.

Inger opened the door, glanced down the hallway, then motioned Nick inside. "Franton has eyes on him. What's the plan?" Inger asked as soon as the door closed.

"Where is he?"

"Warehouse on third, hiding out. Trent spotted him outside your place. The police gave chase, but lost him." Inger grinned a hard, feral smile. "Trent let us have him."

Nick nodded and paced the room, rubbing his hands. "I got some shit in the car, but we'll need more. Can you get a kiddie pool, rope—"

"Yeah, don't worry about that crap. I had that shit handled the day I arrived. Motherfucker is gonna pay, but where?"

"Might be I got a lead on that." Nick told Inger about the canyon.

"Right, Franton and I will take this prick and see where we can hold our party. Trent is making sure Mike is surrounded by eyewitnesses twenty-four-seven. It's gonna be hard as shit for you to sneak away."

"Let me worry about that. And thanks. I can't wait to get my hands on that cocksucker."

Inger slapped his back. "Dude messed with the wrong hombres. Fucker shoulda knowed better, he's been out country with us. And what the fuck is up with attacking a woman like that? Any woman, never mind a friend's goddamned wife. Fuckers gotta pay. Can't go letting pervs thinking our wives are easy fucking prey while we're away." Inger spun around and headed to the doorway. "No, we need to make an example of his ass. Play with the bull you get the horns. No one tries this shit again!"

At the doorway, Inger held out a gnarly hand and pushed Nick back. "No, we got this. You go be conspicuously present. Soon as we secure his ass, I'll call you and arrange a visit."

Nick glared, ran his fingers through his close-cropped blond hair and then sighed. "Right, I'll be at the hospital."

In the car headed to the hospital, a grin flitted over his lips. He couldn't wait to get some payback

Trent stood beside Pauly outside the door to Ashlee's room. "Trent." Nick slapped his back and squeezed his shoulder, thanking him with his eyes.

Trent smiled tight and cold.

"How're things here?" Nick gestured to the room.

"Her mom came and screamed and cried until the doctors made her leave. That woman… she needs a psychiatrist or something. For ten minutes she ranted on the wages of sin. Ashlee didn't hear a goddamn thing. They got her sedated. The doc put a tube in her lung to drain the fluid. Mike is with her. Why don't you go get some rest? If you can't sleep at home, come on over. The key is under the mat. Buddies of mine will be there tonight if you need company. Wherever you go take security with you. We got a list of volunteers a mile long."

Nick nodded. "Yeah, I'll rest after I see her for a few minutes. And thanks, Trent, for everything."

"Oh, by the way, that truck Mike was looking at to replace his heap is no longer for sale. Guy down the road from me bought it. Don't know why. Dude never uses it. Maybe he plans on bringing it to Mexico next time he goes."

Nick's eyes lit, and he leaned forward eagerly. "He go there a lot?"

A hard expression on his face, Trent smiled grimly at Nick. "A few times a year. Has family there. He goes for a few weeks at a time. Probably smuggling relatives back, but what do I know?"

Nick smiled, slapped Trent's shoulder again, and headed into the room.

Mike glanced up when Nick entered, and his eyes narrowed. "You're looking awfully happy."

Nick smoothed his expression. "Just glad to be here. It fucking sucks having to work all day. How was she today?"

Mike snorted and stretched in the chair. "How the fuck you think?" He waved a hand in the air, then rubbed his stubbled cheek. "Sorry, man. No worse, but no better either. When she wakes, she asks for you. She's afraid Steven will kill you and come back for her. Trent came in. Took me a fucking hour to convince her Trent wasn't here to harm her."

Mike rose and began pacing in small circles. "She was scared as shit. This is such bullshit! How the hell do we get over this, Nick? My friends terrify her. Mason comes in, and she's calm. The doctors and nurses don't scare her, but one of the guys peeks in the room, and she freaks."

"Don't let them in. What else can we do? Give her time to recover." Nick kissed Ashlee's brow and stroked her hair. "I need to get some rest. I'll stop in again before work." Nick kissed Ashlee again, gave Mike a quick hug and left.

At their apartment, Nick packed up his clothes and uniforms. Cardboard cartons half filled with cookware sat on the counter. Mike and Ashlee's closet was empty. Mike's uniforms were gone from the hall closet.

Someone had packed her books in boxes

and piled them in the hallway. Stacked by the door, instead of the coat closet, the cases of wine she'd bought on their pseudo honeymoon formed a sad pile. Everything from that closet was packed up and neatly labeled. The house felt empty and lifeless. These few boxes, the remnants of three people's lives.

When Ashlee came home, he was taking her shopping, and they were buying stuff. Stuff she liked, pretty, frivolous things. Decorations he could look at and be reminded of her. Things that made her laugh.

Nick rummaged through the pots and pans. Even these weren't good enough for her. The joy she took in cooking should be celebrated with fancy, beautiful cookware, not these serviceable, cheap pans.

He and Mike were used to leading small lives with no possessions, traveling light. Ashlee came to the marriage with few things of her own, dorm living also not conducive to collecting things, but that was going to change.

He would surround her with beauty and safety. Both he and Mike had savings, living frugal lives, banking most of their pay with no real bills to speak of. They could afford nice things for her. *How selfish I'd been with her, taking comfort and happiness but not returning it. Not even noticing the lack, letting her give everything to me. Without her, my life is shit. The least I should've done was support her dreams.* Angry at himself, he grabbed the box of pots and pans and threw them in the dumpster behind the apartments before driving to Trent's.

- 15 -
MI CASA ES SU CASA

The key was right where Trent told him it would be. Nick let himself into Trent's house and hung his uniforms in the spare room. The black duffle bags with his civilian clothes and supplies he left on the closet floor. Security bars blocked the bedroom window, screwed in on the top and bottom.

Nick ran downstairs to Trent's workbench and grabbed the electric drill, all charged up sitting beside the silicone spray in the center of the bench, and in five minutes had the bars unscrewed. A can of WD-40 sprayed liberally around the window frame, and the window slid easily without making a sound. Two minutes later, he'd loosened a wire in the hall light, ensuring it wouldn't work.

Nick put on a dark blue sweat suit, wiped the tools off and replaced them. A quick search of Trent's workbench and he helped himself to a thin file, wire cutters, four lengths of wire and a small multi-tool that he stuck in his waistband under his sweatshirt and taped down with duct tape. Outside, he committed the yard layout to memory before jogging down the street, heading south.

Two blocks away he spotted the house. Gonzales was written in bold yellow script on the mailbox. A pile of newspapers lay by the front door. A glance in the detached garage window revealed an old, dark-blue pickup truck with Brothers Landscaping written on the door. Nick headed into the backyard while pulling on medical gloves he'd stolen from the hospital.

He broke a window pane with an elbow and let himself in. In less than a minute he'd disabled the alarm. *If I have time, I'll come back and fix the window, or maybe Franton can do it,* he thought as he rummaged through drawers searching for the truck keys. It took him thirty minutes to find the keys to the truck.

The garage remote hung on the truck keyring. Two minutes later, he drove straight to Frank's storage locker and parked the truck inside. He walked off the storage yard then ran to the nearby mall and called a cab, taking it to a restaurant near Trent's place and then jogging to Trent's. When he arrived, Trent was home with Mason and four other men.

Trent glanced up as Nick came through the door, a frown forming on his face. "Don't go jogging alone. From now on, take one of us."

"Steven isn't after me; he's after Mike."

The frown on Trent's face changed to a look of exasperation. "Still— better to be safe than sorry."

"Sure, whatever you say. I feel like I'm gonna jump out of my skin. I need to burn some of this off. Wanna go box for a while?"

Mason stood. "I'll go."

"Neither of you are going." Trent pointed to the sofa. "Sit and relax. Dinner is in thirty minutes. You haven't eaten a meal in days and need sleep."

"Fine. Mind if I shower before dinner?"

"Go ahead, *mi casa es su casa*. Clean towels are in the hall closet. Get a good night sleep, and things will look better."

Nick showered quickly. The paint splashed sweatshirt he placed in his supply bag now on his back, he sat beside Mason and drank a Powerade while waiting for Trent to finish making dinner.

Men came and went, Trent's friends from work checking in. Nick was surprised by how concerned everyone seemed. Concerned and angry. After dinner, Mason left, but an MP Nick didn't know parked his jeep out front.

Nick retired to his room where he stayed up late painting magnets. The day's newspaper spread on the floor of Trent's spare room, he drew out the large white magnetic squares and painted them using the stencils he'd bought. A half-finished blue Powerade sat beside his elbow. He heard Mason come in after his shift and headed to the bathroom, mumbling a quick hello.

Mason nodded and headed to his room. Nick wished he'd invited him to the games. If he'd had the chance to meet Ashlee, Nick was sure he'd be helping now too, but Mason had just relocated here, and Mason and Trent had just become partners.

Nick shrugged and stepped over the still drying signs littering his floor. *Fooling one MP shouldn't be that difficult,* he told himself firmly as he flopped on the bed.

❋ ❋ ❋

In the morning, Nick headed to the hospital. Pauly straightened from where he'd been leaning against the wall when Nick entered.

"All quiet, Nick. Mike's in with her now."

"Has she woken?"

Pauly glanced away and rubbed his palms on his pants. "Yeah, and I sort of wish she hadn't."

Nick nodded, swallowing back the bile that rose in his throat.

Pauly moved aside.

Nick straightened his shoulders and entered the room.

Ashlee shut her eye, her body relaxing as soon as she recognized him. The red, puffy cheek had purpled with a tinge of green. The eye had blackened even more and remained swollen shut. Black stitches held the ragged cut closed on the edge of her cheek. Clean, new butterfly-tape covered the slice on her cheekbone.

Mike's hand rested on the nape of her neck, one of the relatively uninjured spots he could reach. An oxygen mask, speckled with small red splotches, covered the lower half of her face.

"Hey, sweetheart," Nick murmured as he leaned over and kissed the crown of her head. A dull-blue eye flickered open and squeezed shut.

Mike cleared his throat. "Doc says time is all our girl needs now. No more surgery."

Ashlee stirred and moaned, then bit her lip and coughed, straining against the urge. Blood flecks sprayed the oxygen mask, and she trembled. Tears leaked, clotting in her lashes, but she didn't moan again.

"Shh." Mike rubbed her neck. "She can't speak to you, Nick, it makes her cough."

"Okay, sweetheart, rest. You'll be better soon, and all this will be behind us. I love you, and you're safe. Mike and I will stay with you." The heart rate monitor began emitting loud beeps. Two other machines began to chatter and whine. Ashlee moaned again and coughed hard, spitting up phlegm tinged with blood.

A nurse raced in the room and hit the red button on the machine that was now shrilling. A doctor ran in and leaned over Ashlee, listening to her breath through a stethoscope while the nurse gave her an injection.

"Mrs. Evans we're going to roll you a bit." The doctor paused and gave directions to the nurses, then resumed speaking to Ashlee. "The fluid buildup in your lungs will be uncomfortable. You might feel like you're drowning, but I assure you, you won't. The new position will make you cough, but you need to get the fluid out. Once it lessens, you'll be much more comfortable."

"Wait," Nick said as the nurse called for assistance. "Can't you drain it with a tube or something?"

"Normally, yes, but the amount of bruising on her left side makes that procedure a last resort. Mrs. Evans has a pleural effusion. That means fluid is building up in her chest cavity and pressing on her lungs, making breathing difficult. The added fluid inside the lung itself compounds the difficulty. A drain is already in place in her right lung."

Nick drew the doctor aside. "The last resort?"

"No unbruised flesh remains in the area. An incision brings a serious risk of infection, a very serious risk."

"Can you sedate her at least?"

"Sedation will weaken her breathing, leaving the potential she chokes to death. An iron lung in her condition… No, as unappetizing as this is, it's the least harmful option. Ideally, she'll cough hard for a minute or two and rid herself of enough fluid to give the medicine time to work."

"And, if she chokes?" Drained of color, Nick turned his white face to Mike.

"Then we proceed with the drain and hope for the best."

Lips tight, Nick returned to the bed and took Ashlee's hand despite the IV.

"Nick and I are here, honey. A few minutes and it's all over." Mike continued to murmur endearments and encouragement as the nurses shifted her under the doctor's supervision.

Over the last day, her back and the backs of her legs had turned black with purple and green streaks with the occasional angry red. Scabbed welts and swollen flesh interspersed the livid bruises. Not an inch of unbruised flesh remained on her back. The front was better. Lacerations, bruising, and burns marred the left side only. A large bruise showed low on her ribcage and bruises ringed a small incision where the doctor had operated on her spleen and kidney.

Ashlee moaned and panted as they adjusted her and fought the cough as long as she could. "Mike," she gasped between hard hacks and choking. "Mike." Her thin voice rose and quavered.

"How much longer, Doc?" Mike turned a grim face on the doctor while Ashlee heaved, choking and gasping and began to struggle against the nurses hold, her pleading, terrified gaze locked on her husband's face. Ashlee swung her beseeching stare to Nick and tried to call his name, not able to utter more than 'Ni' before choking.

"That's enough. Stop already." Nick glared at the doctor, reaching out to pull the nurse nearest him away.

Ashlee coughed up a wad of phlegm and vomited greenish bile. The doctor nodded to the nurses, and they resettled Ashlee on her stomach, tipped slightly on her side and held in place by foam wedges. Shudders wracked her body and tears streamed from her good eye.

The doctor listened to her breathing. "You're doing well, Mrs. Evans. We won't need to do that again. Rest. Try to take small shallow breaths."

"Nurse Tilgen, send samples to the lab. Let's see what we have. Nurse Hendricks, two CCs of Salbutamol and fifteen-minute checks. Call me at once if anything changes. Sergeant Rossi, if you could stay and visit for a moment while I speak with her husband?"

The doctor gestured Mike to proceed him out the door while Nick took Mike's seat.

"Did I ever tell you how Mike and I met?" Nick kept his voice calm and light. A fine tremble shook the hand in his, slowing as he spoke.

A commotion in the doorway caused Ashlee to crane her head and the hand in his to clench. Her terrified gaze met his; she tried to speak and began to cough. Her mother burst through the doorway, slapping at Mike's grasping hand.

"Ashlee Claire Conner, tell the doctor you're coming home with me." Cold, blue eyes drilled into Nick. "This man is no good, surely you see that now? Flaunt Gods will at your peril."

"Get out!" Mike grabbed her arm and yanked, pulling her from the room.

"This is what happens when you lead an immoral life, fornicating with heathen men without the sanctity of marriage!" Unrelenting in her harangue she yelled imprecations as Mike dragged her out.

Alarms around the bed again sounded. Ashlee continued to cough and strain. The doctor returned followed by MPs.

"Keep that woman out!" Cold and hard, Nick's voice shook with anger. "Her mother doesn't recognize the marriage because it wasn't in a church and Mike isn't Catholic. Ashlee needs peace and quiet. When she's well, she can work things out with her mother, but now isn't the time."

Muffled by the walls and other people hollering, Margret could be heard ranting on the wages of sin and screeching at Mike to release his devilish hold on her daughter to save her eternal soul.

A scuffle broke out in the hallway, and more men yelled for both Mike and Margret to come along with them. The noise died away, and Ashlee calmed as Nick smoothed her hair and murmured endearments.

❋ ❋ ❋

Trent sat beside Mike and sighed. "I get it, man, but you aren't helping yourself with this."

Mike snorted and rattled the chain holding his hand to the desk. "That goddamn bitch is lucky I didn't break her skinny neck. "

"As mother-in-laws go she's a doozy, I grant you that. She's still screaming about the wages of sin."

"Can you keep her away? Ashlee doesn't need any additional stress."

Trent slapped a folder of paperwork on the table between them.

"Fill out these forms. You should've done this when you married."

Mike winced and ran his free hand through his hair.

"Register your wife on base. Don't worry about the insurance. Yours covers her, but this should've been done months ago."

"Yeah, but we didn't think there was any hurry. She didn't need the school benefits, and well, I thought they might give me a hard time 'cause we married so quick. And I wasn't sure how her dual citizenship would affect my postings."

Trent rolled his eyes and tapped the folder with one thick finger.

"Don't be a moron. Just fill the paperwork

out. It's not like your superiors don't know all that already. Talk to a lawyer about getting a restraining order against Margret. And meanwhile, keep your cool so she can't get one against you."

"Can she do that?" Mike leaned forward, his eyes wide.

"How the fuck do I know, but why make it easy?"

"Gimme a pen." Mike sighed and held out his hand.

Trent handed him a pen.

Mike began filling out forms.

Trent glanced at his watch. "Just sign them, Mike. Nick can fill them out. I can't leave you with a pen, and I gotta get going."

Lips tight, Mike scribbled his signature in a furious scrawl and slid the papers to Trent. "Thanks, Trent. And I hate to ask, but could you find me a good lawyer?"

"Yeah, I'll talk to Nick about it. And don't hesitate to ask. Ashlee is my friend too."

"I'm sorry she freaked when you came in." A blush crawled across Mike's cheeks.

"No worries, man. I understand, and I'm sure in time she'll realize Steven had nothing to do with the rest of us." Trent slapped the table with his palm, the noise loud and echoing in the small room. "That goddamned bastard!" He took a deep breath and rose, gathering the papers and pen and headed to the door. "The captain will let you go with a minor misdemeanor, disturbing the peace. Mrs. Conner will beat you out. We'll do our best to keep her away. Ashlee asked for no visitors except you and Nick, but we can't stop her from going to the hospital, just into her room."

"Thanks, do what you can." Mike offered his hand and glared when the chain jerked him up short. Trent rapped the table with his knuckles, then banged on the door with his fist. Mason let him out.

✳ ✳ ✳

Mike entered the hospital room and leaned over Ashlee to kiss her brow. "More x-rays, hun. The doc wants to make sure your ribs stayed in place."

Nick glared at Mike and put his lips on Ashlee's brow. "Relax, no one will hurt you. Stop straining, sweetheart. You're hurting yourself. X-rays won't hurt."

"Your mother returned to Ireland. Don't worry about her, honey," Mike added.

Mike and Nick exchanged relieved glances as the machines hooked to her steadied into slow, even beeps.

Three hours later, they sat by her bedside as she slept. "I finished most of the paperwork."

Nick pointed at the pile on the small table by Ashlee's bed. "The lawyer Trent found called and wants to meet. No hurry, I guess, if the shrew went home."

"Thanks, I'll finish and file."

"Might be a problem as Ashlee can't sign them. The doctors had to cut off both rings, and her fingers are too swollen to sign anything at all. Ask the lawyer, maybe he can witness it or something."

Nick paced the small room, pausing at the door, the bed, and the bank of machinery. "I fucking hate this." Nick glanced at his vibrating phone and stilled, his body quivering with eagerness. "I have to report for duty. Call me if anything changes." He gave Ashlee a light kiss on her forehead and stalked out the door.

- 16 -
MOAN FOR ME REAL GOOD

Two men wearing desert camouflage strode over to Steven Wrint. Bound and gagged, his terrified gaze darted between them. Both men wore black ski masks and surgical gloves. Another man entered and handed one of the men a clear plastic poncho with New York Yankees emblazoned on the back.

Steven began to struggle against his bonds. Wild-eyed and panting furiously, muscles strained as he yanked on the rope holding him.

Two of the men left after slapping the one with the poncho on the back. As soon as they left, Nick pulled off his mask. "Well, Steven, seems you got a bit carried away, no?"

Steven shook his head rapidly, gaze darting over the room.

Nick squatted and removed the gag. "Nobody is around to hear you, but I'll be annoyed if you scream."

Steven licked dry lips.

"Tell me where and how many recordings you have."

"None… Ashlee—"

As hard as he could, Nick punched him in the face. "Never speak her name again."

Steven nodded and licked the blood from his split lip. "Something came over me, man. I had no intention of doing any of that, but she was so stubborn. I'm okay with you being in charge, Nick. Now I see where I went wrong, I should've killed Mike first."

Nick hit him again. "Stop talking. Tell me where the recordings are."

"I told you— I don't have any."

Nick reached into a pocket, drew out a blade and slashed Steven's cheek. Blood spurted, splashing on the poncho as Steven jerked his head back. "That's one, Steven. One hundred forty- three to go, but I'm willing to go the extra mile here."

"What… stop. Come on, Nick. I'm one of you. Yeah, I screwed up, and I'm sorry. I really am. For real, I didn't mean to kill her or even hurt her that bad. We can get another girl, Nick. How about a beautiful blonde? There's this real hot chick…"

Nick ignored his babbling, pulled a pair of

pliers from his pocket, and grabbed Steven's hand. A short struggle ensued, ending with screams and two fingernails laying on the ground.

"Fuck… you fucking bastard!" Steven tugged against his bonds, swearing and panting.

"Let's see, where to start? Seeing as you won't talk, I might as well start with cutting out your tongue, but then I don't get to enjoy your screams." Nick tapped his chin a moment and then smiled. "First things first."

Not acknowledging Steven's protests, threats, and struggles, Nick cut off Steven's clothing. "My friends return soon. It's important to me you have the entire experience, so they're bring me supplies. What will we need, Steve? Water for sure, and lots of it. Tell me, what did you beat her with?"

Steven clamped his lips together and stared at the rock wall.

"That's cool. I'm up for some adlibbing; it's a recreation, after all, doesn't need to be exact. What I don't understand is why? Why kill her?"

Steven choked back his laughter and glared at Nick.

"Fucking bitch would spread her legs for everyone except me. Thought she was too good or something. Her roommate, Sydney, told me stories, and I saw how much she liked it. Fuck, man, I didn't mean to kill her, wanted to teach her a lesson. Wanted her to beg me for it. Uptight, snotty little bitch wouldn't give in, so I had to persuade her hard. Kill me, Nick, cause nothings gonna change the fact she moaned for me real good."

A furious glitter in his gray eyes, two red spots bloomed on Nick's cheeks as Steven spoke. "Think it's that easy, do you? Get me mad, and I'll kill you quick? No, you'll beg me before I'm done." Nick stood and nudged Steven with his boot. "You'll moan for me real good. Let's start with this." Nick strolled to the cave entrance and opened a black bag, taking out a small first aid kit. "Don't think I'm getting soft; I just don't want to you to bleed to death when I cut off your dick."

Nick laughed when Steven swore and struggled, his testicles shriveled tight. Nick grabbed the man's limp penis, yanking hard and twisting, in his hand was a tool for calf castration.

"Gotta admire Inger's imagination and ingenuity. Wonder where the hell he got this from? When I get a second, I gotta see what other fun toys he brought me. See, normally, Steve, this little elastic thingy goes around the balls. The calf screams but settles down quick enough, and in a few days the balls rot and fall off, but I had a better idea." He sat on Steven's chest to restrain him and used the castrating gun on Steven's penis. Steven screamed long and shrill as the elastic band snapped closed.

"Yeah, that ought to do it. Now, where were we? Oh, yeah. Ready to tell me what you beat her with or where the pictures are?"

Steven moaned, cursing and thrashing as Nick stood. The restraints on Steven's hands wouldn't let him reach his crotch, although he kept attempting too, cutting into the skin of wrists in his attempts.

"Let's see if you're tougher than my wife. Going to break your hand to get free? Maybe I'll even let you go if you do. Hell, do it quick enough, and you might even save your cock."

Nick sat on the ground, his back to the rock wall and watched Steven struggle and curse.

Voice thick with tears and hate Steven snarled, "The original recordings are in my apartment, so I assume the police have them. Copies are in the garden shed two doors down from me in a fake paint can on the shelf. Copies of everything are on a hard drive with the letter you wrote her."

Nick buffed his nails on his shirt and inspected them, then glanced at Steven and rose an eyebrow. "And?"

Steven strained at his bonds until the veins in his forehead stood out. Spittle flew from his lips he yelled so harshly, "My belt, goddamn it! I used my belt. But I didn't hit her all that hard. The bruises surprised me. She was just kind of red at first. I didn't realize she would bruise that easy."

Nick removed his belt and slapped it on his palm a few times and then drew back his arm. The leather whistled through the air, connecting with a sharp crack and Steven screamed.

Nick made a line of welts spaced four inches apart across the front of Steven's body and stopped. "Don't want to kill you quite yet. How many times did you water-board her?"

Steven didn't answer. Limp and trembling, moaning and sniffling, he cowered on the dirt.

"Doesn't matter. I'll just do it till you die." Nick glanced at his watch. "Well, gotta run for now, but I'll be back. Don't go anywhere. Unless you got the balls to pull your hand free like my wife did." Cold gray eyes examined Steven once more before Nick left.

Nick loped through the woods and jumped into the stolen truck. Homemade magnets stuck to the side identified the truck as a water company vehicle. Before he pulled onto the main road, Nick pulled over, removed the magnets, and wedged them under the seat, replacing them with ones that said Easy Rental. Then he drove to the storage shed Frank rented and parked inside to change his clothes. He jogged down the street for two miles and got in his car, which he'd left in the mall parking lot.

Once in the car, he removed his sweatshirt and drove away. Before he arrived at work, he'd kicked off the sneakers, shimmied out of the sweatpants, revealing his fatigues, stuffed his feet into boots, tied them, and donned the button-up shirt.

After work, he visited Ashlee for three hours, then went to Trent's house where he greeted Mason and two other officers before retiring to Trent's spare room.

In the bedroom, Nick stuffed a rolled blanket under the covers and positioned the pillows over a blond wig. A prosthetic arm with a lifelike hand he stole from the hospital fit into the sweatshirt with the distinctive paint stains, and he arranged it on the bed. The small nightlight he took from his bag and plugged in the corner gave enough of a glow to make out the bed, but not enough to see clearly. The light dimmed randomly giving the illusion of movement. Unless someone shook his fake shoulder, they should assume he was asleep in the bed.

A dark blue sweat suit and black sneakers on, Nick eased the bars in the window, which he'd previously unscrewed, out, and lowered them to the ground outside, then climbed out. After replacing the bars in the window, he jogged down the street where Inger waited.

Inger dropped him off at the canyon, and he ran back to the cave where he'd left Steven.

"Ah, I see my friends were here," Nick said in satisfaction.

Nick rapped the metal stretcher set in the plastic kiddy pool with his knuckles, the tinny sound echoing in the rock room. "Did they have some fun with you?"

Steven glared from a blackening eye. The gag on his mouth prevented a reply. The beating Nick had given him had left blue bruises across his chest and thighs, and his cock was a dark purple. Nick poked it with a gloved finger and laughed when Steven screamed.

"Man, I bet that hurts. Let's get you on the table; I'm sure you're thirsty by now."

Nick untied his feet while Steven kicked at him, sharp grunts and screams coming from behind the gag. Hands on his hips, Nick sighed. "Man, you're an idiot. What do you hope to accomplish?" A hard grin on his face,

Nick went to the bag in the corner and rummaged through it, removing a blow torch, which he weighed in his hand for a moment and then set it aside for a hammer.

Steven's eyes widen, and he shook his head, making a high keening moan behind the gag as he tried to speak.

"Yeah, yeah, I know, you never used one of these, but see, I don't have all day and night like you did. I only have six hours to play with you tonight. That means I can't be as artistic. While I would love to hold a candle to your foot and burn it in small increments, I just don't have the time. You see my dilemma, right? That was real imaginative by the way, using a candle on her feet and the hot wax on her breast like that. Did she beg you to stop or did you gag her?"

Steven groaned and thrashed his head, nodding as hard as he could.

"Nodding won't help, dumbass."

Nick jumped forward and grabbed both Steven's legs, using his weight to hold them down then used the hammer on Steven's toes. While Steven moaned and sobbed, Nick dragged him to the stretcher and tied him. Once Steven was secure, Nick took out the pliers and one at a time pulled out Steven's fingernails and toenails.

"Three extra for good luck," Nick said as he dropped the last nail on the floor. "Let's rinse you off a bit; you're starting to smell." Nick tipped the stretcher and poured water over Steven's face then stopped and slapped himself in the head. "Wait, I forgot. The ribs, Steven, how many did you break or don't you know?"

Nick waited a moment, grinning a manic grin at Steven before speaking. "Well, I know. You broke four. So, that's eight for you, plus a few for luck, I think." Nick returned to the bag and grabbed a mallet, a chisel with a round end, and a thick piece of padding.

Steven whimpered and begged as Nick turned him over.

"I'm betting my wife didn't beg. Of course, she didn't realize what you were doing, or did she? Did you tell her? Did you enjoy her terror? Doesn't matter what you say, as she said, it's all lies anyway. But, I'll ask her. Oh ho, I shocked you. Yeah, she isn't dead." Nick struck the mallet on the chisel hard and laughed when Steven screamed. After taking three more hits, he flipped him over again and did two more on the front bottom ribs.

"That ought to do it. Now, let's rinse you off."

Nick left Steven tied to the stretcher crying and choking. "Ta, ta, be back in a few."

Nick ran from the cave and met Inger who drove him back to Trent's.

"If we just disappear the fucker, we can avoid all this," Inger said as he pulled to a stop down the street from Trent's.

"If we disappear him, Ash will worry the rest of her life. Besides, this will send a real clear message."

Inger nodded and drove away.

Nick snuck back into the bedroom and changed into light-gray sweat pants and the stained shirt, tucked the wig deep into his bag with the prosthetic arm, and unrolled the blanket. A glance at his watch showed he had forty minutes, so he stretched out on the bed. At six, the alarm sounded. He slapped the buzzer and pushed himself out of bed. Hiding a yawn behind his fist, he headed to the bathroom, nodding good morning to Mason who sat at the kitchen table drinking coffee. In thirty minutes, he left for work and signed in right on time.

He managed an hour and a half nap at lunchtime and stopped for fast food, which he ate on the way to visit Ashlee after work. By her bedside he dozed, holding her hand, a bottle of blue Powerade by his feet. Mike left when he arrived. At eleven, Franton and Pauly escorted Nick to Trent's.

Mason glanced up when he entered. "Two guards will be outside tonight. Trent's already asleep. We haven't spotted Steven again, but we won't give up. We located the room where he kept her and Ashlee's DNA is all over his apartment. Seems he went home to clean up afterward and didn't bother getting rid of the bloody clothing." Mason flushed and glanced away. "The man had over a hundred hours of video from your house. As far as I know no one watched it yet, but any day now."

Nick's lips tightened.

"Get some rest. Nothing you can do about that now."

Nick poured himself a Powerade and sat beside Mason on the couch. "Guards probably aren't necessary on me, just Mike."

Mason shrugged. "Can't hurt and it's not like we have a shortage of manpower."

Nick nodded. The entire base was in an uproar. Thousands had volunteered for guard duty. "Well, I'm gonna hit the hay, I'm beat. Ash had a rough night, and I want to visit her before work tomorrow."

"I'm on duty tonight, three to eleven, want me to wake you?"

"If you're in the neighborhood, a four-thirty wake up would be good."

"No problem. If I'm not here, one of the

guards will make sure you're up."

Nick thanked him and headed to the bedroom where he repeated the same procedure as the night before. Except, this time, he eased from the window and slunk across the yard, hopping the fence into the neighbor's yard and crawling along it until he reached the far corner.

At the corner of the five-foot privacy fence he hesitated, then jumped over and crawled along the bushes, swearing to himself when he put his hand in dog shit. As best he could, he wiped his hand on the grass and continued his crawl. At the end of the bushes, he stood and jogged along the street.

Franton picked him up.

"Jesus!" Franton made a face and rummaged in his glove compartment, emerging with a box of wet-wipes.

Nick snorted and scrubbed his hands. "Pick me up at three."

"No problem. I spent some quality time with him today. Seems to like me. Begged me not to go. Please. Don't. Leave me alone." Franton snickered.

Nick snorted again. "Let's see if I can make him love me more."

At three, Franton picked him up, raising a bushy eyebrow at the blood splattered on

Nick's face and handing him the wet wipes again.

"Don't kill the fucker," Nick said as he exited the car.

Franton nodded and drove away.

Nick crawled back through the window with ten minutes to spare. The last thirty minutes he'd spent sweating, waiting for his guard to move on so he could get in the window. The guard was too damn vigilant, pacing back and forth in the yard in a random pattern, flashlight in hand.

Nick had finally resorted to picking up a rock with his shirttail and throwing it through the neighbor's window. Once inside Trent's spare bedroom, he set a speed record for changing into the paint-splattered sweatshirt and raced into the living room as if he'd just woken.

Next door, the neighbor's alarm blared. "What's going on?" Nick tried to sound sleepy and confused.

"No idea," Trent said. "Stay here. I'll check it out." Gun in hand, Trent headed out the door. From the doorway, Nick waved at the men outside, making sure they saw him, before closing the door. As soon as the door shut, he ran to the bathroom and jumped in the shower. He was showered, shaved, and dressed for the day, wig and fake arm hidden in his bag when Trent returned, followed by Mason and the two guards.

"Could be nothing. A vandal threw a rock through a window next door. Police are on the scene. They'll dust it for prints, but…."Trent shrugged. "Keep your eyes peeled, Nick. Could've been Steven checking response time."

"We'll give you a ride to the hospital."

"No need. Besides, how will I get to work with no car?"

"We'll follow you there then and make sure you get inside okay."

Nick nodded, thanked Trent for his hospitality, and headed out.

In the end, Steven begged Nick to kill him, and Nick complied. A gun in each hand, Nick stood over him. Beaten, bloody, and only semi-conscious, Steven's terrified brown eyes stared into Nick's cold gray ones.

"Be afraid, Steven, for Hell surely awaits you."

Nick pulled both triggers. Inger and Franton also shot, the sound deafening in the space. Nick picked up another gun and shot again. "Those first shots were for me and Ashlee, this one's for Mike, you, sorry son of a bitch."

Once the bleeding stopped, Nick poured

water over Steven for the last time. Dirty, bloody water collected in the kiddie pool. Inger and Franton cleaned off the stretcher while Nick slapped bandages on the bloody wounds and wrapped the body in a sheet.

The three men threw the body on the stretcher, carried the stretcher outside, and dropped it into the back of a truck where they pulled a tarp over it.

Inger's worried gaze traveled from the corpse to Nick. "This is crazy, Nick. Just leave him on the side of the road somewhere. Someone will find his sorry ass, and she'll know he's dead."

"Don't worry. I gotta plan, and if I'm caught, you were never there."

The three men bumped fists and split up. Nick drove straight to Frank's storage shed. Inside the shed, Nick stuffed the body in a box marked, 'Appliance Keep This End Up' he borrowed from the corner where Frank had stashed an old refrigerator and heaved it into the back of the stolen truck with homemade magnet signs on the side claiming to be from Easy Rental. An unboxed flat screen, he also borrowed from Frank's stuff, was placed on the floor of the truck and then he took out a makeup kit.

Usually, when he used this kit, he attempted

to resemble an Arab. Many times he'd snuck close and even walked through towns wearing a disguise to get in range of a target. Tonight, he aimed for an overweight white man. He donned the clothes Inger had dropped off, old jeans and worn, black polo shirt with the name Clearance over the pocket, topped off with an equally shabby baseball cap over a disheveled brown wig. He glanced at his watch after he finished applying his disguise, and smiled. Right on time.

He would go through the base gates during evening rush hour.

Steven had taken Ashlee to an unfinished apartment complex on the south corner of the base. Intended to be single efficiency units, the building was only partly constructed behind the maintenance hangers. Incomplete for two years, construction had halted over safety issues. The contractor had used substandard materials, and the housing was condemned and slated for removal as soon as the case passed through appellate court. On the edge of base, weeds smashed by police encroached the entrances of the abandoned building. Yellow police tape crossed the doorways and windows.

Nick pulled up to the side entrance and rolled the box containing the corpse out and into the building, leaving it right inside the doorway. He returned to the truck, drove up the street, to a finished apartment complex, parked, and walked around the building and back to the deserted apartments. After glancing around, as he pretended to tie his shoe, he headed into the building.

Inside, a trail led through the dust, leading to the room Steven had kept Ashlee. Nick dragged Steven behind him on the hand truck, down the stairs, and into the dark basement.

He hadn't been here before. A slice of light from the open doorway landed on the bed in the otherwise pitch-black closet off the main basement. An old, rusty-metal headboard, showing new scratches, almost filled the small space. The sight of the blood-stained mattress infuriated him. A pile of chains lay beside the bed. A stack of half-full, five-gallon water containers laid outside the door. Initially intended to be a storage closet, the space had no windows and just the one door.

Nick wished he could hurt Steven again. Torture him for years until the sound of his screams erased the sounds in his head of his wife crying.

Panting with rage, he dragged Steven from the box and arranged him on the damp mattress, using the chains artistically. He paused to admire his work, then left, making sure he broke the tape surrounding the doors so the police would investigate.

Back in the storage shed, he changed clothes, bundling the clothes he'd worn over the last few days into separate, small paper bags that he weighted with rocks. Inger would be by later to gather and dispose of them. Franton would clean up the cave, removing the tools and spraying the floor and walls with lime. Tomorrow, Nick would return the prosthetic limb.

A quick stop followed at a do-it-yourself car wash where he vacuumed the truck and washed out the bed and wheels. Two blocks away from Trent's, he returned the truck from where he'd borrowed it, a hair cleaner and a few extra miles on it. Even if the owner noticed, there was nothing to link it to Nick.

At Trent's house, he used the spare key to let himself in and headed to the basement where he found the electric screwdriver on the workbench right where he'd left it four days ago. A few minutes later the security bars were firmly screwed in place, the screwdriver wiped down and returned. He called Trent to secure his alibi and asked him what he should make for dinner.

Thirty minutes later, Trent showed up with

Mason and two other men. For the first time in days, Nick really relaxed. Ashlee was safe. All that remained was retrieving the tapes and letter he'd written from the garden shed, and he could do that at his leisure. That night he slept like a log. Trent had to shake him awake over the alarm clock blaring in the morning.

- 17 -
Get Her Back Legal

"Well, this is a poser." Mason put his hands on his hips as he examined the room before him.

Broken crime scene tape dangled in the doorway. On the bare mattress, from which crime scene investigators had snipped patches when they'd examined the scene days ago, a naked corpse was spread eagled and tied wrists and ankles with loops of chain. A square of gauze taped over his heart barely covered a ragged hole. Red and purple lines, crusted with blood, crisscrossed the corpse head to toe with exact precision. Chains wound around the man's hands. Bloody clotted stumps of fingernails and toenails accented smashed hands and feet. Black eyes set in a swollen, cut up face. A scabbed bloody mess festered on his groin where his penis used to be. A large burn, blackened and crisp, covered his left deltoid, the left nipple burned away.

Trent kicked the foot of the bed the corpse lay on. "Fucker deserved everything and then some."

Mason snorted. "Still a murder, partner. Although I can't argue the justice of it. Bet if we counted there are a hundred and forty-four knife slashes."

Trent made an appreciative sound and grinned. "Bet when the coroner flips his ass over, every damn rib is broken. But no blood on the bed, so he wasn't killed here. This many wounds would've left a horrible mess."

"Why put the fucker here, why not just disappear him?" Mason heaved a sigh. "Never mind. Stupid damn question. He disappears, and she's afraid forever. Better call this in."

Trent smiled and pulled out his radio.

"What the hell are you smiling about? Your friend is going to prison."

"Pfft, no way. Mike isn't dumb. I guarantee he left no evidence behind. But don't get your panties in a knot, we do this by the book."

Mason continued to frown, his hands on his hips. "And, we're in a world of shit. We destroyed evidence that would implicate Nick. This could be him, not Mike. Hell, it was probably both."

* * *

The coroner slapped his report on the chief's desk. "You won't be making the golf game this week."

The chief flipped through the report, his brown eyes narrowing.

The coroner sat in the chair with easy familiarity, crossing his legs and leaning back. "A laundry list of injuries, but bottom line, time and cause of death. Mr. Wrint was dead one day before he was found. My best estimate is the injuries took place over a number of days."

The chief snorted. "Yeah, four. A rookie could've told me that. What killed him?"

"Gunshot to the heart. Five of them to be exact. All from different guns at close range. Impossible to tell which gun fired first. Could've been one man with five guns, or five men, or any combination. Not one hair on his body except for hers. Same with blood, none except his and hers. As her alibi is airtight, you need to look elsewhere."

"Airtight— on her death bed. I tell you, it turns my stomach. If it were up to me, I'd give whoever did this a goddamned medal." The metal office chair squeaked as the chief swiveled side-to-side. "So, no physical evidence?"

"The bullets, the rope, the gauze, but

nothing we have can pinpoint anyone. Crime scene is still combing the bedroom and officers are searching for the kill sight, but obviously, this was her husband."

"Except most of the time he was at her bedside."

"He must have left to eat and sleep, no?"

"Yep. Went home at least five or six times over the last week with guards." The chief smiled while the coroner frowned. "And, not just his own men, but MPs and other men. Seems the base wanted to make sure Steven didn't get a shot at him while he slept. As alibis go, it's pretty tight."

"So, his squad?"

"Seems likely, but good luck proving a damn thing." The chief flipped through the report. "Damned if we do, damned if we don't, here. The base is in an uproar. Every single one of our men has motive. They all wanted Steven Wrint dead, and are glad a message was sent deterring any other would-be rapists that get ideas while they're away."

"So, how we playing this?"

The chief straightened in his chair, folding his hands on the desk before him. "By the book. Dot every I, cross every T, no mistakes. If we make an arrest, there better be no doubt. Our men even think we're trying to brush this under the rug with a quick arrest they're going to riot."

The coroner nodded and stood. "I'll leave you to it then."

The chief called Mason and Trent into his office. "Bring the husband in for questioning. Let's see what he has to say. And his squad. All of them. And Sergeant Rossi. As of this moment, they're confined to base. All leaves canceled."

❃ ❃ ❃

Nick and Mike sat beside Ashlee, both haggard. The doctor had just placed a drain in her left lung. In a medically induced coma, wrapped in a cooling blanket with her feet in ice water in an attempt to lower the fever, Ashlee lay pale and unresponsive.

Four MPs entered the room. "Sirs, if you would come with us please?"

Mike jumped to his feet. Nick rose slowly.

"What's this about?" Mike asked as he followed the officer from the room.

"The body of Steven Wrint has been found, and you're wanted for questioning."

Mike stopped dead and grabbed the man's shoulder, his face intent. "The body? That cock sucker is dead?"

"As a doornail." The MP smiled a moment before assuming a professional air. "Please, sir?"

Mike grinned and nodded, both hands rubbing together.

Nick followed. "Did he off himself?"

"No, I'm sorry, sirs, please save your questions."

Nick slapped Mike's shoulder as they got into the back of a Jeep.

Twenty hours later, the grin had died from Mike's face, replaced with a scowl as he paced the small interrogation room.

"I get it, of course, we're suspects, but how the hell do they think we managed that Houdini trick? Both of us were under constant surveillance." Mike kicked the chair into the wall.

"Just sit down. Keep acting all crazy, and they'll hold you longer."

Mike glared at him and kicked the chair again.

Nick sighed and grabbed the chair, setting it down hard and pointing. "Sit and stay there. Let our lawyer handle this."

Released twelve hours later, they returned to the hospital to find Ashlee gone.

"What do you mean transferred?" Mike shouted at the nurse. "Who transferred her? She was in a fucking coma!"

"Sir, I'm sorry, sir. I had nothing to do with it. Perhaps you'd like to speak to her doctor?" The nurse scurried away, peering over her shoulder at Mike's furious face.

Nick stood against the wall, his lips pressed together as Mike screamed at the doctor, forgetting rank and military discipline in his aggravation. "Where the fuck is my wife and why wasn't I consulted?"

"I'm sorry, sir, but her mother removed her yesterday evening. I can only assume she brought her home. Mrs. Conner presented legal documents. As you were incarcerated at the time, we had no choice but to release her. I assure you, medical procedure was followed. A private ambulance picked her up, and two physicians attended. The fever had receded, although she hadn't woken from the coma."

"What the hell do you mean her mother had legal documents? What legal documents? Why wasn't I informed? I'm Ashlee's next of kin."

"Not according to the Army. Mrs. Conner is Ashlee's legal next of kin until the paperwork is filed stating otherwise. While the marriage is legal, the right of the parent supersedes the right of the spouse if said spouse is accused of a felony and serving time. At least that's what our lawyers say."

"What horse shit. I wasn't accused or serving

time. I was held for questioning!"

Nick grabbed Mike's arm and yanked him away from the doctor. "Cut it out. Let the doctor go. Thank you, Major." He shook Mike when he protested, giving him a pointed glare. "Who the fuck cares why? Just go get her back."

Mike turned to the retreating doctor, and Nick grabbed him again. "No, he won't know where she is, but it doesn't take a genius to figure it out. She'll be taking her to Ireland."

Furious, Mike snatched his arm away and glowered. "And we can't fucking follow. We're confined to base, remember?"

Nick nodded. "Go home and get any paperwork you can find proving who you are and that you're married to Ashlee. Grab the wedding pictures and anything else you can think of. Copy everything while I find out exactly where she is. So help me God, if Ashlee is hurt by this, I'm going to kill that woman." Nick spun around and ran from the room.

In two hours, Nick had located Ashlee on a flight to Dublin. Margret had whisked her from the hospital to the embassy where she lied her ass off about Ashlee's medical condition, claiming she was in an irreversible coma and offering fake medical records to get her sent home. Ashlee's passport and paperwork still contained her maiden name. Her mother had no problem at all claiming to be her guardian.

Mike was nowhere to be found.

In Trent's house, Nick paced. "That goddamned idiot. Jesus Christ, Trent. Mike's going to get himself arrested, and I can't get her back without him."

"Sit, you're wearing out my rug."

Nick sat so hard the couch in Trent's living room let out a loud oomph. Elbows resting on his knees, Nick cradled his head in his hands. "How did my life become shit so fast?"

"Calm down. I grant you this sucks, but it's a minor setback. Apply for leave and go get her."

"How? I have no legal right to her. Unless she's conscious and can say for herself, I can't get her back."

"Yeah. Right." Trent rubbed his forehead with two fingers. "Well, she'll be conscious soon, right? The doctor said…" Trent got himself a beer and handed one to Nick, who took it absently.

"Sure, right, if the goddamned flight doesn't kill her. What are the chances I'll get permission to leave the state, never mind the country?"

Trent winced and sipped his beer. "Not

good. Not until they investigate anyways. It's not like they can keep you here permanently though without charges."

Nick glanced up. "Will there be charges?"

"For you, probably not. Mike on the other hand, maybe? And if he went AWOL, I can practically guarantee them." Trent leaned forward. "Take my advice, Nick, keep your head down and let this blow over. You run off, they're gonna throw the book at you. And God forbid Margret dies while you're over there. Leave a trail of dead bodies and someone is sure to notice. Unless you want to run forever with Ashlee, get her back legal."

"Legal," Nick snarled. "Ashlee needs me, and the law will crucify me if I go to her. I'd do it too, but she needs medical help."

"So, let her get the help she needs. Right now, she doesn't know from nothing. When she wakes, call her. She understands you're under military discipline and can't just leave. She can have herself sent back to you."

Nick leaned back and rolled the cold bottle over his forehead. "You're right, but damn it's hard."

Two days later, Mike was returned in handcuffs, thrown into a cell, and charged with going absent without leave.

"What the hell is wrong with you? Thirty fucking days now, Mike! Are you fucking retarded? Is all you had to do was ask for leave!"

Nick ran a hand through his hair. Lips pressed tight together, he glared at Mike. So angry he could barely contain himself, Nick grabbed the back of a metal office chair, leaned forward, and yelled in Mike's face, "Jesus, the CO would have given you leave as soon as he could. Now you look guilty as hell. You're lucky he isn't court-martialing your ass!"

Mike returned the glare. "Don't be such an ass. What was I supposed to do? Let her mother have her?"

"Mike…" Nick rubbed his face and sat in the chair hard. "Margret does have her. Be smart and get her back legal. When Ash wakes from the coma, she'll insist on coming home. Send her a ticket." Unable to sit still, Nick jumped to his feet and paced the room, resisting the urge to kick the metal chair or beat it against the wall. "File the paperwork so her mother can't take her again."

Mike sat in the other emetal chair with his arms crossed and his booted feet spread. "I want to kill that woman. Ashlee needs me… us." In a sudden violent movement, Mike rose and kicked the chair he'd sat in into the wall, then leaned on the table with both hands, his head hanging. "When I think of my wife waking alone and afraid, and we don't go to her…"

"Which is why you should've listened to me! I can't bring her back, Mike. Only you can. Not until she wakes at least. What did the doctor say about that? How long till I can get her?" Worry over Ashlee's condition dulled his anger at Mike.

"Three weeks before she can return safely, and that's assuming traveling didn't hurt her. The doctor is concerned with the air pressure affecting her lungs. The longer they have to heal, the better." Mike spun away, picked up the chair, and slammed it upright by the table. "That woman doesn't care if she kills her daughter as long she keeps her from us."

Nick straightened, his face pale. "Fuck, Three weeks? I can't get that much leave now. Not with this investigation hanging over my head." Dazed, Nick sat again and rested his head in his hands. In a soft, hard voice, he whispered, "Mike, I promise you, if she kills Ashlee, she won't live long herself."

For a moment, Mike was quiet. "What are we going to do, Nick?"

Hands spread flat and pressed hard on the table top, Nick glared at Mike. "Keep our heads down. Follow the rules. File the paperwork, and pray. The minute Ashlee can safely come home, we bring her back."

Mike scowled then sighed and grabbed the chair he'd thrown. Without bothering to raise it, he sat and slid it to the table. The loud squeal it made echoed in the small room. "You're right, I'm an idiot. I'll call the hospital where Ashlee is and see if I can get control from here."

Nick glanced up, then away, still so angry he wanted to hit him. "How many calls can you make a day?"

"One officially, but maybe Trent can sneak me his cell. I'm not under arrest. I'm being held at the CO's discretion, ordered to remain here while the investigation is ongoing. He gave me thirty-day confinement without pay for going AWOL. Since we dumped the apartment, I have no official residence, so I have to stay here. He would've given me longer if he could have. I can fight this. Thirty days is extreme for being gone less than two days, and I had a real good reason."

Nick leaned back in his seat and tapped his fingers on the table top, his eyes narrowed. "While I'm sure Trent or one of the guys would put you up, I'm telling them not to. Shut up!" he snapped when Mike opened his mouth.

"Obviously, you can't be trusted to use sense. Locked in here, you can't try that shit again. If I didn't need you so bad, I wouldn't give a shit if you ruin your career. But I do need you, and so does Ashlee. Serve your time like a good boy. Step one foot out of line and I'll smack you down hard! Am I clear here, Mike?"

"Crystal." Mike gave him a cold glance. Nick didn't care.

Nick rose and banged on the door. Mason opened the door, glanced at Mike who sat with his arms crossed fuming, to Nick, who wore a deep scowl, and let Nick out.

- 18 -

FUCKER GOT WHAT HE DESERVED

The room Mike spent his days in contained a camp bed, the same kind he had when deployed. A small bathroom with no door that connected to the main room and held a shower, sink, and toilet, much nicer than he had when deployed.

In the main room, a table was bolted to the floor with a metal chair before it. He was allowed books, newspapers, and visitors. No electronic devices, no television, and one twenty-minute phone call a day. A row of bars formed the door to the room, allowing the guards to check on him whenever they wished. If you ignored the bars, the room resembled officer quarters on forward bases.

The first day he wasted his call trying to get ahold of Margret at the hospital. The second day he tried again, this time calling hospital admissions, but ran out of time before he accomplished anything. Nick had hired a lawyer though. Mr. Wilson sat across from him in the small conference room he was escorted to when visitors arrived. The same room he'd spoken to Nick in.

"Sergeant Evans, I've spoken with your friend Sergeant Rossi, and he's explained the situation." Mr. Wilson opened a file he'd brought with him and spread it on the table. "As I understand it, Mrs. Conner, your wife's mother, has assumed custody and transported your wife to Ireland without your consent or that of Mrs. Evans?"

When Mike nodded, Mr. Wilson continued. "The situation may be trickier than you anticipate. There's no denying you're next of kin, but Mrs. Conner has her in custody. First, we must prove Ashlee didn't go voluntarily."

"How could she have? She was in a coma." Mike rubbed his fingers together on top of the table.

"Right now, it's Margret's word against yours that Ashlee never spoke to her. As you're being held for questioning on a murder charge Margret's grounds are pretty strong. At least until Ashlee herself can refute them."

Fingers now clenched tight, Mike leaned forward. "Which she can't do while in a coma."

"Therein lies the dilemma. Sergeant Rossi explained that even if Ashlee agreed to come home, it's unsafe for her to travel at this time. We need to proceed with those facts in mind. Let her mother care for her till such time as it's safe to retrieve her."

"No fucking way! That woman is crazy."

Mr. Wilson cleared his throat and lifted an eyebrow. Mike flushed. "Excuse me, sir, but you don't know the woman."

"No, but I do know you don't have much choice. From what I gather, your wife has no other relatives. Do you want her alone in a strange hospital till she is well enough to leave it then alone— where? A hotel room, till she is well enough to travel?"

Two spots of red appeared on Mike's cheekbones. "Mr. Wilson…" Mike trailed off and took a deep breath. "My wife can't be alone. There must be a way for me to go to her, or Nick. Three weeks... No. You have no idea how afraid she is."

Mr. Wilson's expression darkened. "I assure you, I'm entirely familiar with the case. Every aspect of it. Sergeant Rossi has engaged my services for both him and yourself. My firm has contacted an associate in Dublin to handle things on that end, and we've started the process to assert your guardianship, but like I said earlier, even if you receive full custody, you can't go there or she here."

"Did Nick contact Stacy, Ashlee's old roommate?"

"Yes, and Miss Blake agreed to go, but as of this moment, Mrs. Conner is denying visitors, so there's no point in sending Stacy until you have legal access."

"How long will that take?"

"Hard to say as we're dealing over such a long distance, but I wouldn't think more than two weeks, tops."

Mike took a deep breath, searching for patience. "Can you at least get medical information to me? Regular updates on her condition?"

Mr. Wilson rose. "I'll see what I can do."

Mike stood and shook his hand. "Thank you. Please keep me informed. It's urgent that I be able to speak to her soon."

Mr. Wilson clasped his hand a moment. "Believe me, my firm is doing everything possible. I can only imagine how stressful this is for you and your wife."

The guard at the door let Mr. Wilson out, then escorted Mike to his room. Three hours later, Nick visited.

"I hired a PI to get us reports on Ashlee's condition and called her old roommate Stacy.

The PI tracked Stacy down for me. The address and number Ashlee had was obsolete. The letter Stacy sent telling Ashlee she moved is unopened in Ashlee's stack of mail. Stacy will go as soon as Ash wakes to stay with her and keep us informed, but she can't stay indefinitely."

"Yeah, okay." Mike sat at the table as if exhausted.

"I'll get her back Mike, as soon as I can."

Mike nodded but didn't glance up from the tabletop.

❊ ❊ ❊

Six days later, Inger sauntered down the hallway of St. Vincents Hospital in Dublin, a clipboard in his hand, and a hurried, impatient look on his face. Dressed in blue hospital scrubs and trying to appear busy and important, he headed to Ashlee's room. She'd been out of the coma for thirty hours but hadn't called home. Nick had asked him to go to her and assure her that he would come for her.

Margret still denied all visitors, accepting no phone calls. Money, notes, and an open ticket home for Ashlee sat in Inger's pocket.

The hallways were dim and quiet, nurses going about their business with a minimum of fuss and noise. Ashlee's room was lit by a light near the doorway, leaving the room shadowed. This afternoon, when he arrived, he'd attempted to visit.

While Inger paused in the open doorway and glanced inside, Margret read aloud.

"But the fearful, and unbelieving, and the abominable, and murderers, and whoremongers, and sorcerers, and idolaters, and all liars, shall have their part in the lake which burneth with fire and brimstone: which is the second death."

Her voice was so full of self-righteous relish, Inger wanted to slap her.

Ashlee didn't acknowledge her. Machines surrounded her, beeping and humming. Strapped face down on a bed inclined at a shallow angle; she didn't stir at all. Inger retreated.

Outside of the hospital, he took a seat facing the main doorway and opened a newspaper and waited, debating the possibility of breaking Ashlee out. He'd reluctantly decided it was impossible. Ashlee needed medical help. More help than he could provide. Promptly at five minutes after eight, Margret marched out the door.

"Jesus, wonder if she read aloud the entire time? Poor Ash," Inger muttered as he stuffed the paper in the trash can and headed back inside. An orderly stopped him right inside the doorway. Inger didn't argue. He nodded politely and left. After a trip to a nearby department store, he returned dressed in scrubs and followed a group of chatting nurses into the building.

Now Ashlee's room was empty, and she appeared to be asleep. Inger eased the door shut and squatted to see her face. A hole in the mattress allowed her to lay flat but made communication difficult. With a gentle hand, Inger rubbed her shoulder encased in the white hospital gown. "Ash, honey, wake up."

The machine above her beeped faster as Ashlee stirred.

"Ashlee, Mike sent me. Your husband wants you to –"

Before he could finish his sentence, Ashlee began to scream and thrash. The machine above her shrilled.

"No, Ash. It's me— Inger. Calm down, honey." Inger sank lower so she could see him clearer. "Tell the nurses you want to go home okay?"

Inger bit his lip. She neither saw nor heard him. Eyes squeezed shut, she strained as hard as she could against the strap holding her in place. Harsh pants interspersed her screams for help. Inger ran into the nearby bathroom and out the adjoining room as the door to Ashlee's room opened. Sweat trickled down his brow. *Damn, he should have known better than that.* He'd wait until morning and try again.

In the morning, Ashlee was heavily sedated. Inger changed back into civilian clothes and went to the nurse's desk. "Excuse me, Ma'am, could you tell me the best time to speak to Mrs. Evans? I tried this morning, but she didn't wake."

"Mrs. Evans isn't receiving visitors," the nurse said without looking up.

"Yes, I know her mother is refusing to let her have them but is Ashlee refusing?" Inger leaned over and used one finger to slide the folder the nurse was reading away.

The nurse glanced up, a frown on her face. "Mrs. Evans has refused visitors except for two people, her husband, and her best friend."

"Her husband sent me. He can't get leave—"

"Mrs. Conner informed us," the nurse interrupted. Her aggravated expression hardened. "Mrs. Evans is ill and needs rest, not whatever games her husband is playing." She held up her hand when Inger began to speak. "No, I didn't believe everything her mother said. Anyone can see she is a bit, um, overwrought. But regardless of whether her husband did or did not harm his wife or anyone else, Mrs. Evans needs rest."

Inger gave her best puppy dog look. "Ashlee is a good friend of mine. I serve with her husband. Her mother is making it impossible to get in contact. Could you tell me her condition?"

"I'm not at liberty to say." The nurse's expression softened as Inger gave her his best pleading eyes. "Stable. That's all I can say." She glanced around, then leaned closer. "She had a bad night, a really bad night, and the doctor has sedated her. I can't say officially or anything, but I expect he'll keep her sedated a few days at least. She hurt herself, almost killed herself. No, not on purpose," she added hurriedly when Inger straightened in alarm.

"The doctor has her strapped down to keep the tubes in place. She tried to move and dislodged them. Her, uh, mental condition isn't good." The nurse glanced around again and lowered her voice more. "In my opinion, someone needs to keep her mother away from her. That woman gives me the creeps. Every time I go in the room she's reading a bible verse about hell or sin."

"Could you get Ashlee a message? Tell her a ticket home is ready anytime she wants it, and her husband wants her to return, and if he weren't confined to base, he would be here."

"Yes, I'll tell her. When she's well enough to use a phone, I'll see she gets one."

"Thank you," Inger said, slid the folder back to her, tapped the desk twice, and left.

✱ ✱ ✱

Franton let Inger into his small efficiency apartment and returned to the shabby chair in the corner.

Nick stood. Inger's expression showed the news was bad.

"No good, man. The dragon has her sewn up. I snuck in easy as anything, and your girl nearly died of fright." Inger wiped his brow. "Wish I could see Steven again; I'd like to pay him back for that. Ash used to greet me with smiles and make my favorite food. Now she screams and cries, so afraid it turns my stomach. Try sending a stranger to her instead. No calls or letters will get through."

"How is she? Physically, I mean?"

"Weak, sick, hurting. I stole and copied the doctor's notes. I didn't understand a damn thing on them. The bruising looked better, the little bit I saw. The doctors there strapped her face down on a table. For that alone I wanted to kick her mother."

"She's awake though and aware?"

"Not really, semi-awake and drugged to the gills. Believe me, that's a good thing. Margret sits by her side reading the Bible aloud, all hellfire and condemnation. Man, I was tempted to break her out, but she needs medical help."

Nick rubbed his forehead. "A private detective there has agreed to send me reports on her condition. The minute she's out of the hospital, I'm going for her."

"And then what? Don't be stupid. Wait and do it legal. Send a lawyer. How much longer are they gonna keep you confined to base?"

"No fucking idea."

Franton spoke up from his chair in the corner. "Don't waste this time. Use it getting ready for her return. Find her a new home, a safe place to live. Line up doctors for her."

"Yeah, you're right. Between Mike and I, we can afford a nice place for her."

Franton stabbed the newspaper in his lap with his finger. "Look online, and me and the boys will scope them out and make sure her home is secure."

"Thanks… for everything."

"My fucking pleasure." Franton heaved himself to his feet and grabbed a beer. "I would invite you to stay with us, but Trent's home is better. Gives the impression of law and order."

Nick snickered. "Trent's a stand-up guy."

"Go see Mike. He's going outta his head."

Nick sighed, sat back in the chair, and pinched the bridge of his nose. "Tomorrow. Man has no patience at all."

Franton leaned over and clinked his beer to Nick's. "Some things are worth savoring."

Nick snickered again and drank his beer.

✻ ✻ ✻

Mike glanced up and then threw the newspaper across the room. "You, goddamned asshole, letting me rot in here with no news."

"Stop being so melodramatic. Trent's been here every day. If you weren't such a hothead, you wouldn't be in here. Before you ask, I have no real news. Inger went to see her, but couldn't get in official like, so snuck in and almost gave her a heart attack. We just gotta wait till she's better. If you weren't such a goddamned idiot, you could've ordered her returned, but now...." Nick turned away furious all over again.

Mike sighed and pulled his hair. "This place is making me crazy. I need to get out."

"I'm sure the lawyer told you that's not happening until the investigation is finished. Mike, they arrested you in New York boarding a plane to London, fleeing the goddamn country. Yeah, the CO knows why you did it, but you still look guilty as sin. As much as this sucks, if you just hang tight, it will all blow over. No real charges have been brought. Thank your lucky stars this is just an article fifteen and not a court martial. If you hadn't gone AWOL, you would be waiting on base like the rest of us while they investigate. Now, you serve your goddamn month for that, and then however long it takes them to decide you couldn't possibly have done it. You had nothing to do with it, and a hundred men can testify to your whereabouts almost every moment since you returned home. Our CO is bending over backward here to help us. Don't make it any harder on the man."

"You're awful sure I didn't do it."

"Unhuh," Nick turned away.

"Fucker got what he deserved and then some," Mike said in satisfaction, his narrowed eyes on Nick.

"That fucker could've been tortured a hundred years and it wouldn't be enough." Nick glared, gripping the edge of the table before him, wishing it was Steven's neck he squeezed. "Every teardrop should be repaid in blood. Every cry in screams. For her nightmares, there is no justice. Whoever killed him... Well, I like knowing he suffered as much as humanly possible."

"As much as humanly possible?"

Nick nodded and spun away. Short, sharp

strides took him to the edge of the room and back. "Mike, our girl won't be the same after this. Don t kid yourself about that. If this is too much for you, if you—"

"No, of course, I know that. I'm not an idiot. I realize you two are closer than me and her. Especially now when she doubts me. Doesn't matter, you still can't have her. She's my wife. Mine! Yeah, I love the sex, but that isn't all she is to me. Any way she needs, I'll be there for her."

"Good, glad to hear. Whatever she needs, we do."

- 19 -

NOT HER HOUSE, BUT HER MOTHER'S

One crusted eyelid peeled open with a soft sucking pull, the other sprang open as if on a spring. The room swirled in muted colors and suppressed sound. Panic built as she recognized the sensation.

The drugs Steven injected her with did this. Soon the pain would begin. Pain and humiliation such as she'd never imagined. His gloating voice whispering Mike's words of love while he cut her skin. The knife in his hand transforming into melted silver, dripping hot globules under her drugged gaze.

Instinctively, she lashed out and was shocked to find herself unfettered. The room around her spun, refusing to take a shape she recognized. Familiar edges morphed into nightmare images. A sob lodged in her chest. Afraid to make a noise and drag Steven back into the room, Ashlee closed her eyes and used her sense of touch instead.

Agony raced up her spine when her feet contacted the floor, so she dropped to her knees.

On her hands and knees, she inched from the room, praying to find a wall. Her head found the wall first, impacting with a dull thunk. The sob escaped before she could contain it. Both hands walked her way up the wall, and she felt the way ahead, using the wall to keep herself upright, ignoring the pain from her feet as best she could.

An open space met her questing hand, and she risked a glance. Bright light and white flooring that dipped and swayed alarmingly met her eyes. As she stepped forward, something tugged her back. Not unfettered then, but tied by her right arm. The left hand, encased in a heavy bandage, weighed a ton, and she couldn't force it to grab the rope holding her. Another sob, this one louder, changed to hysterical pants as she yanked the arm that was keeping her from freedom. A loud crash and alarm sounded. Desperate now, she jerked again, using the doorframe as leverage and fell headlong when the rope broke free from her arm. She smacked her face hard into the casing around the doorway.

A scream burst from her lips as she lost her balance and slid to the floor. Eyes squeezed shut, she grabbed at her cheek, which felt freshly rebroken, grinding agony beneath her hand. Knife-like stabs of pain shot from her feet to the crown of her head. Footsteps approached, squeaking and muffled, while garbled voices yelled. The alarm behind her filled her senses with its blaring.

"No, no, no," she shrieked as hands grabbed her. Her entire being strained to get free, fighting wildly, teeth, knees, and elbows. The agony in her feet escalated until they no longer supported her.

Above her, a man ordered her to calm down. A needle pierced her skin and grasping hands forcing her to stillness. The world faded, and she hoped she would never wake again.

"What the hell happened here, Nurse?" The doctor glanced over to the two nurses as they lifted Ashlee back into the hospital bed.

"She must have woken sooner than expected. Ten minutes ago, she was resting peacefully."

"Keep her in restraints until such time as she's got a full shilling about her." The doctor held up a hand as the nurses exchanged unhappy glances. "As distasteful as restraints are, it's for her own good. The IV needle has broken off in her arm and look at her poor feet. No, keep her restrained. When she is physically well enough, we can send her to the psychiatric ward. They have the facilities there to deal with her unrestrained. Our priority is getting her well."

The next time Ashlee woke, the room spun in the usual sickening swirls of color and light. Both her hands were tied at her sides, and her ankles were constrained. The desire to scream built, but if she wanted to escape, she needed to be calm and wait her chance.

In an hour or so the drug haze would lift and she would be able to see around her. If she were lucky, Steven would remain away and give her a chance. She'd broken free once, she could do it again and surely this time Mike and Nick were looking for her. If they weren't already dead… tears trickled down her cheeks, and a mechanical hum turned into a steady beeping. *Oh, dear God, has he strapped me to a bomb? Have I set if off somehow?*

Afraid to move at all now, she opened her eyes and tried to force the spinning to stop. Instead of stopping, the motion made her ill, and she vomited as hands grabbed her arms. Not able to speak as she wretched, she shuddered in his grasp.

Gradually, she realized it was a woman

speaking and smoothing her hair back. "Sydney, please, help me, please," she gasped between heaves. Steven had spoken longingly of Sydney and her, with him and Nick. But surely Sydney wouldn't help him no matter how much she disliked Ashlee.

"I'm Martha, dear. Martha Allen, your nurse. Sydney isn't here."

Ashlee tried again to look, but the woman's face melted and blurred, clear one second, showing kind brown eyes in round face, then a travesty of a face. An Escher painting of mangled features.

"Relax, dear, the medication is making you ill. You're safe in hospital." Martha continued taking Ashlee's vitals while she spoke.

Safe. The word echoed then lost meaning.

"Safe?" Her voice cracked hoarse and rough.

"Perfectly safe. Rest, take slow breaths. Your mam will be here soon."

"My ma? Is Mike here? Can I see my husband?" Hope flared.

"Sorry, dearie, but he isn't here. The only visitor you've had is your mother and a gentleman your husband sent."

"No!" Wild and shrill, her scream shocked them both. "No, don't let him near me. Promise me!"

"No one will come into your room, except

the doctors, nurses, and your mam. This is a secure floor. You're perfectly safe. I'll release the restraints if you can remain calm."

Ashlee nodded. The nurse released her and cleaned her off, talking the entire time. "Your mam comes every day, she's that concerned about you, dearie. The doctor is right pleased with your progress."

"Can I go home?"

"Soon, dearie. Give us a day or two. You've only just woken from a coma."

"My husband hasn't come? Or Nick?"

"Sorry, dearie just your mam." The nurse helped Ashlee sit and examined her back before replacing the soiled hospital gown. "The bruising is looking scads better. A nice brownish green. I expect it to be gone in a week or so. Try to remain on your right side as much as possible. Give the back a chance to heal up."

Ashlee lay back in the bed.

"The doctor will be along to examine you, but do you have any pains?" Martha gently palpated Ashlee's abdomen. "The surgery sites have healed nicely."

"Can I have a phone to call my husband?"

"Once the doctor has seen you, I'll bring one in." The nurse continued her examination, checking Ashlee's breathing and reflexes and rebandaging her arm and feet. "The arm will be sore and the feet too, I'm afraid. But we can give you something for the pain."

"Don't make me sleep. Whatever you're giving me now is making me sick and the room spin."

A frown on her face, the nurse took Ashlee's temperature and retook her vitals. "Will you be okay alone a moment?"

"Yes." Ashlee cracked her eyelids and peered at the nurse, closing them again as the room dipped alarmingly.

The nurse left her in peace. *Why wasn't Mike with her? Why hadn't he visited? Maybe he had to return to duty, but what about Nick?* Dread dried her mouth. "Please, God, let them be alive," she whispered. Hands folded under her chin, she continued to pray.

The sharp tap of high heels announced the nurses return. Ashlee opened her eyes and closed them again. Her mother, not the nurse.

"Ma, where is my husband?"

"You have no husband, girl."

Ashlee sat in alarm. "Ma?"

"He's no dead, he just doesn't care. The man's a complete waster. What, you thought now that your looks are ruined he would still want to slake his lust with you? Don't be ridiculous. Men are all the same. Give them a pretty face and a willing body, and they're content. Take those things away, and they're on to the next girl. Did you think you were special? I tried to warn you."

"No, Ma, Mike loves me, and Nick loves me too—"

"So foolish you are. If that were true, where are they? Now, daughter, don't take on so."

Ashlee cried and couldn't stop, her mother's voice was a whining drone in her ear. The doctor and Martha returned. A needle pierced her arm, and the world faded.

A period of foggy ache followed. Mental pain and long bouts of tears filled her days, and through it all Margret's voice lectured and bossed.

The doctors kept Ashlee sedated, and she welcomed the numbness. In a moment of clarity, she saw the doctor standing beside her bed. He was an Indian man with a thick accent she needed to concentrate on to understand— or maybe it was the drugs. His words seemed far away and unimportant.

"Mrs. Evans, we can release you into the care of your mother. Or, if you prefer, we can place you in a convalescence home."

"Home? I can go home?"

"Your mother's home, yes. You require care, and I recommend seeing a psychiatrist to help you deal with your situation. Drugs are a temporary fix. Now that your body is recovering, it's time to work on your mind."

Ashlee heard nothing else he said. She could go home.

"Send me home, please. I want to go home." While the doctor spoke, she drifted to sleep with a smile on her lips.

When next she woke, she lay on a bed in her mother's living room. She didn't remember the trip to Ireland at all. Not her house, but her mother's. The room hadn't changed since she'd left it six years earlier. Perhaps the fabrics were a bit more faded, but the wood sparkled under layers of lemon wax. Mullioned windows broke the gray light into small squares.

Outside this open window, the herb garden still grew. The breeze brought the scent of rosemary to her.

The horsehair sofa pushed against the wall, to make room for the bed she lay on, still had shiny worn spots from generations of Leigh ancestors. This estate had been in her mother's family since being built in 1803. The acreage surrounding it had shrunk. No longer a working farm, only twelve acres remained. The only gardens were small, not the flourishing fields her mother remembered from her youth. Her mother had sold the land and lived a hermit's life in the house, building barricades to keep the world out.

Now the walls comforted Ashlee. Thick stone walls encased the house, and high iron bars surrounded it. Steven would have a difficult time stealing onto the property. *Surely her mother would have alarms put in to protect me.*

The memory of Steven and what he wanted caused sweat to bead on her brow. Sweat followed by crying that escalated to deep sobs and gasping breaths.

Her mother came and gave her an injection, and she slipped into a troubled sleep.

A hand shook her awake, and she thrashed and groaned.

"Ashlee Claire Conner, stop it this instant. We have guests." Her mother slapped her cheeks lightly. Not Steven her mother. Her racing heart slowed, and she took her mother's hand, pressing it to her cheek, containing the sobs that wanted to force their way from her throat.

"Officer?" Margret said in a cold, haughty voice. "As you can see, my daughter is most upset over your intrusion, please be quick."

"Mrs. Evans?" A man asked.

Ashlee tried to raise herself but lacked the strength. Weak and disoriented, the room swam in front of her eyes.

"Aye."

"Are you here of your own free will? Shall I call an ambulance for you?"

"No ambulance, I want to go home. My ma is taking me home." The effort to speak exhausted her. She drifted to sleep while her mother spoke.

"My daughter needs rest. What ridiculousness. The man is in jail. How can he care for her? Anyone can see she needs her mother now. Are you satisfied I'm not forcing her to stay here?"

"Yes, Ma'am, but –"

"No, she is my daughter, and I will care for her. Go! And don't return without a warrant. This is my land. No visitors are welcome. I have a restraining order against that man. He may not step foot on my property. If my daughter chooses to see him, she will need to do it elsewhere. But, that isn't a problem, is it gentleman, when the man is under arrest for murder."

The officer sighed, removed his cap, and scratched his balding head. "No, Ma'am, it isn't a problem. We can see ourselves out."

The two officers hurried from the house and got in their car.

Margret opened the gate remotely and locked it behind them. "Well, girl, the devil has his talons in ya, there's no mistaking that, but I'll pry them out," she said to Ashlee's sleeping form.

It took a month before Ashlee could walk any distance on her feet. A month of listening daily to her mother rant on the wages of sin. Tired of begging for a ride to a telephone, Ashlee stole her mother's clothing and walked to the nearest neighbor.

It took her three hours to walk a mile, and when she arrived, the woman wouldn't let her use the phone. Ashlee pressed on, the burns and cuts on her feet throbbing and beginning to bleed. An hour and a half later she reached the next home. The woman there took pity on her and let her use her phone.

No one answered her call. The house phone was disconnected, and Mike's cell went right to voice mail. The woman's lips tightened every time Ashlee dialed, so she didn't call Nick. Cheeks red with humiliation, Ashlee thanked her after she hung up. An overseas call she had no way of paying for except with thanks was too much to ask.

She limped to the neighbor's house and called Nick from there after more humiliating begging and explanations.

Nick didn't answer either. Dejected, she

headed home. The walk was terrifying. Every moment she expected Steven to leap out at her.

Bereft of the comfort of her high walls she felt exposed and defenseless. If Steven appeared, she couldn't run; she could barely walk. Only pride kept her on her feet instead of crawling home. Each step was a new agony.

Blood soaked her socks and stained the bottom of the shoes she'd stolen from her mother. The hard, cold look in her mother's eyes as she helped rebandage her feet pierced her heart.

"See, girl? This is what comes of flaunting God's will. How many times must God show you the folly of your ways? How much clearer can he be? Turn your back on the Lord at your peril. He's reaching out to you, daughter."

Ashlee said nothing, biting her lip against the pain in her feet.

Her mother handed her two pills, which Ashlee gratefully swallowed.

"Tomorrow, you move into your bedroom upstairs. If you're well enough to hike miles in pursuit of sin, you're well enough to walk downstairs."

"Yes, Ma. Did you call about the alarm?"

"Better, I got you this." Margret went to the coffee table and opened a box from which she removed a shiny revolver. "This will give you what you deserve."

The gun tumbled from Margret's hand, landing in Ashlee's lap. Six bullets followed, dropped one by one like tear drops.

- 20 -
STOP HIM OR I WILL

Mason sank into the chair and slapped a sheaf of papers onto the desk in front of him. "Found this on your coffee table. What the hell are you doing about it?"

Trent frowned and pushed the papers to Mason with one finger. "Nothing. What do you want me to do?"

Mason leaned over the desk and lowered his voice. "Nick's gonna do a runner any day now." Mason snatched the papers and shook them in Trent's face. "That detective reported Mrs. Conner took Ashlee home from the hospital. No visitors are allowed in the house, and he's quit sending reports. So, what, you think Nick is gonna be content with that?"

"What do you think I should do about it?" Trent repeated and stood.

Mason jumped up and grabbed Trent's

shoulder. "Stop him or I will."

Trent jerked away. "Stop him how? By all means, if you can stop him, do so."

Mason leaned over and hissed in his ear. "If I go in the chief's office and tell what I know—"

"And ruin your career? With what proof?"

Mason shook Trent's shoulder.

Trent slapped Mason's hand from his shoulder and pulled him into a nearby interrogation room. "Look, sorry, just what do you expect me to do? The only thing that will stop him is iron bars."

"Exactly."

Trent lurched back. "Why do you even care?"

"Because he's a damned murderer, getting away with it, and it's my fault."

"How do you figure? And what the hell were you doing at my house anyway? I thought you moved all your things out."

"If I hadn't agreed to destroy evidence—"

Trent threw his hands in the air. "For the millionth time that wasn't evidence. That's their own goddamn business. The fact Nick's sleeping with her is irrelevant and no one's business except theirs. Get over this obsession, it's not like Nick isn't being investigated hard."

Mason spun away, speaking with his back turned. "Trent, Nick did it. Everyone knows he did it."

"Okay, Sherlock, how did he do it? When did he do it?"

Mason whirled back. "Not alone obviously, but he was involved."

"Oh sure, fairies came and whisked him away under the noses of us and the guards. Or, maybe while he was at work. No, I know, Nick, Mike, and Ashlee snuck out of the hospital past the guarded door and snuck back in without being seen ten hours later."

Mason snorted, and Trent continued.

"Wait, I have an even better theory. Maybe they kept Steven chained in the hospital basement." Mason jerked his head up, and Trent laughed. "Or mine. Is that why you were at my house? Did I drug you somehow, Mason, and then Nick and I slipped downstairs for a little torture?"

When Mason flushed, Trent laughed. "You checked." Trent sat in a chair and crossed his legs on the table top. "Did you check for tunnels and trapdoors? Or the helipad on the roof?"

"Nick must have snuck out of work. I saw him with my own eyes at your house. Checked on him and everything and he was always there. No way did he have time at night but during the day…."

A grin on his face, Trent crossed his arms behind his head. "Nope, I admit it's a neat theory, and I'm not denying they would've loved to kill the man, but neither had time enough even assuming Steven was kept ten minutes away."

"Then who did? Every single member of their squad has alibis and not just with each other."

"Doubt we'll ever know, and honestly, I don't care. Good riddance, I say."

"Not arguing that, and if I didn't mess with the damn evidence, I wouldn't care either."

Trent slammed his feet to the floor and stood. "Jesus, man, if it bothers you that much, let's turn ourselves in. But it won't accomplish shit other than getting all of us court-martialed. Not to mention Ashlee's humiliation in the press. But, by all means, let's ease your guilty conscience."

Hands on his hips, Mason glared. "You know; you can be a real dick."

Trent smirked and rose an eyebrow. "You just hate it when I'm right."

Mason held up his empty hands. "Fine, I'm dropping it, never to mention it again. But that doesn't mean I'm giving up on proving Nick did it."

"Sure, keep looking for the killer, but don't

hang your hopes on Nick and Mike. If Mike did it, he went without sleep for four days. Did you see him a drink one coffee in all that time?"

Mason looked thoughtful.

Trent rolled his eyes. "Ask the nurses at the hospital when you go to check the basement."

Mason glowered, then laughed and left.

Trent returned to his desk, grabbed the Powerade he'd taken from his refrigerator that morning, and chuckled as he drank it.

Two days later, Mason arrested Nick, using the file he'd stolen from Trent's house and a plane reservation in his name. Nick's CO locked him up for thirty days for planning to go AWOL. Since he hadn't actually gone, he received an NJP of thirty days, and no criminal charges were laid.

Nick knew he could fight it, but that would alienate his commander who thought he was doing Nick a favor, saving him from himself.

Trent met with Nick in the small conference room. "You know why he did it."

Nick snorted.

"I hate to say this, but it's for your own good. Not that I put him up to it," Trent added hastily as Nick lifted his head and glared. "Serve your month, and by then, hopefully, the other matter is finished, and you're cleared and can get leave. Nick, what were you going to do? Go there and kidnap her? Kill her mother? Come on, man. I'll keep trying to call for you."

"Shit, don't bother. No call will go through. Keep in touch with my lawyer though, please. There must be a way to circumvent the woman and get a message to Ashlee."

A sad frown on his face, Trent leaned on the table. "Not that this is a comfort, but the detective said Ashlee was pretty out of it. Now that she's released, and doing better, she can call you."

"Keep our cells charged, Trent, and keep checking for messages."

"Will do. The phone at your old apartment is off, but the phone company said they'll forward calls to my number for two months. Since you'll be unavailable, I'll get the guys and put your stuff in storage."

"Don't bother. Throw everything away. Save Ashlee's things, but the furniture and house stuff throw out or give away. Mike and I will buy her new stuff."

"Right, I'll keep her things with yours in my spare room, and you can decide what to do with them when you get out."

❋ ❋ ❋

A week later, Trent snuck Nick's cell phone in to him. "Ashlee left you a message. I called the number, but the woman on the other end wouldn't take a message. She didn't want to speak to Margret. The entire village hates that woman. Can the lawyer help?"

Nick played the message, his eyes filling with tears. Ashlee's brogue had thickened, and her voice was sad and despondent with a hysterical edge.

"Nick, please come get me. I love you. We have no phone at our house, and I think my ma is destroying my mail, at least I hope she is. I hope you're trying to reach me. I can't reach Mike either. Please come get me, Nick. Please, I miss you so much."

"If you speak to her, Trent, tell her I will as soon as I can."

"Will do, man."

The next message Ashlee left infuriated him. "Nick, it's okay if you don't want me anymore, but please help me get home. I don't know who else to call. Stacy moved, and Kurt is home not at school, and I don't have his home number or address. Please, help me get home, and I'll never bother you again. This place… I hate it here, Nick. If you send my passport and driver license, I could access my bank account from here. Ten minutes to send it and you never have to speak to me again." Choked sobs interrupted her. "I'm so sorry I ruined your life." She cried for a moment before hanging up.

Nick left an away message on his phone telling Ashlee to call Trent or the police, and he would send her a ticket.

Trent sat across the metal table from Nick, his hands folded on the table before him. "Why can't your lawyer get there? Someone must be able to talk to her and give her a plane ticket home."

"No one can get on the property. Stacy went and couldn't reach her. She sat outside the fence yelling for Ashlee until the police came. Mrs. Conner has a restraining order on Mike and an injunction on the lawyer. Since the police spoke to Ashlee, they won't interfere. They searched the house and spoke to her doctor and got medical reports sent to Mike. The lawyer claims he's sending letters, if Ashlee can just call him, or the police, or anyone who can tell her how to get the ticket we sent..." Nick trailed off and put his head in his hands.

"I'll go. I can sneak by the old bird."

"You'll scare her to death. How can I send a stranger to her when a friend terrifies her? A strange man sneaking into the house... No, I can't do that. I don't know what to do, and Mike says she still needs medical care. Could I trust a stranger to kidnap her and get her here safely, without scaring her to death? Inger is going, he'll sneak into her room and leave her letters, IDs, the ticket, and money, it's the only thing I could think of."

"I'm sorry now you're locked up here. AWOL would be better than this."

Nick nodded tiredly and closed his eyes, rubbing his face.

"A few more weeks, Nick."

"Yeah."

- 21 -
To Live with Her Nightmares and Dreams, or Not

Weeks had elapsed with no word from either of her husbands. The first month passed in a haze of drugs and pain. No one returned her calls. She'd stopped trying two weeks ago. The walk was too long, the begging to borrow the phone and pitying looks too hard to bear. She cursed herself for not memorizing any of her friends numbers, but she never imagined she'd be without her phone.

The nearest neighbor wouldn't answer the door when Ashlee knocked, and the quiet country roads were terrifying to walk alone. At first, she'd been grateful when her mother gave her the gun.

Since she'd gotten released from the hospital, her mother hadn't said one kind word to her, Bible quotes and prayers being her only communication. Face turned to the wall as she lay on the bed in her mother's living room, Ashlee closed her eyes and remembered happiness and horror. Terror would overwhelm her until her mother came with the needle and the world floated away.

Her mother quit coming to her room to preach when Ashlee took to reading Psalms aloud. Furious, but unable to bring herself to take the Bible from Ashlee, Margret retreated to the kitchen, leaving Ashlee in peace.

The house remained silent now, the two women unspeaking for days on end.

Margret delivered her meals and medicine and left her alone. Ashlee began sitting by the front gate in the hopes the lawyer would come again, and she would beat her mother there. Even if he were serving her divorce papers, it would be contact. Surely, Mike would help her return to the states even if he no longer wanted anything to do with her. Or Nick, if she could reach him. Tears filled her eyes, and she cried again. Why didn't he come? Their life was a lie, a sham, a sin like her mother said.

She was there by the gate when the postman came and signed for the letter with hands that trembled. A certified letter that Mike had sent. In a voice that cracked from disuse, she thanked the man.

He tipped his hat and turned away, but before she even turned from the gate, her mother had snatched the letter and ran to the kitchen. Ashlee chased her, slow on her hurt, swollen feet. By the time she'd reached her, the letter was a pile of ash on the gas range.

Ashlee spun away after one furious shout of, "Mother!"

"Stop this foolishness now, girl. The priory of Saint Anne's has agreed to put you up until such time as you can fend for yourself. I explained your soiled condition, and the abbess assures me she has helped many wayward girls to see the light. In a weeks' time, I'll escort you there. God knows I've tried my best. Ashlee. Daughter, you'll see in time this is for the best."

Ashlee said nothing, turning away and trudging to her room one hard stair at a time. On her bed, she stared at the ceiling, wondering what Mike had said in his letter. Goodbye, good riddance, good luck… come home. She would never know. A week, she had a week to decide to live with her nightmares and dreams, or not.

Ashlee stood on the windswept shore, gun in hand. Every day she came here and gazed into the sea.

The crash of waves and wild violence of the spot was somehow soothing despite the gun in her hand. The gun her mother had given her, "To give her what she deserved." Said in such a way as to be ambiguous.

Do I deserve protection or death? Protection or death? The thought rattled through her head. *Why do I stay*? she asked herself for the millionth time. *Where would I go*? That thought stumped her. Sick, weak, and jumping at shadows with no money of her own and no other family, what was she to do? The sea beckoned.

From the top of the cliff, the postman paused on his rounds, gazed down, and frowned. The girl needed help.

"Your mam is a crazy old tarter, a regular shrew. Always with the ranting and raving, preaching hellfire and damnation isn't she, girl?" he mumbled as Ashlee knelt in the sand.

Wind whipped her brown hair and waves crashed, the spray catching the light and forming rainbows that disappeared before they could truly form.

Mind made up, he rummaged in his truck for the clipboard and flipped pages until he found the receipt he was looking for. Paper in hand, he straightened his shoulders, and lips in a firm line, he went to break the law.

First, he copied the number and address on the receipt, then ripped it up. On his break, he called the phone number and left his name and number on the machine that answered. Three-thirty the next morning he received a phone call from America.

"Hello, Mr. McNeary? You called me earlier while I was out. I just now received the call."

"To whom am I speaking?" Mr. McNeary fumbled for his light switch and rubbed his bleary eyes.

"Michael Evans, you called me six hours ago, but only left your name and number. Did you call about my wife?"

"Your wife?" Mr. McNeary knitted his brows. "I called about a failure to deliver a letter. Well, that's not quite true, I delivered the letter, but the recipient had no chance to read it."

"The old bitch took it from her?"

McNeary snorted back a laugh. "Aye, that she did. You say Ashlee is your wife?"

"Yes, could you get a message to her, please?"

"Mayhap. I can try. Mrs. Conner won't let anyone in the house, so I need to catch your wife outside, but she goes to the shore almost daily." McNeary paused. "Your wife's in a bad way. On the ragged edge if you know what I mean. Chills run right up my spine every time I see her there, gun in hand."

"Tell her I'm coming for her as soon as I can."

"Well, young man, I wouldn't dawdle were I you."

"If it were up to me, I would leave today. Unfortunately, I need to wait for leave. God, this is such a rotten mess. Please, Ashlee… her damn mother is filling her head with poison. If you can speak with her, tell her I love her and would've been there if I could."

"Aye. I will. God willing, you can speak to her yourself soon."

"Thank you, Mr. McNeary. I can't tell you what it means to me. Every time I try to write or call, her mother blocks me. I would be most indebted to you if you could help Ashlee contact me."

"Aye, Mrs. Conner is a hard woman. If the chance arises, I'll inform your wife she may use my phone or I will send a letter anywhere she desires."

✳ ✳ ✳

Mike returned the cell phone to Trent, both relieved and terrified. *What the hell did she need a gun for?*

"Call my lawyer for me, please. He needs to get me out." Mike grabbed the bars separating him from the rest of the world and leaned his forehead against them. "I need to go there and speak with her."

"Nick will stop by today after his release. Talk his sorry ass into staying on base. He goes AWOL… When they find him, they're throwing away the key, if they don't hang him outright."

"What's the word on me, Trent?"

"No idea. Sorry, man. The squad has been cleared and returned to duty. Someone is sure to stop by tomorrow and fill you in."

"Keep checking your phone. That call was the mailman who tried to deliver my letter, and he says he'll try to speak to her."

Trent heaved a sigh. "Man, I would go myself if you think she won't freak."

Mike winced. "Thanks, but I can't take the chance. Soon, I should be able to go. They can't keep me much longer without charges. Our lawyer is working on getting access and assures me Margret can't block him much longer from speaking to Ashlee on a regular basis. The police spoke to her when her mother brought her home from the hospital, but she was all drugged up. Because she said she was there willingly, they can't do a damn thing. She couldn't have known her mother wouldn't let us talk to her then and now it's too late, they won't go again."

Trent glanced around and lowered his voice. "Every USB and I fragged his computer."

"You're a better friend than we deserve. Thanks, man."

"I did it for Ashlee. No one needs to see those recordings. Who would it help? The bastard is dead. May he rot in hell."

Mike nodded and whispered, "Did you…"

"No, I had nothing to do with it, but I wish I did." Trent chuckled suddenly. "Someone painted, 'I had nothing to do with that motherfucker's death, but I wish I did,' on the side of the apartment building, and in two days one hundred people wrote 'me too' on the wall. If you can keep your cool and avoid going AWOL, this will all blow over for you."

Mike spun and paced in the small room. "Ha, this will never be over for me. You think my wife is just going to go, okay, he's dead, let's live happily ever after?"

Trent winced. "Sorry, man."

Mike rubbed his forehead. "No, I'm sorry. I've written to my CO and asked for leave and permission to go get her and bring her home. What I'll do with her once she's home I don't know. How can I leave her and go overseas?"

Trent cleared his throat. "Won't, um, Nick be with her?"

"If he can be, but can he be without raising suspicion? Then they investigate him."

"They already are." Trent held up a hand as Mike whirled in alarm. "Nick hasn't been subtle about his friendship with her, so of course he's a suspect. Add in he led that squad for six years and he's a prime suspect." Trent glanced around, leaned forward and whispered. "Did he do it?"

"He says not." Mike shrugged. "I want to hug whoever did and kill them for taking his death away from me. Does Ashlee even know he's dead?"

"That I don't know, but I doubt it. Her mom had her outta here at the first opportunity. Heads are still rolling over that. She shouldn't have been able to have her moved."

"For a crazy old bitch, she's damn clever."

"Never saw a woman so full of hate. How the hell did she manage to bring up a girl as sweet as Ashlee?" Trent glanced at his watch. "Sorry, man, I gotta go. Hang in there."

Mike snorted and flopped onto the thin mattress

Trent patted the bars and walked away.

The next day, Nick met with Mike and their lawyer, Mr. Wilson.

Mr. Wilson tapped his pen on the table in front of him. "They'll release you tomorrow, cleared, but don't expect things to return to normal. This incident will follow you. Expect slow to no promotion after this. The consensus is you must have been involved somehow, and every commanding officer you have will know that."

"I'll be free to go?" Eyes bright, Mike clenched his hands together.

"Not at all. You'll be free to leave confinement and resume your duty. If you go AWOL, expect the full sentence."

"Damn it—"

"Calm down. I spoke with your CO, and he's cutting the orders to grant you leave, but you need to wait to get them. Go off halfcocked, and you'll be back here for good."

Nick laid a hand on Mike's shoulder. "I booked us on a flight for Friday. Five days, Mike. Ashlee will be in contact with the lawyer in seven days even if we can't go. The minute she steps foot off that property our man will give her a ticket home and our letters."

Nick took Mike's hand and squeezed. "Don't screw this up or I'll fucking kill you. Keep your temper in check. Ashlee needs you. I need you. I have no legal right to her. If I go there alone, her mother can have me thrown out. If you go, you can demand she let you speak with your wife."

Mike jerked his hand away, debating telling Nick about Ashlee's trips to the shore, but Nick would go right now. The only thing stopping him from rushing over there was Nick believed she still needed constant medical care and her mother could deny him access to her home. To see her, he would need to break in. Add to that, he would need to go AWOL, and he'd waited, but he wouldn't wait much longer.

"How'd you manage to get leave too?" Mike asked.

"Mr. Wilson." Nick turned to the lawyer. "Thank you, for everything."

Mr. Wilson scrutinized them both with narrowed eyes. "Five days. Do nothing stupid. If you have any problems, call me. Murder cases never go away. If new evidence comes to light, charges can be filed fifty years later. Keep my card, you might need it."

"Thank you." Mike offered his hand, and the two men shook. Mike hesitated again, tempted to tell Nick he could reach Ashlee away from her mother's house, but he wanted to go to her.

Nick was edging him out a bit at a time. Ashlee turned to Nick, calling for him when Mike was right there. *Goddamn Steven's soul to hell for making her even contemplate I would give her away or harm her.* Five more days, surely five days after nine weeks wouldn't matter.

Mike remained silent.

On the windswept shore again, Ashlee knelt on the damp sand, the gun clutched in both hands. Sunrise lit the sky a delicate rose-tinted gold. The tide had receded, leaving pristine sand studded with weeds and shells.

Overhead, gulls wheeled and called, darting down on the newly exposed crabs crawling in the seaweed. The ocean was a soft ripple, comforting, a never-ending sound.

Ashlee laughed and spun the cylinder, put the gun to her head, and pulled the trigger. A sob followed by another laugh and she pulled it again then again, then dropped her hand to her lap. Perhaps God wanted her to live. Or, like her ma said, she needed to suffer for her sins to truly repent them.

Head in her hands, Ashlee laughed sadly. The problem was she didn't think loving her husbands was a sin. Stupid maybe, believing they loved her, but on her part, she'd loved them. Despite what her mother said, she knew she wasn't a whore for letting them touch her.

A whore would've let Steven, and she never had, not once, no matter what he said or did. That had to prove to God she wasn't, didn't it?

Tomorrow, she would give God a fair chance to send her to Hell and pull the trigger four times if once wasn't enough. If he didn't take her before Saturday, surely that meant he'd forgiven her. In two days, she would go without complaint to the Abby. The Abby sounded good. A place away from everything. Maybe there she could regain her courage while she straightened out her life.

She sat unmoving on the shore till the waves touched her skirt.

The next day she came at noon. The sun peeked from behind gray clouds. A soft mist fell, weighing her hair. The wool of her sweater repelled the water in small beads that dripped onto her skirt, saturating it. Before she could lower herself to the sand an older man approached. Ashlee backed away, headed to the cliffs.

When it became clear the man planned on approaching her, she raised the gun. "Stop!"

"Aye, lassie, I mean ya no harm." Mr. McNeary held up his hands, showing they were empty.

"Leave me be!" Ashlee's voice was shrill. The birds echoed her, rising in whirling shrieking flocks.

"Mrs. Evans, your husband sent me."

Ashlee pulled the trigger and screamed when nothing happened.

Mr. McNeary took a step back. "Please,

Mrs."

Hands shaking, Ashlee clutched the gun in two hands and pulled again. The retort was deafening against the cliffs and knocked her back in surprise.

Mr. McNeary turned and ran back the way he'd come.

Ashlee fumbled in her pocket and reloaded the gun with hands that trembled. She filled every chamber. As messages from God went that one was clear. She was already in Hell.

- 22 -
You're Never Coming Back Here

Mike scanned the house with binoculars while Nick fumed beside him. "Why the fuck didn't you tell me she goes to the shore? I could've come for her days ago."

Mike glanced at him, then resumed his perusal. "Cause I just fucking found out. Stop whining, you're giving me a headache."

"This is utter bullshit. Just go inside and get her."

"And if she doesn't want to come? You think I should beat her mother in front of her and force her? What are the chances that crazy old bat says a polite hello and lets me speak to her? My plan is better. We avoid her, and talk to Ashlee."

The distant sound of a gunshot made both men start.

"Yeah, you're right, but the wait is

agonizing." Nick rubbed his face hard with both hands, his gaze on the seagulls that flew in a squawking flock over the house.

Mike paled and slapped his knee. "Stay here; I'll be back."

Mike headed to the shore, leaving Nick in the car with the binoculars.

Wind fluttered the black dress Ashlee wore against her legs as she limped down the beach. She paused with the cliffs at her back. Dark clouds hung low on the horizon, shadowing her face and chilling Mike. She fell to her knees in the sand and lowered her head, clenching the gun with a hand that shook.

The hair on Mike's arms rose.

"Ash?"

The surf competed with his soft question, but she heard him. Clumsily, she stumbled to her feet, dropping the gun and scrabbling for it. A hoarse gasping groan came from her.

"It's me, honey."

Sand covered hands rose as though to fend him off as she straightened.

"Mike?" Joy lit her face as she stepped towards him, then uncertainty, and she halted.

His hands outstretched, Mike approached slowly, afraid to spook her. "God, I've been trying to call— to write— I even sent Inger."

Horror filled her eyes, and she took a step

back.

"To talk to you, just talk. Your mother blocked every attempt I made."

The scar on her face showed starkly when she paled. Wind whipped her brown hair around her face, obscuring the deep lines etching her forehead. She tucked her hair behind her ear, then flushed and shook her hair loose, hiding the scar.

Mike traced the mark with his fingertips. "Means nothing to me. I still think you're the most beautiful girl I've ever seen."

"Oh, aye, but you've been busy. Things to do, people to see." Tears filled her eyes and anger made her voice tremble, exaggerating her lilt. "Too busy to call me back. Never mind it took me a day to walk to a nearby house to use the phone and made my feet bleed for two. And much too busy to visit."

As she spun away, she stumbled, landing on her hands and knees.

"Don't!" she yelled when Mike reached down to help her up.

Caught between anger and hysteria her voice rose and fell oddly.

"Why come now? I was moments from peace. Am I so evil God must torture me?"

He squatted in the sand beside her, as she sank back on her heels.

"I didn't return your call because I couldn't. Nick and I were arrested the day your mother took you. I came as soon as I could. God had nothing to do with it."

Her bottom lip quivered. "Arrested? For what?"

"Murder."

She swayed and landed on her hands again. "He's dead then?" Soft and low, her voice was a bare murmur of sound, so full of hope it almost broke Mike's heart.

"Deader than a doornail and roasting in Hell."

A tremor passed over her. Mike pulled her onto his lap.

"You…" she trailed off and began to cry.

"No, I didn't kill him. I was with you. I wish I had though. Nothing's changed how I feel for you. I love you, honey. God, when your mother took you, I went crazy. They were holding Nick and I for questioning. Your mother got the doctor to release you into her care and immediately had you at the consulate and sent back home. I tried to follow and got caught at the airport, then was confined while they investigated."

She leaned into his neck breathing deeply. "You're sure he's dead?" she asked with a quaver in her voice

"Shot five times in the chest," Mike said with satisfaction.

"I'm safe," she said it wonderingly, laced with hope.

"Come home with me, honey. I missed you so much. God, for weeks I didn't even know if you were alive or dead. Why didn't you come back to me?"

"How? I have no money, no passport, no nothing. I couldn't even walk till last month. To call you, I had to beg people to use their phones."

"Why didn't you use the ticket we sent? Inger said you got it. He saw you pick it up and run to the door."

Ashlee was silent a moment. When she spoke, her voice was thick with anger. "Oh, aye, I did sort of get it. I found the packet in my room, but my ma took it from me before I opened it. I thought Steven left it for me and I freaked out a little. She should've given it to me when she saw it was from you. Instead, she lied, said she dropped it that morning when she brought my medicine."

"You should've called Franton or Trent, they would've come for you…" he trailed off as she began to shake.

"No, no, no, don't, don't!" Gasping, she pushed away from him and vomited in the sand.

He reached for her, and she shrieked and tried to run, jumping to her feet, then falling again. The shriek rose in volume when he grabbed her.

"What? Stop, honey. Calm down."

"Let me go! Let me go!" Sobbing now, she strained in his hold, her gaze darting wildly around the empty beach. "Oh God, please, let me go. Please. Nicky, help me! Someone!" Her shriek echoed off the cliff. Seagulls screamed as if mocking her while she panted and struggled, flailing at Mike. With surprising suddenness, she went limp, a dead weight in his arms.

Mike fumbled for his phone, holding her tight around the waist as he called Nick. "Get down here. We're on the beach, and she's freaking out."

Ashlee moaned and tried to straighten. Terrified blue eyes met his. Mike pressed the phone to her ear. "Talk to her, Nick."

"Sweetheart, I'll be there in one minute, okay?"

"Nicky? Don't let him give me away. Don't. You won't 'right? Please help me, please." Tears streamed across her face as she strained in Mike's grasp.

"No, Ash, I never would, never. I swear to God." The cell-phone tumbled to the sand as

Mike used both hands to subdue her. "Those men are friends and wouldn't harm you. I'm so sorry Steven did, but I didn't tell him to."

Eyes with pupils so dilated they appeared black stared at him. "I didn't believe him— I didn't— but my mother is right, how did he know about Nick and I if you didn't tell him?"

"Because she did."

Both hands rose to cover her mouth. Wide eyed she stared at him as a bewildered expression crossed her face. "My ma?"

"Honey, she probably just vented, not meaning any harm, well, not harm like she caused."

Nick ran up and snatched her from Mike. She began crying again and threw her arms around Nick's neck, begging him to take her away.

Nick scooped her into his arms, whispering reassurance and endearments. Mike rose, grabbed his phone, and searched the sand for the gun. After emptying it, he tucked it in his waistband. A scowl etched his brow. Anger grew as he followed them. In the car, Ashlee huddled into Nick still crying. Mike hesitated; he wanted to yank her away and comfort her himself. For a moment, he was furious with Nick, but it wasn't Nick's fault Steven had terrorized her. Clearly, she needed Nick. This was his fault. If he hadn't talked her into loving Nick too, none of this would have happened.

✳ ✳ ✳

Teary blue eyes stared into Nick's gray ones. "My ma told him?"

Guilt burned like acid on Nick's soul. He flicked a glance at Mike who watched anxiously and smoothed her hair back. Mike's eyes pleaded with him, and his guilt deepened. Nick could use this to turn Ashlee against him and steal her away, but this was his fault. He was the one who'd told Steven, but telling her that truth would destroy them.

Mike's eyes filled with tears as Nick hesitated. He knew Nick could turn this to his advantage.

Nick released Ashlee to squeeze Mikes' shoulder as he released his dream. Ashlee needed them both.

He leaned down to kiss her brow and said, "I swear to you; Mike didn't give you away. He never did. He shared you with me because he loves us both. Your mother ran into Steven the day she left. Steven was coming over to tell you that Mike had gotten leave. If I had arrived home just ten minutes earlier, she wouldn't have spoken with him."

Mike gave him a grateful glance and Nick told himself he hadn't really lied. Margret had told Steven, he'd just confirmed it. As he tried to ease his conscious, Ashlee spoke.

"I need to go home. To my mother's house," she corrected as she rubbed her face with both hands.

"Ash…"

"My medicine is there, and I need it."

"Whatever you want, sweetheart, but you can't go in there alone."

She nodded against his chest. "Why didn't you come for me?"

Nick glared over her head at Mike. Mike bit his lip and dropped his eyes. *Later*, Nick told himself. He'd deal with Mike's lies later. *Ashlee needed peace, not fighting.*

"God, I wanted to, Ash, but at first I was confined to a cell, and then to base while the investigation was ongoing. If I had come, what could I do? I had no legal right to you. I couldn't even demand to see you or speak with you. For a while, I contemplated coming and kidnapping you, but I thought you were too ill to fly home. Those were the longest months of my life."

"You have to marry me, Nick, legally. You have too! No more pretending and no law separating us."

"Okay, we'll go to Vegas and marry. There are lots of Mormons in that vicinity. We'll find somewhere to marry legally."

"I love you, Nicky," she murmured as she kissed his neck.

"I love you too."

Mike crawled into the backseat and stroked her hair. "I love you too. And I agree, Nick needs a legal right to care for you. We'll work it out."

✳ ✳ ✳

They huddled together in the back of the car for an hour. Finally, Ashlee pulled away. "I need my medicine."

"Mike, give me the gun." Nick snorted at Ashlee's alarmed look. "No, I'm not going to shoot the crazy old bat, although it would be a kindness to put her out of her misery. I'm going to wipe it down and leave it here. Get caught with a gun here and its serious jail time."

Mike slapped the gun into Nick's hand and scrounged in his pocket for the bullets, then handed them to Nick.

"I'll drive us back." Not bothering to exit the car, Mike crawled to the front seat.

At her mother's house, Ashlee glanced from one to the other, her pale face tear streaked and her eyes wide.

Mike ran a gentle hand over her hair and across her shoulder. "Stay here, honey. I'll get your things."

"No, I want to say goodbye. I never want to see her again. I hate her. God, I know that's wrong, but I do. The things she said about me – us— why does she hate me so much?" Ashlee took a deep, trembling breath. "When you didn't come, I believed her when she said you didn't want me anymore, but she knew you couldn't. All this time she let me be afraid when she knew Steven was dead."

Nick laid a hand against her face. "Ash, your mother is sick. Not a sickness we can help with because she likes being sick. Say goodbye and never look back. I'm your family now and forever; I swear on my soul. The messages you left broke my heart. Never doubt me again. Never!"

Ashlee kissed him.

Mike took her hand and banged on the door of her mother's house.

The sharp staccato of high heels on a wood floor approached, and Margret opened the door. Margret hadn't changed. The same black dress as the one Ashlee wore came to her calves. Her graying black hair was in a neat bun, and her blue eyes were so full of venom that Nick moved in front of Ashlee.

Margret trailed her contemptuous gaze over them and pursed her lips. Two small patches of red bloomed on her cheekbones. "So, you've decided then? A life of sin and an eternity of damnation."

"Ma, did you tell Steven about Nick and me?"

"Don't blame me if your lovers abuse you. A whore gets what she deserves. God knows I tried to save you, but you always were willful and full of the devil. The blood that courses through your body is evil. From the moment of your birth, I knew it. How could it not be, being his daughter? But, I saved myself and I tried to save you. I too fell for Satan's lies. Men with their sinful lusts—"

"Did you tell him, Ma!" Ashlee shouted.

"I have no idea what you're going on about. I spoke to you and your other paramours. Told them God would make them pay for eternity for slaking their lusts with you. You're damned, but maybe the men around you can be saved. And he tried to save you, to make you repent your evil ways, but you seduced him."

Ashlee put her hands over her ears as tears streamed down her face.

"There's no hiding from your sin, girl. God will forgive—"

Mike slapped her. "One more fucking word and I'll kill you. Move out of the damn way."

He halted and swung back. "Where are the tickets and her IDs?"

Margret pressed a hand to her red cheek and glared at Mike. "Bottom drawer of my dresser."

Body rigid with anger, Mike pushed passed, dragging Ashlee with him.

"Take her and —"

Nick grabbed Margret's arm and yanked her to a halt. He slapped his hand over her mouth mid-yell, jerked her against his chest, and kicked the door closed with one foot.

"Listen good," a menacing whisper breathed in her ear, Nick's voice was full of hate. He shook her with one hand, keeping her mouth covered with the other. "I have three confirmed kills and twenty-seven unconfirmed, but I've killed way more than that, some sanctioned, some not. Believe me when I tell you I could snap your neck and sleep like a baby. Go near my wife again, call her, text her, write her, communicate in any way, and I'll be back here, and they'll find your corpse the next day." Nick forced her fingers around the gun handle and lifted the gun to her temple.

Eyes rolling in her white face, Margret tried to get away. Nick pulled the trigger. The click of the empty round was loud in the silence.

She screamed, the sound muffled by his

hand.

The hand over Margret's mouth pressed down harder as he forced her to pull the trigger again. "One word, one peep, and I load this." The hand on her mouth moved to her neck, and he squeezed while she gasped and scratched at him. Before she passed out, as her eyes fluttered back in her head, he released his grip.

"See how easy killing you would be for me?"

Eyes wide, Margret rubbed her throat, drawing deep, hoarse breaths, and nodded.

Nick pushed her roughly away. "Go away. I never want to see you again." Two at a time he ran up the stairs, headed to the only room with a light on.

Mike was stuffing clothes in a pillowcase he'd taken from the bed.

Ashlee stood in the doorway, watching Mike and biting her lip.

"Where's your medicine?" Anger at her mother made Nick's voice harsher than he meant it to be.

Ashlee started and rubbed her hands together, twining her fingers. "Ma keeps it her room."

"Stay here with Mike; I'll get it." Nick kissed her brow and hurried to the next room, finding it unoccupied, he went to the next. Her mother's room lurked in the back of the house.

A weird odor of incense and mothballs filled the room. He waved a hand before his face in a futile attempt to block the scent.

Nick flipped on the light and winced. Religious paintings hung on the walls and a life-sized statue of Mary, arms outstretched, stood at the foot of the bed. On the dresser, an assortment of pill bottles sat on a wooden tray beside a stack of red candles and an incense burner. Some of the bottles were for her mother, though most were for Ashlee.

The letters he and Mike had sent were wrapped in newspaper along with her passport, license, ticket, and money, right were Margret said they would be. Nick ripped a pillow case off the bed, snatched the medicine, and ran back to Ashlee.

"Where did you get a gun, anyway?" Nick hugged Ashlee who was holding Mike and crying in the middle of her small bedroom. Even with the light on, the room seemed dim. No color softened the room. No happiness filled it. Cold and austere, no childhood mementos in sight, her room appeared more a prison than a bedroom.

"Ma gave it to me." A hysterical laugh burst from her, and she pushed away. "To get what I deserve. What do I deserve, Nicky? I thought

God sent me a message right before Mike came…" Ashlee trailed off, making a sound halfway between a laugh and a cry.

Nick pulled her close, hugging her tight while her body trembled against his. "Love, sweetheart. Safety, happiness, and love. None of this is your fault. Steven was sick, not an agent of God. Your mom is sick too, so twisted up inside with hatred she can't think straight. Wait here while I make sure this is all the medicine." Nick kissed her cold cheek and ran downstairs.

Margret sat at the kitchen table with a Bible before her.

"Is this all her medicine? What was on your dresser?"

Her icy blue eyes fixed on him as she nodded, but didn't speak.

Nick fished in his pocket and pulled out a bullet. He rubbed it on his pants a few seconds, shining the brass. Using the tail of his shirt as a glove, he placed the bullet in front of the Bible before Margret. "This will bring you peace and to your reward. The one you know you deserve. It wasn't the sins of the father you were trying to save Ashlee from, but the sins of the mother."

Margret trembled and snatched the bullet, knuckles white on her clenched fist.

A hard, satisfied smile on his face, Nick ran back upstairs.

Neither had moved in his absence, still huddled together, hugging in the cold room. "Let's go. Leave this crap. We'll get you new clothes."

Ashlee nodded and hugged him. Automatically, Nick put an arm around her.

"Can we take the blanket? My gram made it for me when I was little."

"Take whatever you like. You're never coming back here." In his arms, Ashlee trembled. A mix of thankfulness for her presence, guilt over what he'd told Steven, and furious anger at Margret and Mike for keeping her from him made his head pound.

Mike grabbed the blanket from her bed. Made for a child's bed, dull with age in shades of cream and gray it didn't quite cover hers. "Did you want anything else?"

Ashlee shook her head, and they headed to the door.

With the tail of his black t-shirt Nick wiped off the gun and threw it into the living room as he passed.

Ashlee fell asleep in the backseat on the way to Dublin minutes after she took the medicine. Three different pills taken with water and a look of relief.

Mike sat in back with her while Nick drove, fuming and horrified over the tale Ashlee told of her last trip to the shore. It not only scared him to death, it angered him. Ashlee's tears and fear, her desperation and need to be safe was a physical pain, and Mike had goddamn known Nick could've gone to her earlier. Now he had a suicidal wife and a lying friend to deal with.

A glance into the back seat showed Ashlee sound asleep. Nick pulled over at the first rest stop he passed.

"Get out," he said as he slammed the car door. Heavy cloud cover dimmed the moon's radiance, leaving them in darkness. Gravel embedded in the hard-packed clay, almost smooth from use, was interspersed with thick, short tufts of grass that crushed under his feet giving off a fresh grassy smell. Arms crossed on his chest, Nick stared into the dark fields, his fury growing as he waited for Mike.

"What's up?" Mike asked as he quietly closed his car door.

Without warning, Nick slammed Mike into the side of the car. He grasped the front of his shirt and drew back. Mike grabbed the descending fist and twisted while using his feet to send Nick off balance.

"You, goddamn motherfucker! You fucking

knew exactly where she would be and didn't tell me," Nick snarled as he swung again.

Never in his life had he been this angry with Mike. This punch connected but did little damage as Mike turned with it.

"Cut it out! You're going to wake her," Mike hissed as he lifted both palms to block the next punch.

Nick dropped his fists and aimed for the gut, connecting with a solid hit. A load oof escaped Mike, and he dropped his hands. Nick sprang forward and hit him with his shoulder, grabbed both Mike's wrists and twisted, using momentum to throw him. He followed him to the ground, kneeling hard on his groin, both hands squeezing Mike's neck.

Mike grasped Nick's hands and tried to force them off.

So furious his breath came in harsh pants, Nick leaned over Mike. "Your selfishness could've fucking killed her. This isn't about what you want. We do whatever we have to for her, like it or not! I thought you got that, but apparently, I need to beat it into your thick skull."

Mike dropped his hands to his sides, making no resistance. "No, you're right. And if it'll make you feel better, hit me. How close she came to killing herself makes me sick." Mike shuddered and tried to rise, but Nick's body blocked him. He sagged and took a deep breath. "Nick, it never occurred to me…"

Nick switched his grasp to Mike's shoulders and smacked his head twice on the ground, then crouched on his heels at Mike's feet.

Mike sat, one hand rubbing his crotch, the other his head. "How could I know her mother was encouraging her to use the damned gun on herself? Ashlee is my wife! I just wanted to see my wife first."

"Mine too. Did you think I was playing, Mike? Were you?"

Mike turned away, avoiding Nick's hard stare. "I guess I was. Partly anyways. She loves you, but I thought I would always be first in her heart, not equal." Mike's breath caught. "Or lesser." An expression of loss on his face, Mike turned back to Nick. "Steven took her from me, and I don't think I'll get her back, not like it was. The poison her mom spewed will take a lifetime to cure. Do you think losing her to you is easy for me?"

On his feet now, Nick stood with his hands on his hips. "Ashlee is my wife as much as yours. If it were my choice, I wouldn't share her with you. That's always been true. But I see she needs you. For her sake, I won't take advantage here and turn her against you when we both know I could, and easily. But you need to do what's best for her. Not you— her!"

The skin on Mike's wrists reddened as he rubbed them and glared up at Nick. "I wish I'd never shared her with you."

"Too late and don't pretend you didn't realize when we started this. We both told you. It's not our fault you're so arrogant you couldn't imagine her wanting me more."

"Who's cocky now?" Mike surged to his feet with his fists clenched. "Just because she calls for you when she's frightened—"

"Does it matter why she does? If you try to keep her from me again— for any damn reason— I'll kill you. I love you, Mike, but I love her more."

"You really would, wouldn't you?" Mike stepped back, his face pale.

"Are you saying you wouldn't do the same if I risked her life for myself?"

Shoulders rigid, Mike took short, sharp strides away, then relaxed and turned back, straightened, and held out his hand. "Everything you said is true. Forgive me, and I promise to never attempt to come between you again."

Nick hesitated.

Mike dropped his hand. 'Nick..." Laced with sorrow and longing the one word hung in the air between them.

Nick stepped forward, gave Mike a quick hug, and then grabbed Mike's shoulders again, his gaze intent on Mike's face.

"Whatever she needs, we do. If that's staying with one of us and not the other, we do that. If she needs to be alone or leave the States or have one of us sit by her side every minute, then that's what we do."

Mike nodded.

Nick hugged him again.

"I love you too," Mike mumbled and squeezed him a second before stepping back.

"Don't get all gay on me." Nick tousled Mike's hair hard, laughed a strained, forced laugh, and turned away.

Mike chuckled, sounding sad and relieved and then straightened his shirt.

Both men got into the car where Ashlee slept on undisturbed, the sedatives making her sleep deeply.

- 23 -
WIFE NOT FEELING WELL, SIR?

Dawn light filtered into the backseat of the car. The gray sunshine illuminated enough to read by. Nick had the medicine bottles spread out, examining the labels. Across his and Mike's laps, Ashlee slept. Mike dozed, his hands buried in his wife's hair, his head leaning back at an uncomfortable angle on the seat.

"Mike."

Mike's head jerked up, and he tightened his grip on her hair for a moment before relaxing and freeing his fingers to smooth it.

"Hmmm?"

"This medicine is different types of sedatives and pain medicine. No antibiotics or anything else that I recognize. We need to get her to a doctor ASAP."

Mike rubbed his eyes and glanced at his watch. "Flight leaves in six hours. Can it wait till we're home?"

"Guess so." Nick handed the bottles to Mike. "Meanwhile, what do we give her? No way can she have all this stuff, it will kill her."

Mike removed each bottle from the bag, examining and then dropping them on the floor of the car one at a time. "These three here are from this month. Looks like pain medication and two types of sedatives. The white pills she took last night and an injectable one. I'm guessing that's a stronger version."

Furious brown eyes met Nick's. "Jesus, that woman. What the hell is wrong with her treating her daughter like this?" Mike shook the pill bottle containing the pain medication. "Oxycodone is some strong shit. Our girl is likely addicted."

Nick snorted and took the bottle from him. "I knew that when she made us go back for it. The sedation worries me more. A million clinics and programs are available to help kick an addiction, and God knows our girl is strong and determined. But why do you suppose the old bitch was sedating her?"

Mike closed his eyes and leaned his head back. "The motherfucker is dead. Now that she knows, maybe she won't need it?"

Nick snorted again, and both men were quiet while the sun climbed into the sky, burning off the dawn gray.

Mike glanced at his watch again. "Find a store, Nick. Somewhere we can buy her comfortable shoes and a pretty dress or something."

Wrapped in the gray blanket, Ashlee's head laid on Mike's lap, her feet on Nick's. Two pairs of wool socks cushioned Ashlee's tender feet and kept the ugly black sneakers from slipping off. The black dress she wore fit her badly, being tight on the top, leaving gaping buttons that a nappy black sweater covered.

While she slept, Nick had slid the dress up, exposing her left leg. Silvery-red scars crisscrossed the pale, firm flesh. No bruises remained. Most of the scars were thin lines that would fade in time. Afraid to wake her, he'd left the thick socks alone. The feet needed a doctor. A limp developed if she took normal strides. Small, slow steps she managed with no limp. *Maybe it was the shoes* he thought hopefully and rubbed his eyes. Nick took out his phone and opened the GPS.

"Stay in the back with her, I'll drive." Nick eased from the back seat, closing the door as quietly as he could, and got in the driver's seat. Ashlee stirred but settled as Mike murmured to her. "Before clothes, we need a restroom. The first diner I pass, I'm stopping. We can eat and use the bathroom, then go shopping."

In the parking lot of a nearby diner, they waited for her to wake. Nick glanced at his watch and then into the backseat. "Wake her, Mike. She can sleep on the plane. Who knows how long those damn pills will make her groggy and we need her alert to board."

Mike nodded and kissed Ashlee's cheek as he shook her shoulder. "Wake up, honey."

An indistinct murmur was his answer, and Nick smiled. The sound brought back pleasant memories. A heavy sleeper, Ashlee would cuddle closer when being woken, her soft warmth pressed against his side. As she woke, her hands would trail over him, groggy sleep mumbles changing to interested low moans as her hands fondled him. Not this morning, though. This morning, the sleepy murmur changed to a shriek as she leaped up. A struggle ensued in the backseat as Mike tried to hold her while reassuring her as she flailed to get free.

"Let her go," Nick barked.

He leaned over the seat and placed a hand on her face. Her wild eyes focused on him, and she stopped struggling, breath coming in short, harsh pants that slowed as Nick spoke.

Tears in her eyes, she turned back to Mike and huddled in his embrace.

"Sorry, I was sleeping, and you scared me. I get a little disorientated when I wake." A sob hitched her breath. "I forget where I am."

"Shh, it's okay, honey." Mike rubbed her back and murmured too low for Nick to make out what he said.

"Hungry, sweetheart? The plane leaves in a few hours, and there's a bathroom here." Nick exited the car, opened the back door, and put her ugly sneakers on her. Once she had the sweater buttoned, she let Mike help her out, and they entered the diner.

Mike ordered for her while she used the bathroom. The food arrived before she returned. When she finally appeared, she was pale, and dark rings circled her eyes. She'd attempted to fix her hair, pulling it to one side in a ponytail, trying to hide the scar on the edge of her cheek. Her limp, lifeless hair appeared dull, not its normal vibrant chestnut. Nick patted the seat beside him, and she smiled and snuggled into his side.

A listless hand picked at her food as they devoured their breakfast.

"Want something different?" Mike nodded at her barely touched plate of eggs and sausage. "They have pie here or muffins."

"No, I'm just not hungry."

"Feet hurt?"

When she nodded, Nick handed her a pain pill. "These pills are strong, Ash. Eat a bit more so it doesn't upset your stomach."

A smile on her face, she took the pill and ate the toast. A few minutes later she excused herself to use the restroom again.

The waitress approached and gestured at the untouched plate. "Wife not feeling well, sir? Want me to wrap that?"

Nick gave the waitress a polite smile. "She's a tad under the weather. Travel does that sometimes. Don't bother to wrap it, but thank you. The airline lost our luggage. You wouldn't happen to know a place nearby to buy some comfortable clothes and shoes like yours, would you?"

The waitress giggled and glanced at her feet encased in wool lined boots. "The shops on Grafton Street in Dublin are nice, but you can get essentials in Penny's right down the road a bit in Dalkey. Not quite as stylish, but not as expensive either." She gave them directions as she wiped up the table.

Ashlee returned. Mike left a generous tip and paid while Nick walked her out to the car. The waitress had directed them to a small row of shops. Stone buildings lined a small main street just opening for the day.

"What are we doing?" Ashlee gazed about,

her eyes lighting on a jeweler's sign and brightening.

On impulse, Nick said, "Buying new wedding rings."

Mike glanced up, appearing surprised, then glanced at Ashlee's shining eyes and smiled.

Ashlee's smile faded when they got to the jewelers and found that they didn't open till ten. "Good, time to shop while we wait." Nick grinned at her and pulled her towards the nearby clothing store.

Ashlee hesitated in the doorway. "Nick, look at this place. We can't afford these clothes." Anxious, envious eyes scanned the mannequin in the window wearing a soft wool skirt and a silk shirt that appeared expensive. Leather riding boots hugged the feet in a casual pose, and a black leather duster draped over the mannequin's arm.

"Can't hurt to look; besides we have time to kill."

Still biting her lip, Ashlee followed him in.

Mike picked out clothes while Nick helped her try on boots. "When your feet are recovered, I promise to buy you a pair of boots just like the ones in the window, but for now these are better. Easy to take on and off and you need to remove your shoes at the airport."

Ashlee bit her bottom lip hard and gazed at

her feet. Red and swollen, the burns had left shiny patches intersected by thick white scars. Not too noticeable when she stood, but when she lifted her foot to remove or replace shoes the damage was obvious. Nick handed her a pair of light tan boots with a dense insert of wool.

"Try these. They look comfortable and should slide on and off easily."

Ashlee slid her foot in and smiled, then took the boot off and flipped it over, examining the price. A flush on her face, she gasped and gave the boot back, shaking her head.

Nick turned them over, saw the price, and shrugged. "Are they comfortable?" When Ashlee didn't answer, he sighed heavily. "I'm buying these boots whether you like them or not, but at least make sure they fit, okay?"

A half-smile, half-grimace on her face, she took the boot back and tried it again, pacing in a small circle, then hugging Nick.

Mike spoke with the shopkeeper, and when they left, Ashlee wore the same lilac silk blouse the mannequin sported and soft, gray wool trousers tucked into her new boots. Another outfit was in a large bag with a pair of silk pajamas and two sets of lingerie. A fluffy wool sweater that reached her knees in shades of purple finished her outfit. The happy clerk escorted them out. The clothes Ashlee had worn entering the store were stuffed into the garbage can.

Nick was pleased to see she walked easier, taking bigger steps without tenseness. The jewelry store had opened while they shopped, and the three of them entered.

"What can I do for you today?" the bespectacled man behind the counter inquired with a friendly smile.

Nick took a step forward. "Wedding rings. My wife was in an accident and had to have hers cut off. To replace them, we want something really special."

"But not unique." Mike kissed Ashlee's brow. "We need matching rings."

"I, uh, see." The clerk bit his bottom lip. He tapped the glass case before him a moment, and his eyes narrowed.

Ashlee turned away, a blush flushing her cheeks.

Nick was about to lead her from the store when the clerk spoke.

"Ah-ha, I have just the thing. The very thing indeed." Face wreathed in smiles, the clerk gestured to them. "A bit pricey mind you, but beautiful and appropriate." A grin on his face, he led them to a small case that stood alone with a spotlight over it. "The Claddagh wedding ring made by artisans right here in Ireland and stamped by the Irish Government Assay Office in Dublin Castle."

Nick glanced at Ashlee's face and smiled. "Perfect. Can you size them here?"

An hour later, they left the store wearing matching rings, thick gold bands with rounded silver edges, with the Claddagh design engraved across them. Small diamond chips adorned the rings Ashlee wore on each ring finger. The jeweler had inscribed them with their names, apologizing the entire time for his shaky penmanship. Usually, a man hired just for that did it, but they didn't have time to wait.

"I can't believe we paid so much," Ashlee mumbled as she admired her rings and then kissed the band on Mike's finger.

Mike laughed and hugged her. "I would pay a million times that to see you smile."

Nick glanced in the rearview mirror and smiled himself at her happiness. Color in her pale cheeks, and laughing quietly in the backseat, she snuggled in Mike's arms. Nick was relieved. He turned his attention to the road and drove them to the airport.

With no bags to check, they breezed through security with time to spare. Nick gave Ashlee another pain pill and one of the sedative tablets. A stewardess took the medicine and locked it a small box for the duration of the flight. Ashlee held both their hands.

By the window with Ashlee beside him, Nick put an arm around her and held her hand, ignoring the glances from the passengers in the seat beside theirs as Mike did the same.

"Ireland is beautiful, but it will nice to be home." Mike leaned over and kissed her cheek. "We missed you so much. Without you there, it isn't home."

Ashlee bit her lip and glanced away. "About that, I can't live in that apartment, Mike."

Nick tightened his grip on her as he kissed her cheek. "We figured and already got a new place off the base. A condo right on the beach with a full-time doorman. We're renting now, but if you like it, we can buy it. The kitchen is real nice. Trent found for it for us."

The hand in his tightened. Nick released her and smoothed her hair. "Trent is a good friend, but if you never want to see him again, that's okay."

"I…. I like Trent and I know it's stupid to be afraid of him, but… I'm not sure. And it isn't fair of me to say you can't have friends. We can't live in isolation."

"No need to decide anything now. Or ever. Let's see how you feel when we get home. No one will come to our place that you don't invite, okay?" Nick searched her eyes for her response and was reassured when she met his gaze and smiled.

Mike put his chin on her head and hugged her. "When we get home, you need to see a doctor for your feet and…" He took a deep breath. "I was thinking a therapist. Someone to help us all cope with this?"

Ashlee nodded slowly, and took a deep quavering breath before straightening. "Oh aye, I do need help. Nightmares haunt me, and I jump at shadows." Soft and low, her voice shook with self-disgust.

"Nightmares haunt me too," Nick said and pulled her close, whispering in her ear, "I can't bear the memory either. Not being able to stay with you when you needed me is the worst one. For that, I'm sorrier than I can say."

Ashlee kissed him, the kiss deepening until she pulled away breathing harder. A nervous hand smoothed her hair as she licked her lips. Then, with determination, she grasped his shirt, pulled him close, and kissed him again. The kiss ended, and she cuddled as close as she could, pressing herself against him, her warm breath caressing his neck.

Over her shoulder, the passenger in the seat beside theirs gawked. Nick narrowed his eyes, and the man glanced away, but his gaze was drawn back as Mike leaned over, hugging Ashlee too and kissing her neck. After a moment, Mike straightened and flicked a newspaper open, resting one hand on Ashlee's knee.

Ashlee seemed oblivious to anyone else, content to hug Nick and rest in his arms. They both dozed off.

- 24 -
SHE'S WORTH WAITING FOR

Nick glanced at his watch and frowned. Dublin airport had been an easy boarding. London airport, where they switched plans, was nightmarish. Crowded and confusing, a long layover followed by an extended wait to leave had everyone on this flight cranky.

Ashlee needed her pain medicine. Cramps in both feet made the simple task of walking to the bathroom on board difficult. The last trip left her pale and shaking. Unable to stretch out or raise her feet, they'd both swollen. Nick rose and approached the flight attendant for their section.

"Excuse me, Ma'am, I wonder if you might help me. My traveling companion has medicine the flight attendant confiscated when we boarded and needs it. If you could bring her one of the oxycodone pills, please?"

The flight attendant nodded and hurried away.

Nick glanced back at their seat. Ashlee had moved to his seat and had her feet in Mike's lap under the gray blanket. Head tipped back against the window, her eyes closed and her face pale and strained, she grimaced as Mike rubbed her feet.

A few moments later the stewardess returned with a water bottle and the bottle of pills. Nick pointed to Ashlee, and the stewardess brought her the medicine. After checking her passport, the woman handed Ashlee the water and the pill and waited to ensure she swallowed it before returning to the front of the plane where Nick waited.

"Sir, if you would like to sit elsewhere so she can keep her injured foot elevated there are free seats in the back."

"Thank you very much. I might take you up on that offer, but let me speak to my friends first."

Nick smiled his thanks, and the woman returned his smile, a slight blush on her cheekbones. At one point in his life he would've pursued her interest, invited her for drinks or dinner and enjoyed her company for an evening, but those days were over. The only company he wanted now was Ashlee's.

Happiness filled him when he gazed at her. For a time, he'd thought she would die from her injuries, and now here she was. Sick, yes, but getting better. Happy at moments and content with them. The smile on her face when she ran her fingers over their rings made him smile too.

"Stay there," Nick motioned for Ashlee to stay seated as she straightened when he arrived. "The stewardess assures me a seat can be found for me somewhere, but I'll use yours. I don't mind your legs in my lap." A smile tilted the edge of his lips. He leaned closer and whispered, "I can't wait to feel your legs around me again."

To his delight, she smiled and blushed. After glancing around, she kissed his neck.

Nick used his hands to frame her face and kissed her lips, curling his fingers in her hair. Breathless, she pulled back and rested her forehead on his, making a small contented sound that filled him with heat. Unable to resist, he kissed her again. A minute later, he realized he'd pushed her against the side of the plane, and his hand was on the bare skin of her stomach under her shirt. Hastily, he drew back.

"Sorry, sweetheart, got carried away."

She giggled.

Mike groaned and then coughed. "Stop, you're killing me; it's been months."

Ashlee giggled again and put her feet in his lap.

A heated look passed between them, making Nick smile. *Recovery from the attack would take a lifetime, but this was a good start*, he thought as Ashlee took his hand and kissed his fingers one at a time as she flexed her feet in Mike's lap under the blanket.

Nick shifted in his seat and leaned closer.

Eyes bright, she smiled at him.

Gaze intent on her, he lifted her hands and kissed the ring on her right finger and then the one on the left. Slowly, he sucked her finger into his mouth, licking along the length. Her lips parted as she leaned forward.

He removed her finger and kissed her hand again. His voice deep and low, he whispered, "Do you want to play cards?"

She giggled again and nodded. Nick grinned at her, lowered the small table, and took out the pack of cards with shamrocks on them they'd bought in Dublin. In London, they'd bought two packs, the Tower of London, on the backs of one, and Big Ben on another. Ashlee had spent an hour browsing the postcards. Mike had bought her a stack, earning a big smile and a hug. Nick had no idea she liked things like that but made a mental note to have Mike pick up postcards and decks of cards for her when he traveled.

Two hours later, they arrived in Vegas tired and hungry a day earlier than when they'd left Ireland.

It took them forty-five minutes to rent a car and another thirty to reach the strip. Once out of the congested airport the traffic wasn't bad.

Ashlee wanted to see the sights, so Mike drove down the strip. Eleven at night and the place bustled with activity. Bright lights blinked everywhere, infusing Nick with a false sense of energy.

"Let's stop somewhere and eat, I'm starving," Mike said. "What hotel shall we stay at, Ash?"

"What are my choices?" Fingertips resting on the window, she continued to gaze at the bright lights, a smile turning up the corner of her bottom lip.

"Any one you want," Nick said and handed her the map he'd picked up at the car rental counter.

"How about a small place tonight and tomorrow one of the big ones to celebrate our wedding?" Eyes anxious on Mike's face, she bit her lip, waiting for his answer.

"Sure, but first food." Mike grinned at her

and drew her closer. A happy sigh escaped him when she kissed his neck. One arm around her, the other on the wheel of the car, he pulled into a brightly lit restaurant. Neon lights flashed, outlining a giant steak, while white light bulbs blinked in sequence around another sign proclaiming, 'All you can eat steak dinners ten ninety-nine, all day, every day.'

Ashlee giggled and turned shining eyes on Nick. Her happiness made him laugh aloud. The men each took one of her hands. The walk to the restaurant hurt her. Small slow steps and a tight grip on his hand revealed her pain. Before Nick could pick her up, Mike scooped her up in his arms and kissed her. She shrieked and laughed and asked to be put down.

Mike nuzzled her neck. "Too slow, woman, and I'm starving." When she opened her mouth to speak, he kissed her and stopped moving.

Nick waited by the entrance.

"Well, I guess I'm not that hungry," Mike murmured as her hands wandered over his chest.

A smile on her face, she pulled his head to hers and kissed him again. "Let's eat. I don't want you fainting from hunger."

Nick held the door for them, and Mike set her down when they entered.

The food was good, but the crowd made

Ashlee nervous. Every time someone passed behind her she jumped. Nick gave her another pain pill and one of the sedatives. Half sitting in his lap, leaning on his shoulder, Nick and Ashlee watched Mike eat his third steak.

"You're going to get sick," Ashlee said.

"Uhh un." Mike shook his head as he swallowed and gestured with his fork.

Ashlee laughed, and Nick smiled, perfectly content. By the time Mike finished, Ashlee dozed against Nick. She woke for the walk outside, but Nick carried her to the car and climbed in the backseat with her. "Find somewhere quiet, Mike. Our girl needs a good night's sleep."

In minutes, she fell asleep in Nick's lap.

Mike glanced at them in the rear-view mirror. "Damn, guess I should've eaten after, but I guess one more day won't kill me."

"Poor Mike, this must be the longest dry spell of your life," Nick said with real sympathy.

"She's worth waiting for."

"That she is," Nick whispered and kissed her brow.

Mike pulled into a small, dark motel. Ashlee murmured and turned, but didn't wake. "I'll go see about getting us a room with a late checkout." Mike hurried into the shabby office and returned a few minutes later swinging a key around his finger. "Number seven, by the end. I asked for a quiet, private room where no one will bother us," he said as he started the car and pulled up to the end of the building.

He parked and opened the back door still speaking. "The clerk offered some advice and gave me a list of chapels we can take her to."

Ashlee's eyes fluttered open, and she screamed. "No, don't!" A fist hit Nick in the jaw, and she flailed, pushing away and smacking at Nick's hand's as he tried to grab her.

"Sweetheart, wake up. It's me!" Nick yelled.

"No! Don't take me anywhere! Let me go!" Shrill and panicked, her voice was a gasping shriek.

Nick released her.

Huddled as far from him as she could get in the back seat, she rubbed her eyes with both hands.

"Nick?" The terrified wail when she lowered her hands and saw him shriveled his soul.

He reached out to her, and she threw herself into his arms sobbing.

"Oh God, Nick, I hate those dreams..."

White-faced, Mike held the door open. "Sorry, honey, we'll be more careful waking you."

Still crying she reached for Mike. When she stepped from the car, she moaned and fell into his arms unable to walk. "Don't let me go," she begged as Mike carried her. One hand reached to Nick for a moment before she withdrew and huddled in Mike's arms sobbing, begging Mike to not let anyone take her.

Nick rushed to the door and opened it, then returned to the car and grabbed her medicine.

A man two doors down let the curtain slide closed.

In the motel room, Ashlee continued to cry. Nick knelt before her with his hands on her knees. "Sweetheart, I can give you a shot to calm you if you like?"

"Help me, Nicky, I feel so bad," she whimpered and clutched him around the neck.

Lips pressed together in a grim line, Nick gave her half a dose. Mike pulled her into his arms and whispered in her ear as the medicine took hold. Five minutes later they exchanged uneasy glances over her sleeping form.

"Jesus, Nick, what the hell are we going to do?"

"For starters, don't talk when we wake her. I'm sure she heard you, and it got confused into her nightmare. Say her name, your name, and you love her, that's it until she's awake."

"You think the sedatives are making her

dreams worse?"

"No, but they're probably making it harder to wake, so we need to be careful."

"Should we undress her or let her sleep in her clothes?"

"Put her in the pajamas we bought and keep a light on in here. I shudder to think what will happen if she wakes up in a strange place in the dark."

Mike nodded, bit his lip, and began undressing Ashlee, unbuttoning the silk blouse and undoing her pants.

Nick returned to the car and grabbed the bags. "You got this if I go take a quick shower?" he asked as he handed Ashlee's bag to Mike.

"Yeah, take your time."

Nick had just stepped into the shower when Mike started swearing in the other room. Naked and dripping he ran out. Blue and red lights strobed through the room and someone pounded on the door.

- 25 -

Don't Let Him Take Me from You

"Las Vegas police! Open up!" a woman yelled.

Nick ran back to the bathroom as Mike headed to the door. He returned with a towel wrapped around his waist in time to see the door open and a police officer motion with her gun drawn for Mike to step outside. Half-naked, Ashlee lay on the bed with one arm dangling limply to the floor. Harsh hotel light revealed her scars and sedated state.

"Keep your hands where I can see them." The officer gestured with her pistol for Mike to walk forward and glanced through the doorway. Her eyes narrowed, and she nudged her radio with her chin. "Dispatch, this is Charlie thirty-seven, I have a two-oh-seven-A in progress and require assistance." The gun now clutched in two hands, she stepped back and yelled for Mike to get on the ground.

Nick didn't wait to be told; he laid on the dirty carpet and laced his hands over his head.

"What the hell?" Mike glared at the officer and blocked the door.

From his spot on the floor, Nick yelled, "Mike, get on the floor. Let the officer do her job."

Mike continued to stand in the doorway. The police officer backed up, pointing her pistol. Sirens sounded in the distance, drawing closer. Sounding angry, her partner hollered at Mike to drop to the ground.

"Mike, goddamn it, get on the damn ground right now before they wake Ashlee and we really have a problem!"

Mike glanced over his shoulder at Nick, then Ashlee, and lowered himself to the ground. A furious light in his eyes, and his lips pressed together, he let the officer cuff him.

The female officer approached Nick with her cuffs in hand as her partner covered him.

"If you check our wallets, you'll see she's his wife." Nick gestured with his chin to his pants on a chair in front of the bathroom door. "Ashlee is sedated. If you wake her, she's going to freak out."

"Yeah, I see. I also see the scars. You have the right to remain silent..." The woman read him his rights as she cuffed him and hauled him upright.

Four more officers showed up, sirens blaring, as the officer walked him to the door.

Mike yelled from the floor. "Look, she's my wife, and we're helping her, not hurting her. Her passport is in the glove compartment of the car. Call my lawyer, his card is in my wallet, or call the precinct on my base and ask them. The medicine is prescription. But please, don't wake her."

"Don't think they can," Nick said, "At least for a while. She hasn't twitched. Calm down, Mike, and we'll get this straightened out, and Ash will be fine."

The woman officer handed him over to a pair of the newly arrived officers, entered the room, and put her hand on Ashlee's neck, feeling for a pulse. An ambulance pulled in as Nick was pushed into the back of a police car, losing his towel in the process. The officer who pushed him in threw the towel over his lap and slammed the door.

The female officer gestured to the paramedics and pointed to the vial of sedative and needle on the nightstand. "Is she in danger?"

The medic picked up the vial and read the label. "Not if they used it correctly, but..." He shrugged, replaced the bottle, took Ashlee's pulse and listened to her heart.

"What do we got here, Barb?" another officer asked as he entered the room, his gaze traveling over Ashlee's half naked form. Mike had thrown her shirt over her when he answered the door, but the silvery red scars on her left-hand side were clearly visible.

"Neighbor called it in. Two men dragging a crying woman into the room. She was screaming for them to leave her alone. Unresponsive so far, but one of the men claims to be her husband."

"Doesn't make this shit right." The officer nodded to the scars covering Ashlee. "Sick fucks like this really get me mad."

"The man claiming to be her husband says she needed the sedation and if we wake her, she'll freak. Told me to call his base. Something is familiar about her, but I can't put my finger on it. Might be she was reported kidnapped." Barb turned to the paramedic. "Can that be right? Will it harm her to wake her?"

"Medically no, but if sedation is for a mental problem, then yes."

"Is it safe to leave her here while we straighten this out? Say, thirty minutes or so?"

"I can't recommend that as I'm not a doctor, but her vitals are fine."

Barb hesitated before nodding decisively.

"Get her in the bus. Without waking her if you can."

The paramedic nodded as Barb grabbed Nick's pants from the chair and went through the pockets, removing his wallet. Inside the wallet, she found his ID, a picture of Ashlee, another picture of the three of them, and a picture of Nick and Ashlee, arms around each other, smiling into each other's eyes.

Mrs. Evans passport was in the glove compartment right where the man said it would be. Her husband's wallet contained the same pictures, except he stared into Ashlee's eyes smiling. A frown creased Barb's brow. Her gaze traveled the scene once more before she dialed the base in California.

"This is Officer Barbara Stertan from Las Vegas. I need some information regarding Sergeant Michael Evans, Nicolas—"

Before she finished her sentence, the man on the other end of the line asked her to hold.

A man came on the line in moments. "Hello, I'm Sergeant Mason, how can I help you?"

"This is Officer Barbara Stertan from Las Vegas, and I'm hoping you can clear things up for me. I got a call about a possible abduction and found an unconscious woman with two men. A Michael Evans and Nicholas Rossi –"

"Ashlee Conner Evans," Mason interrupted.

"Yeah, they're married. You say Ashlee is unconscious?"

"Drugged and unresponsive. The husband claims he sedated her for her own good and if we wake her she'll be upset."

Mason sighed. "Yep, sounds about right. If Mrs. Evans doesn't need medical attention, let it be."

"Are you aware of the previous injuries? My witness is pretty insistent the woman was calling for help."

"I'm sure she was. And I saw more of her injuries then I wished too. The fact that she needs sedation doesn't surprise me. Look, I'll send you the file, but if her husband says she'll be upset if you wake her, then don't. We aren't talking about a little upset here, but the kind that can get you fired."

Barb bit her lip. "Never had a case like this before. Usually it's real clear when a man is beating his wife, or otherwise abusing her, but these injuries are healing scars, and she's sedated, not harmed. If I didn't have a witness…."

"Mrs. Evans could very well have called for help. When the police brought her to the hospital, she called for help almost daily, sometimes hourly. Look, I can't tell you what to do, just what I know. Mrs. Evans was attacked. Her attacker was murdered, we suspect by one or both of those men, but there's no proof. Their alibis are tight. If they did it, they stayed awake for four days straight and snuck around invisible, and I can't figure out how they did either of those things. The attack was brutal and ugly, so I'm not surprised she has issues now. I'm faxing copies of the reports to your precinct."

"Thank you, Sergeant, you've been a help." Barb put her phone in her pocket and gazed at Ashlee uneasily. She remembered the case now. If her husband had killed that man, he was a vicious psychopath. The news was full of experts and vigilantes praising and condemning him. The fact that no proof existed, and in fact he had an airtight alibi, chilled her. Harming his wife seemed like a very bad idea. One that could get you dead.

Mason snorted and hung up. "What the hell are they doing in Vegas?" he mused aloud.

Barb returned to the paramedic who sat beside Ashlee in the ambulance. "Bring her back to the room. Her husband is refusing treatment for her, and the sedatives are prescribed. My partner and I will stay and make sure she really is okay when she wakes. How long will that be?"

"I would guess six hours, but you can

probably wake her in about three. She stirred a few times when we moved her. I might be able to wake her now with nothing more than smelling salts if you like."

"No, let her sleep, but give me the salts. Damn, I hate this fucking call." Barb held her hand out for the smelling salts. The paramedic handed them to her, and then he and his partner carried Ashlee back into the hotel room.

Mike and Nick were released. Mike hurried to Ashlee, glaring at the officers.

Nick sighed and shook his head. "Sorry, he's a bit on edge. We just got in from Ireland tonight, and they haven't seen each other in months."

Barb nodded and waved a hand at his pants that laid on the bed. "Sorry about the mix-up, but we have a witness saying she was screaming for you to let her go and begging for help."

Nick winced.

Mike spun around from where he was crouched over Ashlee. "My wife was yelling for me not to let her go. She had a bad dream."

Nick gave the police officers an apologetic glance as he spoke to Mike. "Calm down. The police are just doing their jobs and Ashlee's fine, she doesn't even know anything happened." Nick grabbed his pants and headed to the bathroom.

"My partner and I will remain on scene until Mrs. Evans confirms she's here willingly. If you don't mind me asking, why are you here?"

Nick stopped by the bathroom door and turned. "Ash wanted to renew their vows," he said before could Mike could speak.

"I see." Barb's thoughtful gaze followed Nick into the bathroom.

Nick took a quick shower and put on his dirty clothes. In the main room, the two officers stood by the door. Mike sat on the bed with Ashlee's head in his lap, stroking her hair, glaring at the officers. In Nick's absence, Mike had dressed Ashlee in the pajama top and wrapped her in her blanket.

"Sorry we're taking your time like this, and thanks for looking out for her." Nick tapped the bottle of sedative. "I gave her a half dose because I wasn't sure how it would react with the other medicine she's taking. When we return home, we'll get her to a doctor."

"Her feet look pretty sore." Barb nodded at Ashlee's red, swollen feet.

"The plane ride was too long. At least I hope that's all it is." Nick turned to Mike. "If you want to go shower, I'll sit with her."

When Mike entered the small bathroom,

both officers relaxed.

"You three are pretty close, huh?" Barb said.

Heat burned across Nick's cheeks. "Yeah, we are." He leaned down and kissed Ashlee on the lips, giving Barb a challenging stare.

"It's nice seeing friends help each other like this. Not many men would travel halfway around the world to escort a friend home, or go to his wedding."

Nick opened his mouth to speak, and Barb held up a hand. She grabbed her notebook, wrote a minute, tore out the page, and handed it to Nick. "For my first wedding I had three hundred guests and just twenty for my second, and I gotta say, I'm much happier now." A smile peeking from the corner of her lips, she pointed to the paper in Nick's hand.

He read it. His eyes narrowed as he nodded.

"That's the lawyer I saw for my divorce. If I had a marriage issue, I'd use him again. As far as I know, to remarry someone needs no special license, but it couldn't hurt to check with him. It would really suck to get arrested for breaking a marriage law."

"That happen a lot around here?" Nick lifted an eyebrow.

Barb and her partner laughed, and Barb said, "More than you'd think. Or maybe not— this is Vegas after all. We arrested a guy this week who wanted to marry his pig."

"His pig?"

"That's not why we arrested him," her partner interrupted. "We arrested him for admitting to fornicating with the animal. If he'd kept his dumb mouth shut, he could've just gone home."

Barb laughed. "And the week before that we arrested two people for trying to marry underage girls and one man for trying to marry an underage boy. Then, let's see, what is it this week? Seven bigamists so far and about twenty assaults from angry spouses who arrived in time to stop the weddings."

Her partner snorted. "Everyone believes that what happens in Vegas, stays in Vegas, but the police record follows you home."

Nick folded the slip of paper and slid it into his pocket. Ashlee stirred on the bed. Everyone stopped speaking and stared at her a minute, but she didn't wake.

"Sorry, I can't wake her. When Mike comes out, he can try. Please keep in mind she almost always wakes up afraid for a few minutes until she's fully awake and knows where she is."

Barb nodded. Her partner narrowed his eyes and moved into the corner of the room with one hand on his gun with the holster unsnapped.

Mike exited the shower bare-chested, rubbing his hair with a thin, damp towel.

"Ash stirred a bit, Mike. Maybe you can wake her?" Nick sat in the chair by the bathroom door.

"Yeah, I guess. Move the chair closer, Nick, so she can see you." A scowl on his face, Mike turned to the officers. "And if you wouldn't mind, don't let her see you or speak to her until she's awake. Strangers frighten her."

Barb moved to the bathroom doorway. Her partner stayed where he was.

Mike climbed on the bed and pulled Ashlee up, sitting her up in his lap. She murmured sleepily and tried to roll onto her side. Mike laughed and rubbed her back. "Wake up, sleepyhead. Open your eyes, Ash."

She murmured again and then snored. Mike glanced at Nick and shrugged. "I don't think it'll work, Nick, it's been less than an hour, and I really don't want to shake her hard."

Nick took Ashlee's hands and rubbed them. "Wake up, sweetheart! I need you to wake up," he yelled and shook her.

"Nicky?" she mumbled and opened her eyes a crack, smiled, closed her eyes, and went right back to sleep.

Nick frowned, glanced from the officers to Mike and shrugged. "Guess you gotta wait another hour or so." Nick flipped on the television.

Mike snorted, turned back the covers and climbed in the bed. When he was settled, he pulled his wife into his arms and went to sleep.

Both officers leaned on the wall by the door, talking in low tones. Nick surprised himself by dozing off. The radio Barb carried woke him when a voice asked for their position.

"Charlie thirty-seven, dispatch, we're still on site," Barb said, her gaze traveling Ashlee and Mike sleeping in the bed.

Ashlee and Mike stirred. Mike sat, glanced at the cheap clock on the nightstand, then flopped back down and closed his eyes.

"We've been traveling with no real sleep for three days now." Nick yawned and stretched, wanting to lay beside Ashlee and close his eyes, but he stayed in the chair.

"Man, I could use a coffee or something," Mike said.

"Go ahead," Barb said.

"Can't, if she wakes and I'm not here… well, I'm not sure what would happen, and I really don't want to find that out tonight. Besides, it would take more than coffee to keep me up. This is a Powerade night for sure."

Barb laughed and rose an eyebrow. "Powerade?"

Mike plumped the pillows behind his head as he spoke. "Stuff works better than espresso. Mountain berry blast, the blue stuff. One of those and your good to go like you drank ten coffees."

Nick shifted in his seat.

"Weird, must be an allergy or something." Barb dropped her hand to her phone. A frisson of fear curled her spine. For a moment, she debated calling Sergeant Mason and informing him she knew how Mike had stayed awake. The problem was proof. How do you prove that? Visions of Steven's mangled corpse competed with the scars on Ashlee's drugged body before her. Did she want to prove that? She dropped her hand from her phone and leaned against the wall again.

Nick shrugged and tried to wake Ashlee again. This time, she opened her eyes and thrashed in the covers. Nick pushed them off her, talking the entire time, telling her she was with him and safe.

Tears trailed down her cheeks as she clutched him. Mike took her from him and whispered in her ear. A moment later he spoke louder. "Ash, are you awake?"

"Uhhuh, what's wrong? Are you sick? I'm sick. My head feels funny."

"No one is sick." Nick stroked her hair. "The

sedatives are making you feel weird. In a minute you can go to sleep again. Someone saw us bring you in here crying and they called the police. Can you tell the officers who we are and why we're here?"

"My husband and we're getting married again, really married." Ashlee turned in Mike's arms, her gaze darting around the room, landing on the officer standing in the corner with his hand on his gun.

"Don't let him take me from you. Don't let anyone, Mike!" Her shrill voice cracked, and her hands gripped his arm tight.

"No one will make you go anywhere, Mrs. Evans. Did you come here voluntarily?" Barb tried to keep her voice soft and her manner unthreatening.

"Aye, I'm okay." Shivers wracked her as she hid her face in Mike's neck.

Mike's glare ratcheted up a notch.

Barb winced as she spoke. "Mrs. Evans, could we talk a moment alone, please?"

Ashlee shook her head wildly, brown hair obscuring her face.

Nick glanced from the officer to Ashlee, his lips tightening. "Sweetheart, the officer needs to know you're okay and we aren't forcing you to say anything. Mike and I will be right outside the door. And you don't have to speak about anything else."

Sobbing now, deep gasping breaths, Ashlee nodded.

Mike glowered at the officers as he left her curled in the bed.

Nick grabbed his arm and pulled him from the room.

Barb waited till the door closed behind them and her partner. "Do you require assistance? Should I call an ambulance for you?"

Ashlee wiped her face with both hands. "I really am okay. I just have bad dreams and a hard time waking. Can my husband come back please?" Huddled in the blanket, Ashlee's hands shook as she rubbed her face again. "Please?"

"Yes, and I'm sorry we disturbed you. If you change your mind, call us."

"Change my mind?"

Barb hesitated. "Sorry, that isn't what I meant. If you need help, call, and we'll come."

"Thank you."

Barb nodded and left.

Mike brushed past her in the doorway.

Nick stopped to shake their hands and thank them again. He tapped the pocket where he'd put the note Barb wrote. "Thanks for everything."

Barb nodded and left, glad to get away from

that mess. The men seemed nice, average even, but the reports of Steven Wrint's death proved one of them wasn't. Her money was on the husband, alibi or not.

- 26 -
This was His Chance

Nick had set his watch alarm for nine. Mike and Ashlee were still sound asleep when he rose.

To keep from waking them he stepped outside to make a phone call, Officer Stertan's note clutched in his hand. Barb's stories were a clear message.

He called the number and talked the receptionist into making them an appointment for late that afternoon. The receptionist confirmed his hunch that it would be impossible for them to marry.

Vegas in early morning lacked the glamor of Vegas at night, appearing tawdry and gray. The motel was shabby in the daylight. Without the neon signs and flashing lights, the building resembled a cheap motel you'd find on any rundown avenue. Not at all the type of place he wanted to take Ashlee.

Tonight, he would pick the hotel. Not to celebrate a marriage, there couldn't be one. What there could be was a plan for the future. This was his chance. Ironically, he need do nothing at all. Unwittingly, Steven had given her to him.

Clearly, Ashlee needed him and the stability of a constant husband. Mike would see that. Even if Mike quit his job to be with her, she needed Nick more. Although he didn't love this part of himself, he wasn't above taking advantage of the situation and pushing Mike out.

Now, he needed to make Mike see it, and the quickest way was to let him be alone with Ashlee when she woke. Granted, that was a risk. She might be fine and not call for him, but the chances were she would wake upset.

After a moment's reflection, he hurried to the nearest store and bought new clothes for Mike and himself, a case of bottled water, and a box of granola bars. Then he headed back but didn't go in. When Ashlee woke and called for him, he would enter after letting Mike try to handle it alone for a few minutes.

He waited outside the door, sitting against the cement wall, sipping the same water bottle for an hour.

✳   ✳   ✳

Mike woke when Ashlee stirred. A glance showed Nick wasn't in bed and the bathroom was quiet. He must have risen earlier and stepped out.

Last night, after the police had left they'd settled down to sleep. Nick had undressed Ashlee, and she'd fallen asleep with her head on Nick's shoulder. Now she curled against Mike's side with her arm around his waist. Unable to resist, he ran a hand down her body. Warm and soft, the familiar curves under his palm felt like home. Tears of gratitude filled his eyes.

So close to losing her, losing my future.

The bed creaked as he rolled onto his back and pulled her on top of his chest. A sleepy murmur as she stretched against him brought back memories. Weekends when Nick and he were home, she would wake slow and kiss them one at a time. Sleepy murmurs changing to excited breathing when they ran their hands over her. Long days spent in bed, cuddling and talking between bouts of love. Mussed hair and crumbs on the sheets, the sound of her laughter while she watched them make the bed so no one had to sleep in the wet spot.

If he slept later than her, she would bring him breakfast and sit cross-legged at the foot while he ate. Or, if she had class, she would trail a hand over him and sigh. The love and lust she felt clear in the sound when she kissed him goodbye.

He wanted those relaxed days back. The sweet, unafraid smile. Uninhibited sex where he wasn't afraid to do or say the wrong thing. He slid the sheet down and eased her onto her back.

No bruises remained on her back. The scars along her left side showed as faint, silvery-red marks. Over the last months her tan had faded, making the scars easier to see on her fair skin. Seventy-two crisscrossed lines too neat to be accidental. In shorts and a t-shirt, they would be glaringly obvious. Burns on her breast had left shiny patches. Her left nipple was a shade darker than the right one now. The surgeries had left small marks that would never disappear. Her feet were the worst. The nails had partially grown in, two looked wavy, the third normal if a bit thin. Swollen to the ankles, puffy and red, her feet were a mess of scar tissue, shiny from the burns with rough ridges from the cuts.

The scar on the edge of her face was jagged and crooked, but not too noticeable and didn't detract from her beauty. A thin, straight, white line scored the left cheekbone. The broken cheekbone had healed with only the slightest of curves, making one cheek bone a hair more prominent than the other.

What must she think when she looked in a mirror? What memories haunted her? Mike pulled the sheet up and closed his eyes. So unfair. So goddamned cruel. And for what? Did Steven think she would agree to be his just like that? That Nick would share her with him? He wished to God she hadn't fought him that she'd lied instead and faked it and made Steven believe she loved him. That he hadn't beaten or scarred her.

And that was Mike's fault, if somewhere in her soul she thought having sex with anyone else would make her a whore, irredeemable to God. Hell, if he'd taken her seriously when she said Steven gave her the creeps… A deep sigh escaped him.

No point in rehashing what ifs. The now they had was what they needed to deal with.

"Ash?" Mike smoothed her hair back and kissed her brow. "Wake up, honey. Time to get up."

Sudden tense stillness was followed by a shriek as she leapt away, tangling in the sheet and falling to the floor hard as she screamed. On her hands and knees, she shook her head and pushed herself up as Mike called her name.

Once she was standing, her head turned from side-to-side, her terrified gaze scanning the room. Tear-filled eyes locked on Mike, kneeling on the bed, holding his hands out and she sobbed, as she crawled onto the bed and fell on him.

"Sorry. Sorry." Bitter and sad, she mumbled apologies into his chest. "Where's Nick?"

"Don't know. He was gone when I woke. Probably went for food or something. Relax, honey, your safe with me. Everything's okay."

Mike laid back down, taking her with him, murmuring endearments till her heart stopped pounding, and she relaxed against him.

"Are you hungry?"

"How can you be hungry? You ate three steaks." She kissed his cheek then squirmed away and limped to the bathroom.

Mike laughed and tucked both pillows behind his head.

She was in the bathroom a long time. Mike flipped on the television. When she emerged, she hesitated in the bathroom doorway scanning the room, her gaze avoiding him.

"Nick's not back yet. Want me to call him? Sometime today we'll go buy you a new phone."

"No, don't call." Both hands twisted

together, and her gaze darted to him and away again.

Mike patted the bed beside him, and she bit her lip.

"I won't hurt you." Mike sat straighter and patted the bed again.

Pale and nervous, she licked her lips as she sat beside him. A flinch when he moved, which she tried to mask as a stretch, made him frown.

"Honey, you don't have to sit near me. You don't have to do anything you don't want to. I won't be angry."

"No, it's not… I'm sorry, Mike." She crept to him and rested in his arms, but her body was tense.

Mike ran a hand down her back. The pajama shirt was damp from her hair. He reached for the buttons on the front, and she grabbed his hand, jerking back from him.

"Can we wait for, Nick, please?" A nervous flutter in her voice, the please caught on a sob.

"That wasn't… yes, we can wait for Nick, but I was just going to take off the shirt because it was wet." A frown on his face, Mike pulled away and framed her face with his hands. "Don't be afraid to tell me what you want. If you want to be alone or snuggle or sleep just tell me. I'm not going to pretend this never happened and I don't expect you too."

He kissed her lips. "When you're ready for sex, I'll be waiting. However, you want to. Just us, just Nick, or both of us. We won't pressure you."

"I love you, Mike, I really do, but the thought of—" a small cry of dismay interrupted her as her breath hitched. "I do want to make to love to you, but if you're both here, both touching me, it won't be him."

"Then that's what we'll do." Mike smiled a sad, confused smile. "You know I don't mind that at all."

A fake smile on her face, Ashlee kissed him and snuggled into his arms. "I'm so sorry, Mike."

"Don't be, Ash. Whatever you need is okay." He kissed her brow again and stood. "I need the bathroom."

The blankets slithered across the bed as she yanked them up, curling in the bed. Mike tried not to mind her relief when he left her.

❋ ❋ ❋

Outside the door, Nick glanced at his watch. He'd wait ten more minutes. The shower had just stopped. She'd calmed quicker than he thought she would when she woke. Now he wasn't sure what to do. *Give them time to talk without him or go inside?*

"Stupid idea anyway," he mumbled and let

himself back into the room.

"Nick!" Her face lit as she sat in the bed. Wet hair made the pajama top cling to her, taunt nipples poking the light material, and he couldn't keep his gaze from her breasts.

Hurriedly, he turned away. "Hey, sweetheart, I bought Mike and I clean clothes." He rummaged in the bag and handed her the box of granola bars and a water bottle. "Mike in the bathroom?"

"Yeah, I expect he'll be a while."

Nick snickered, sat beside her, and kicked his shoes off. He debated telling her they couldn't marry but decided to wait till Mike was present, no point in explaining twice. "How are the feet this morning? Need a pill?" He handed her the pain pill and brushed her wet hair over her shoulder as she took it. Nick traced the scar on her cheek with a fingertip then kissed it.

Tears filled her eyes as he traced the scar on the side of her face and kissed that. His finger slid down her neck and across her collarbone, and he kissed the silvery scar there.

"Don't." Her voice hitched, and her eyes squeezed shut as she turned her face away.

"Ash, do my scars make me ugly?"

Surprised, her eyes flew open. "No, but it's not the same."

"Yours are worse, I agree, but not ugly, Ash." When she turned her head away again, he used one finger to tip it back to him. "Not shameful either. The shame is Steven's not yours. The memories of how you got them will haunt you forever, but that man is dead and will never harm you or anyone else again. Don't let him into our lives, Ash. His words were lies. Mike never gave you to anyone and he never would. Mike doesn't speak of our love life to anyone except us. You have never been, and will never be, the topic of discussion for either of us."

Nick pulled her close, putting his face in the curve of her neck. "If you want to tell me, or Mike, or both of us, what happened, you can. Nothing will change how we feel for you." Nick slipped his hand under the shirt and cupped her left breast.

A shiver raced over her, and she tried to pull back.

"To me, this still feels amazing. If it hurts you, physically or mentally, I won't touch it. But, Ash, don't think because Steven touched you here that I don't want too. If it feels good, let it."

Ashlee leaned forward and rested her chin on his shoulder. "I want to forget. More than anything I want it to be like it was."

Embarrassment and disgust filled her harsh whisper. "I'm afraid I'll feel him when you touch me."

"Can't happen. My hands are full of love." He rubbed the nipple between his thumb and forefinger. "Physical pain could happen, something might hurt, but my hands love you. The intent to love is there. A tender breast, sore rib, or a cramp, we deal with the same as we always did. If we're honest with each other, we can work anything out."

The sheets rustled, the only sound in the room, as Nick stroked her breast.

Ashlee pulled away and unbuttoned her shirt as Nick's eyes kindled. The shirt fell to the bed as she reached for his shirt and removed it.

"You're so beautiful, Ash. The most beautiful woman I've ever seen. Let me make love to you." Nick's voice caught. Both his hands trailed across her body, then through her hair as he kissed her lips.

"Let me touch you, Nick." Eyes closed, and a frown of concentration on her face, her hands skimmed his body, lingering on the muscles of his arms and his hands. In a minute, she was burrowed against his chest crying, running her hands over him.

In slow circles Nick rubbed her back, wondering what she was thinking. Was she comparing him to Steven, trying to force the memory of what Steven felt like away? Or was she attempting to make herself want this, to want him?

"Feel the love in my hands. Not at all like Steven's were."

Still crying she nodded and knelt, taking his face in both hands she kissed him.

The toilet flushed in the other room and water ran in the shower.

Ashlee rested her forehead on his. "Did you kill him?"

"Yes." His satisfaction was clear in his one-word response.

She heaved a deep sigh as her body relaxed against him. "Thank you. You're going to marry me, Nicky, and take care of me forever. No one will ever hurt me again."

Soft and warm she curled against him. Her tone was certain as if she didn't have a doubt in the world he would care for her and she wasn't wrong.

"I can't wait to marry you. Everyone will know you're mine and what will happen to them if they even think about messing with you."

When Mike came out of the bathroom, they were naked and kissing on the bed.

Mike sat on the edge of the bed as Ashlee

drew back from Nick, her face flushed. On her knees, she shimmied backward, using her hands to urge Nick into an upright position. Once he was standing, Ashlee knelt on the bed, her palms pressing Nick forward into her mouth.

Nick's fingers tangled in her hair, the warmth of the nape of her neck and heat of her mouth making a fire inside him. Mike knelt behind her not touching, staring, one hand on his cock, stroking himself slowly, the other balancing against the headboard.

Nick closed his eyes and threw his head back, enjoying the excited sounds she made more than her mouth on him. This excited her with no fear because no other men except he and Mike had ever done this with her. Steven had told him he never tried. He'd believed her when she'd said she'd bite off his dick no matter what he did to her. Smart man, Nick believed that too.

A flash of angry disgust made him sigh hard. Goddamn the man for taking his thoughts now. Steven had no place in his bed. Not when it should be only them.

"Don't stop," he murmured as Ashlee drew back. "Please." Voice thick with desire, he continued to tell Ashlee how much he liked her mouth on him. A minute later his hips were moving, and he pulled away from her.

One hand on his cock, Nick used the other to lift her left breast and came, coating her breast with his semen, as if it were a magical elixir that could erase the scars.

For a moment it worked. Ashlee glanced down and smiled. Nick exhaled a long shivery sigh and ran his hand over her breast, smearing the wet stickiness.

She pressed his hands against her, her head tipped back and eyes closed.

A soft smile on his lips, Nick sat against the headboard and pulled her to his chest, his semen warm between them. Limp, as if she'd had the orgasm not him, she rested in his arms. He held her to his chest and smoothed her hair, his face buried in her neck.

Mike leaned against her back, hugging them both.

After a minute, Ashlee squirmed around, pressing her back to Nick's chest and hugged Mike. They sat entwined together for minutes. When Ashlee ran her hands over Mike's body, he shuddered.

"I love you, Ash." Deep and low, Mike's voice cracked.

"I love you too, husband." Breathy and shy her voice was barely above a whisper. Both her hands placed Nick's palms over her breasts then trailed over Mike again, urging him to his feet so she could take his cock in her mouth.

Mike groaned loudly as he stood and leaned against the wall with both hands.

Nick supported her weight with both his hands on her breasts as she leaned forward.

Mike moaned and thrust.

It wouldn't take him too long to come, Nick thought. And it didn't. A few minutes later, Mike used one hand to push Ashlee back.

Nick drew her against his chest, and lifted both breasts, offering the pointy peaks to Mike.

"God yes, you're so beautiful." Mike finished himself by hand, coming in long spurts across Ashlee's breasts as she made excited sounds. When Mike finished, he dropped to his knees and hugged her, falling backward onto the bed as he kissed her.

Nick laid beside them, running a hand over her body as Mike kissed her. The curve of her ass lifted into his hand. He took it as encouragement and slipped his hand between her legs. Wetness greeted his searching fingers. He smiled and slid one finger inside her. The sound she made encouraged him even more.

He pulled Mike's leg, making room to kneel between his legs as Ashlee slipped astride Mike and thrust her ass further in the air, giving Nick access. Behind her now, Nick slid two fingers inside her while the other hand caressed her breasts. Only semi-erect, his cock wasn't hard enough to penetrate. He needed more time.

"Mike, lay her on her back."

Mike made an indistinct sound and rolled over, letting Ashlee slide to his side, but continuing to kiss her with one hand on her face and the other her breasts.

Nick laid between her legs and used his mouth on her, holding her exposed with both hands.

Mike pulled her leg back opening her wider.

Nick took the opportunity to slip two fingers inside her again. She widened her legs, and thrust against his fingers, pulling away from Mike's kiss and thrashing her head as she began to keen.

"That's right, honey. Nick feels real good, doesn't he?" Mike continued to murmur to her as he stroked her breast with one hand, the other holding her spread so Nick could lick her.

Nick stifled a laugh that turned to an internal snarl. Mike was trying not to use any of his usual phrases, afraid Steven had used them and it would upset her. Once again Steven was in bed with them.

Ashlee seemed to appreciate his efforts

though, her body responding to Mike's encouragement. When she came, she called Nick's name. A long drawn out Nicky. Nick drew her into his arms as she panted.

Mike hugged them both again, resting against her back.

They snuggled together for an hour. Finally, Nick gathered her and rose, carrying her to the bathroom where he set her on her feet in the shower.

Mike joined them.

Ashlee giggled as she tried to wash them as they washed her. From head-to-toe Nick soaped her, massaging her scalp, running the soapy washcloth over her breasts. On his knees, he soaped her legs and lifted one foot at a time, washing her feet, getting in between each toe.

Ashlee gasped and jerked away.

Nick stilled. "Ash, nothing you don't want will happen. Tell us no, and we'll stop right away. If you don't want me touching your feet or anywhere—"

"No, sorry its... I like it, but they're so ugly now." A sob caught in her throat.

"No, every part of you is beautiful. For your sake, I'm sorry you have scars. For mine, they don't matter. I don't even see them. All I see is Ashlee, my beautiful girl."

Nick lifted her foot, making eye contact through the steamy water and sucked her toe. The sound she made went right to his groin. He lowered her foot onto his cock, and she giggled as she ran her toes over it.

"We're clean enough." Mike lifted Ashlee in his arms and set her outside the tub and then turned the water off. "Let's go get dirty again." He grabbed a towel and wrapped it around Ashlee and laughed as she giggled when he rubbed against her, drying himself.

Nick stepped out and toweled his hair then hers, not bothering to dry off in the warm, steamy room. Mike's hard cock bobbed as he pulled Ashlee to the bed.

She glanced over her shoulder to Nick, her anxious expression lightening when he smiled at her. Nick hurried his pace and beat them to the bed. "Lie here, sweetheart." He pulled her across his chest at the edge of the bed. The same position Mike had taken the first night they were together, except this time Nick held her while Mike made love to her with slow, gentle thrusts.

"Oh God, Ash. Oh God." Mike called her name and fell limply over her chest when he was through. Nick nudged Mike away and rolled Ashlee underneath him. Wet from Mike, he slid inside easily. Ashlee's eyes fixed on his, and without meaning to, he surged hard.

"Yessss," she hissed a long-drawn-out sigh and arched against him, tightening her legs around his waist. Before he knew it, they were rolling on the bed, both moaning and grabbing each other.

Head thrown back and yelling, "Yes," over and over Ashlee rode him hard, meeting each thrust with her own. The headboard slammed into the wall. Mike rose and braced the bed with his body.

Nick flipped her again until he was on top and lifted her ass with one hand pushing her legs straight back, plunging into her as hard and fast as he could while she screamed his name telling him to go harder.

When she came, she squirted and screamed.

He stilled, breathing hard on the edge of orgasm as her muscles contracting around him.

"Oh, Nick." Crying, she reached for him, and he came, jerking his hips hard against her. "Oh, Nicky."

Soft and full of love, she repeated his name, and crying and smiling, she hugged him tightly.

Nick almost felt bad for Mike, but he was too happy for himself.

- 27 -

ASHLEE EVANS ROSSI HAS A NICE RING TO IT

Ashlee sat beside Nick, clutching his hand in her sweaty one. A complete stranger would note her stress. White-faced, both her shaking hands clutched him.

"No matter what he says, Ash, I'm not going anywhere, and we'll be together," Nick said.

Tears filled her eyes, and she lowered her head, letting her hair curtain her face. Mike exchanged an uneasy glance with him.

"Look, honey, if we can't—"

Ashlee's breath caught in a sob, and Mike stopped speaking. Suddenly she threw herself into Mike's arms and began crying. "I'm so sorry, but I need him. I need him," she repeated pitifully as she wept on his shoulder.

Mike rubbed her back, kissing her neck, and murmuring in her ear too low for Nick to hear.

Nick glanced over at the receptionist whose gaze darted away, pretending to be busy with paperwork. The lawyers waiting room was empty, except for them. Soft music played. Discreet lighting accented art on the walls, and the furniture was comfortable. Thick leather pieces, gave the impression of a fancy study, not a waiting room. The receptionist sat behind a carved mahogany desk, office equipment encased in matching wooden cabinets tucked out of sight.

The receptionist cleared her throat. "Can I get you anything? Water perhaps? Or maybe coffee or tea?"

"No, thank you." Nick rose and stretched, giving his watch a pointed glance.

"Mr. Cohen will be with you shortly." The secretary returned to her typing as Nick began to pace.

Ashlee had quieted for the moment. Mike glared at him over her shoulder. The anger he accepted. Nick would be angry too if his wife wanted another man, but Mike chose this. He hadn't snuck in and stole her. A guilty twinge made Nick scowl. He'd planned to steal her. To do everything in his power to get here. Of course, his plan included a child, not this fiasco, but he wouldn't lie to himself. The fact that Ashlee needed him so desperately pleased him. Why she needed him filled him with fury.

Mike too— he simmered with anger, trying his best to hide it from Ashlee and not succeeding at all.

The door to the inner office opened, and a portly man wearing an expensive blue suit and a toupee escorted a woman to the door. Ashlee slid off Mike's lap and wiped her eyes.

The sharp clack of the woman's high heels across the hardwood floor drowned out the soft murmurs of the lawyer as he spoke. Plastic surgery and expensive clothing disguised the woman's age. Nick spun away and crouched before Ashlee, taking her cold hands in his.

"No matter what. Remember that okay? We'll work something out."

Ashlee yanked her hands away and pressed the heels against her eyes as she nodded.

Mike ran his hand over her bowed head and glared at Nick, then rose to his feet and turned to the lawyer.

Mr. Cohen stopped before them. "Please, join me in my office." A wide, expansive gesture directed them inside. He paused to speak to his secretary as they entered and settled in the chairs before his desk.

Ashlee stared at her folded hands.

"Now, what can I do for you today?" Mr. Cohen sat at his desk and folded his hands, his polite smile and inquiring gaze traveling over them.

"Officer Stertan recommend we come speak with you. Thank you for seeing us on such short notice." Nick offered his hand and introduced everyone. Mike shook Mr. Cohen's hand, Ashlee murmured hello, but didn't look up.

"From what Officer Stertan said I don't think we can do what we intended. I'm hoping you can advise us as to the best way to proceed." Nick cleared his throat. "We wish to marry each other, all three of us."

"Ahh." the lawyer leaned back in his chair, resting his hands on the chair's wide arms. "Yes, I see, and I'm afraid Officer Stertan is quite correct." His gaze flitted to Ashlee as she let out a low sob, stifling it instantly.

"The only place such a marriage can take place and be recognized would be Africa and some parts of the middle east."

Nick grabbed Ashlee's hand. "Can we join ourselves some other way, legally?"

"How do you mean?" Mr. Cohen leaned forward, looking intrigued.

"Ashlee has health problems, and I'm unable to care for her, make decisions for her. Can we draw legal documents to give her into my care?"

"A full power of attorney would do that. I could draw that up for you today."

Ashlee started crying.

"Sweetheart…" Nick lifted a hand and laid it on her hair.

"Honey," Mike said and cleared his throat. "I would share you with him, I really would, but the law won't let us both marry you. Mr. Cohen can fill out these papers and no one will be able to take you from him again."

"Mike," Nick took a deep breath. "I'm sorry, man, but you have to let her go. Let her marry me. Mr. Cohen can draw up the papers for you. Nothing will change except she'll have the comfort of being my wife publicly. When you come home, you can stay with us for as long as Ashlee likes. And meanwhile, she can live a normal life with me."

"Goddamn it!" Mike jumped to his feet.

Ashlee moaned and slumped.

Nick leaned over and hugged her, staring at Mike as he paced the room.

Mike halted before them and took Ashlee from Nick, holding her close. "I know he's right, but I hate giving you up. The happiest I've ever been is with you, calling you my wife. I'm so sorry I did this to us. All of this. This entire thing is my fault. God, Ash, if I could take it all back, I would." Mike began crying and hid his face in her hair.

Nick rose and hugged them both.

Mr. Cohen cleared his throat. "If I might ask your current state of residence and how long you've been married?"

"California and almost a year, most of which they lived apart," Nick said as Mike groaned.

Ashlee took deep hitching breaths and trembled.

"A divorce in California can take up to year, an annulment on the other hand—"

"No, that means we were never married. No, I won't give him up." Ashlee glared at Mr. Cohen from red, swollen eyes.

"There are options. The fastest being a trip to Guam. In a week you can be divorced. Or, if one of you becomes a legal resident of Nevada, in six weeks I can file the paperwork. No quicker means are available. I see that you're concerned about legal custody and I can draw papers today, making both men your legal guardians in the event you're incapacitated in any way."

"Yes, do that," Nick said. "Mike and I only have four more days of leave. What's required to become a legal resident here?"

"A place of residence and a driver license. Register your car here if you have one. Registering to vote wouldn't hurt either. A signature from a member of the community certifying your intent to make Nevada your home and that you've been living here for six weeks." Mr. Cohen cleared his throat again. "California law requires the reversion to your maiden name. If that will be an issue for you, I can legally change your name."

Ashlee slumped only Mike's grip on her keeping her upright. "Mike…" thin and weak, she wailed his name.

"Forever, Ash, no matter what, right? Whatever you need, I'll do. God knows I want to stay your husband."

Nick laid a hand on her shoulder. "Mr. Cohen can make you legally Mrs. Ashlee Evans Rossi." He felt like a thief, stealing her away, exhilarated and sorry, knowing he was taking advantage.

Mike lifted his cheek from her hair and glared. "Don't, Nick."

Nick dropped his hand and spun away, his lips tight. "Mike, I'm sorry, man, I really am, but I told you when we started this I wasn't settling for part-time, that you would have to share her completely. As long as Ashlee needs you I will never discourage her from seeing you. But she needs me now." He spun to face Mike. "Please— let her have a stable, normal life. Don't force her to hide in the house afraid people will notice how we live. Let her have friends visit and be able to sit outside at night holding my hand on the porch. Is this so much to ask? Or quit your job and do those things with her."

"And do what?"

"Whatever you want. If you quit I'll still be there every day, that won't change."

"Ash?"

"No," Nick interrupted. "Don't make her choose. Man-up and make this choice yourself."

Mr. Cohen spoke up. "These decisions need not be made right this minute. Take your time and discuss this amongst yourselves. I'll get started on the paperwork giving you both power of attorney. Stop by my office tomorrow to pick them up. If you decide to proceed with a divorce, I'll file either here or California, whichever you choose. My secretary will give you pamphlets answering questions on the procedure, and she can help arrange the necessary paperwork."

"Can you arrange legal support for her? Not alimony as I don't qualify, but something?" Nick glanced at Ashlee then back at Mr. Cohen. "I want her as secure as we can make her. Neither Mike nor I have many assets, but we both have good retirement funds and healthy bank accounts. Is there a way to ensure she has access to everything I own? Legal access that I can't rescind?"

"Yes." Mr. Cohen leaned back in his chair and rubbed his chin. "A trust fund would be easy enough to arrange. Bank accounts, retirement funds, all those things can be added with access set to the three of you. In the future, put all purchases directly into the fund. Any purchases not in the fund would be the property of the purchaser. Rules of expenditure can be added and clauses for children."

"Perfect." Nick relaxed in his seat. "Can you draw that up too? Give us all full access."

Mr. Cohen nodded. "Full access is just that, Mr. Rossi. Mr. or Mrs. Evans could empty your accounts legally."

"Yes, that's fine, I understand. Can the access be changed at a later date?"

"If all three of you agree, yes. I recommend requiring all three signatures to access the retirement funds. The standard clause for death should be sufficient, making each other your heirs at least until there are children to consider. I can have that ready for you tomorrow as well. When you return home, send me the signed bank access cards, and I'll file and get the trust set up. It just needs a name. Might I suggest Evans Rossi Living Trust?"

"Yes, thank you. That sounds perfect. When she's taken care of, I'll sleep better at night." Nick placed his hands on Ashlee's tear-streaked cheeks. "Never again will you be trapped somewhere without funds to reach us or go wherever you chose. Mr. Cohen, if you think of anything else that can legally join us…."

Mr. Cohen rose and walked to the doorway. "If you haven't already, put her name as the beneficiary on all life insurance policies, and add them to the trust. If you have no policies, take them out. Not only is it a good way to save money, but knowing your loved ones will be provided for after your death will ease your mind."

He ushered them to the secretary's desk and spoke briefly to her, then shook their hands. "Angela will have your forms to sign in the morning. Whenever you're ready to proceed with the other matter give me a call." He took Ashlee's hand in his and patted. "Be happy, my dear, whichever you choose is a good choice."

Nick sat in the driver's seat and glanced in the rear-view mirror. Mike met his eyes and sighed. One arm around Ashlee, he reached forward and squeezed Nick's shoulder.

"Marriage is complicated as fuck. Why can't this just be easy? Whose business is it if we want to live together anyways?" He glanced down at Ashlee as she rested her cheek on his shoulder. "If we can't all be married it makes sense for Nick to marry you. For now, anyway. Let's take turns. Ashlee can be your wife for a year or two. Lots of people get remarried. Who cares what anyone thinks?"

Ashlee laughed and kissed his cheek. "You really don't mind?"

"I'll admit I was jealous, but you still love me, right?" Mike tipped her chin up.

"Always." Her hand rose and traced his face.

"Okay, then. Let's not let Steven Wrint in our lives. We go on together. The three of us. In three months, I'll dance at your wedding and toast my best friend. Ashlee Evans Rossi has a nice ring to it."

Nick grinned. Ashlee's eyes met his in the mirror, so full of love and happiness tears filled his eyes. Not how he planned or hoped, but she would be his. Once she was his wife, he would never let her go.

THE END